ENTHUSIASTIC ACCLAIM FOR A CRIME FICTION
GIANT—*NEW YORK TIMES* BESTSELLING
GRAND MASTER

TONY HILLERMAN

"Hillerman is a master."
St. Louis Post-Dispatch

"Surely one of the finest and
most original craftsmen."
Boston Globe

"Hillerman transcends the mystery genre."
Washington Post Book World

"What he communicates better than almost any
other suspense writer is a different sense of time,
a different sense of connection to nature,
a different way of being."
Ft. Worth Star-Telegram

"An amazing writer."
Albuquerque Journal

"Hillerman's novels are like no others."
San Diego Union-Tribune

"His Leaphorn/Chee series is one of the most
original and influential in modern crime fiction."
Portland Sunday Oregonian

"We couldn't do better for a true voice of the West."
Denver Rocky Mountain News

BOOKS BY TONY HILLERMAN

FICTION
The Shape Shifter
Skeleton Man • *The Sinister Pig*
The Wailing Wind • *Hunting Badger*
The First Eagle • *The Fallen Man*
Finding Moon • *Sacred Clowns*
Coyote Waits • *Talking God*
A Thief of Time • *Skinwalkers*
The Ghostway • *The Dark Wind*
People of Darkness • *Listening Woman*
Dance Hall of the Dead • *The Fly on the Wall*
The Blessing Way • *The Mysterious West*
The Boy Who Made Dragonfly (for children)
Buster Mesquite's Cowboy Band (for children)

NONFICTION
Seldom Disappointed
Hillerman Country
The Great Taos Bank Robbery
Rio Grande
New Mexico
The Spell of New Mexico
Indian Country
Talking Mysteries (with Ernie Bulow)
Kilroy Was There
A New Omnibus of Crime

NOW AVAILABLE IN HARDCOVER
Tony Hillerman's Landscape by Anne Hillerman

ATTENTION: ORGANIZATIONS AND CORPORATIONS
Most Harper paperbacks are available at special quantity discounts
for bulk purchases for sales promotions, premiums, or fund-raising.
For information, please call or write:

Special Markets Department, HarperCollins Publishers,
10 East 53rd Street, New York, New York 10022-5299.
Telephone: (212) 207-7528.   Fax: (212) 207-7222.

LISTENING WOMAN

TONY HILLERMAN

HARPER

An Imprint of HarperCollinsPublishers

This is a work of fiction. Names, characters, places, and incidents are products of the author's imagination or are used fictitiously and are not to be construed as real. Any resemblance to actual events, locales, organizations, or persons, living or dead, is entirely coincidental.

HARPER

An Imprint of HarperCollins*Publishers*
195 Broadway,
New York, NY 10007.

Copyright © 1978 by Anthony G. Hillerman
ISBN 978-0-06-196776-4

First Harper Premium paperback printing: June 2010
First HarperTorch paperback printing: April 2002
First HarperPaperbacks printing: January 1990

A hardcover edition of this book was published in 1978 by Harper & Row, Publishers, Inc.

Printed in the United States of America

Visit Harper paperbacks on the World Wide Web at
www.harpercollins.com

10   9   8   7   6

LISTENING WOMAN

ONE

THE SOUTHWEST WIND picked up turbulence
around the San Francisco Peaks, howled across
the emptiness of the Moenkopi plateau, and made
a thousand strange sounds in windows of the old
Hopi villages at Shongopovi and Second Mesa.
Two hundred vacant miles to the north and east,
it sandblasted the stone sculptures of Monument
Valley Navajo Tribal Park and whistled eastward
across the maze of canyons on the Utah-Arizona
border. Over the arid immensity of the Nokaito
Bench it filled the blank blue sky with a rushing
sound. At the hogan of Hosteen Tso, at 3:17 P.M.,
it gusted and eddied, and formed a dust devil,
which crossed the wagon track and raced with a
swirling roar across Margaret Cigaret's old Dodge
pickup truck and past the Tso brush arbor. The
three people under the arbor huddled against the

driven dust. Tso covered his eyes with his hands and leaned forward in his rocking chair as the sand stung his naked shoulders. Anna Atcitty turned her back to the wind and put her hands over her hair because when this business was finished and she got Margaret Cigaret home again, she would meet the new boy from the Short Mountain Trading Post. And Mrs. Margaret Cigaret, who was also called Blind Eyes, and Listening Woman, threw her shawl over the magic odds and ends arrayed on the arbor table. She held down the edges of the shawl.

"Damn dirty wind," she said. "Dirty son-of-a-bitch."

"It's the Blue Flint boys playing tricks with it," Hosteen Tso said in his old man's voice. He wiped his eyes with the backs of his hands and looked after the whirlwind. "That's what my mother's father told me. The Blue Flint boys make the wind do that when they play one of their games."

Listening Woman put the shawl back around her shoulders, felt carefully among the assortment of bottles, brushes and fetishes on the table, selected a clear plastic prescription vial, and uncapped it.

"Don't think about that," she said. "Think about what we're doing. Think about how you got this trouble in your body." She poured a measure of yellow corn pollen from the vial and swiveled her blind face toward where the girl was standing. "You pay attention now, daughter-of-my-sister. We're going to bless this man with this pollen. You remember how we do that?"

"You sing the song of the Talking God," Anna Atcitty said. "The one about Born of Water and the Monster Slayer." She was a pretty girl, perhaps sixteen. The legends GANADO HIGH SCHOOL and TIGER PEP were printed across the front of her T-shirt.

Listening Woman sprinkled the pollen carefully over the shoulders of Hosteen Tso, chanting in low, melodic Navajo. From the cheekbone to the scalp, the left side of the old man's face was painted blue-black. Another patch of blackness covered his bony rib cage over his heart. Above that, the colorful curved stick figure of the Rainbow Man arched over Tso's chest from nipple to nipple—painted by Anna Atcitty in the ritual tints of blue, yellow, green and gray. He held his wiry body straight in the chair, his face stiff with sickness, patience and suppressed pain. Listening Woman's chant rose abruptly in volume. "In beauty it is finished," she sang. "In beauty it is finished."

"Okay," she said. "Now I will go and listen for the earth to tell me what makes you sick." She felt carefully across the plank table, collecting the fetishes and amulets of her profession, and then found her walking cane. She was a large woman, handsome once, dressed in the traditional voluminous skirt and blue velvet blouse of the People. She put the last of the vials in her black plastic purse, snapped it shut, and turned her sightless eyes toward Tso. "Think about it now, before I go. When you dream, you dream of your son who is dead and of that place you call the painted cave? You don't have any witch in that dream?" She paused, giving Tso a chance to answer.

"No," he said. "No witches."

"No dogs? No wolves? Nothing about Navajo Wolves?"

"Nothing about witches," Tso said. "I dream about the cave."

"You been with the whores over at Flagstaff? You been laying with any kinfolks?"

"Too old," Tso said. He smiled slightly.

"Been burning any wood struck by lightning?"

"No."

Listening Woman stood, face stern, staring past him with her blind eyes. "Listen, Old Man," she said, "I think you better tell me more about how these sand paintings got messed up. If you're worried about people knowing about it, Anna here can go away behind the hogan. Then nobody knows but you and me. And I don't tell secrets."

Hosteen Tso smiled, very slightly. "Now nobody

knows but me," he said, "and I don't tell secrets either."

"Maybe it will help tell why you're sick," Listening Woman said. "It sounds like witchery to me. Sand paintings getting messed up. If there was more than one sand painting at a time, then that would be doing the ceremonial wrong. That would be turning the blessing around. That would be witch business. If you been fooling around with the Navajo Wolves, then you're going to need a different kind of cure."

Tso's face was stubborn now. "Understand this, woman. A long time ago I made a promise. Some things I can't talk about."

The silence stretched, Listening Woman looking at whatever vision the blind see inside their skulls, Hosteen Tso staring out across the mesa, and Anna Atcitty, her face expressionless, waiting for the outcome of this contest.

"I forgot to tell you," Tso said. "On the same day the sand paintings got ruined, I killed a frog."

Listening Woman looked startled. "How?" she asked. In the complex Navajo metaphysics, the concept that would evolve into frogs was one of the Holy People. To kill the animals or insects which represented such holy thoughts violated a very basic taboo and was known to bring on crippling diseases.

"I was climbing among the rocks," Tso said. "A boulder fell down and crushed the frog."

"Before the sand paintings were messed up? Or after?"

"After," Tso said. He paused. "I talk no more about the sand paintings. I've told all that I can tell. The promise was to my father, and to the father of my father. If I have a ghost sickness, it would be a sickness from my great-grandfather's ghost, because I was where his ghost might be. I can tell you no more."

Listening Woman's expression was grim. "Why you want to waste your money, Old Man?" she asked. "You get me to come all the way out here to find out what kind of a cure you need. Now you won't tell me what I need to know."

Tso sat motionless, looking straight ahead.

Listening Woman waited, frowning.

"God damn it!" she said. "Some things I got to know. You think you been around some witches. Just being around them skinwalkers can make you sick. I got to know more about it."

Tso said nothing.

"How many witches?"

"It was dark," Tso said. "Maybe two."

"Did they do anything to you? Blow anything at you? Throw corpse powder on you? Anything like that?"

"No," Tso said.

"Why not?" Mrs. Cigaret asked. "Are you a Navajo Wolf yourself? You one of them witches?"

Tso laughed. It was a nervous sound. He glanced at Anna Atcitty—a look which asked help.

"I'm no skinwalker," he said.

"It was dark," said Listening Woman, almost mockingly. "But you said it was daytime. Were you in the witches' den?"

Tso's embarrassment turned to anger.

"Woman," he said, "I told you I couldn't talk about where it was. I made a promise. We will talk about that no more."

"Big secret," Mrs. Cigaret said. Her tone was sarcastic.

"Yes," Tso said. "A secret."

She made an impatient gesture. "Well, hell," she said. "You want to waste your money, no use me wasting my time. If I don't hear anything, or if I get it wrong, it's because you wouldn't tell me enough to know anything. Now Anna will take me to where I can hear the voice-in-the-earth. Don't mess with the painting on your chest. When I get back I will try to tell you what sing you need."

"Wait," Tso said. He hesitated. "One more thing. Do you know how to send a letter to somebody who went on the Jesus Road?"

Listening Woman frowned. "You mean moved off the Big Reservation? Ask Old Man McGinnis. He'll send it for you."

"I asked. McGinnis didn't know how," Tso said. "He said you had to write down on it the place it goes to."

Listening Woman laughed. "Sure," she said. "The address. Like Gallup, or Flagstaff, or wherever they live, and the name of the street they live on. Things like that. Who do you want to write to?"

"My grandson," Tso said. "I have to get him to come. But all I know is he went with the Jesus People."

"I don't know how you're going to find him," Listening Woman said. She found her cane. "Don't worry about it. Somebody else can take care of getting a singer for you and all that."

"But there's something I have to tell him," Hosteen Tso said. "I have to tell him something before I die. I have to."

"I don't know," Listening Woman said. She turned away from Tso and tapped the brush arbor pole with her cane, getting her direction. "Come on, Anna. Take me up to that place where I can listen."

Listening Woman felt the coolness of the cliff before its shadow touched her face. She had Anna lead her to a place where erosion had formed a sand-floored cul-de-sac. Then she sent the girl away to await her call. Anna was a good student in some ways, and a bad one in others. But when she got over being crazy about boys, she would be an effective Listener. This niece of Listening Woman's had the rare gift of hearing the voices in the wind and getting the visions that came out of the earth. It was something that ran in the family—a gift of divining the cause of illness. Her mother's uncle had been a Hand-Trembler famous throughout the Short Mountain territory for diagnosing lightning sickness. Listening Woman herself—she knew—was widely known up and down this corner of the Big Reservation. And someday Anna would be famous, too.

Listening Woman settled herself on the sand, arranged her skirts around her and leaned her forehead against the stone. It was cool, and rough. At first she found herself thinking about what Old Man Tso had told her, trying to diagnose his illness from that. There was something about Tso that troubled her and made her very sad. Then she cleared her mind of all this and thought only of the early-evening sky and the light of a single star. She made the star grow larger in her mind, remembering how it had looked before her blindness came.

An eddy of wind whistled through the piñons at the mouth of this pocket-in-the-cliff. It stirred the skirt of Listening Woman, uncovering a blue tennis shoe. But now her breathing was deep and regular. The shadow of the cliff moved inch by inch across the sandy space. Listening Woman moaned, moaned again, muttered something unintelligible and lapsed into silence.

From somewhere out of sight down the slope, a half-dozen ravens squawked into startled flight. The wind rose again, and fell. A lizard emerged from a crevice in the cliff, turned its cold, unblinking eyes on the woman, and then scurried to its late-afternoon hunting stand under a pile of tumbleweeds. A sound partly obscured by wind and distance reached the sandy place. A woman screaming. It rose and fell, sobbing. Then it stopped. The lizard caught a horsefly. Listening Woman breathed on.

The shadow of the cliff had moved fifty yards down the slope when Listening Woman pushed herself stiffly from the sand and got to her feet. She stood a moment with her head down and both hands pressed to her face—still half immersed in the strangeness of the trance. It was as if she had gone into the rock, and through it into the Black World at the very beginning—when there were only Holy People and the things that would become the Navajos were only mist. Finally she had heard the voice, and found herself in the Fourth World. She had looked down through the emergence hole, peering at Hosteen Tso in what must have been Tso's painted cave. An old man had rocked on a rocking chair on its floor, braiding his hair with string. At first it was

Tso, but when the man looked up at her she had seen the face was dead. Blackness was swelling up around the rocking chair.

Listening Woman rubbed her knuckles against her eyes, and shook her head, and called for Anna. She knew what the diagnosis would have to be. Hosteen Tso would need a Mountain Way Chant and a Black Rain Chant. There had been a witch in the painted cave, and Tso had been there, and had been infected with some sort of ghost sickness. That meant he should find a singer who knew how to do the Mountain Way and one to sing the Black Rain. She knew that. But she also thought that it would be too late. She shook her head again.

"Girl," she called. "I'm ready now."

What would she tell Tso? With the sensitized hearing of the blind, she listened for Anna Atcitty's footsteps. And heard nothing but the breeze.

"Girl," she shouted. "Girl!" Still hearing nothing, she fumbled against the cliff, and found her cane. She felt her way carefully back to the pathway toward the hogan. Should she tell Tso of the darkness she had seen all around as the voice spoke to her? Should she tell him of the crying of ghosts she had heard in the stone? Should she tell him he was dying?

Listening Woman's feet found the pathway. She called again for Anna, then shouted for Old

Man Tso to come and lead her. Waiting, she heard nothing but the moving air. She tapped her way cautiously down the sheep trail, muttering angrily. The tip of her cane warned her away from a cactus, guided her around a depression and past an outcrop of sandstone. It tapped against a hummock of dead grass and contacted the little finger of the outstretched left hand of Anna Atcitty. The hand lay palm up, and the wind had drifted a little sand against it, and even to Listening Woman's sensitive touch, it felt like nothing more than another stick. And so she tapped her way, still calling and muttering, down the path toward the place where the body of Hosteen Tso lay sprawled beside his overturned rocking chair— the Rainbow Man still arched across his chest.

TWO

THE SPEAKER ON the radio crackled and growled and said, "Tuba City."

"Unit Nine," Joe Leaphorn said. "You got anything for me?"

"Just a minute, Joe." The radio's voice was pleasantly feminine.

The young man sitting on the passenger side of the Navajo police carryall was staring out the window toward the sunset. The afterglow outlined the rough shape of the San Francisco Peaks on the horizon, and turned a lacy brushwork of high clouds luminescent rose, and reflected down on the desert below and onto the face of the man. It was a flat Mongolian face, with tiny lines around the eyes giving it a sardonic cast. He was wearing a black felt Stetson, a denim jacket and a rodeo-style shirt. On his left wrist was a $12.95

Timex watch held by a heavy sand-cast silver watchband, and his left wrist was fastened to his right one with a pair of standard-issue police handcuffs. He glanced at Leaphorn, caught his eye, and nodded toward the sunset.

"Yeah," Leaphorn said. "I noticed it."

The radio crackled again. "Two or three things," it said. "The captain asked if you got the Begay boy. He said if you got him, don't let him get away again."

"Yes, Ma'am," the young man said. "Tell the captain the Begay boy is in custody."

"I got him," Leaphorn said.

"Tell her I want the cell with the window this time," the young man said.

"Begay says he wants the cell with the window," Leaphorn said.

"And the waterbed," Begay said.

"And the captain wants to talk to you when you get in," the radio said.

"What about?"

"He didn't say."

"But I'll bet you know."

The radio speaker rattled with laughter. "Well," it said. "Window Rock called and asked the captain why you weren't over there helping out with the Boy Scouts. When will you be in?"

"We're coming down on Navajo Route 1 west of

Tsegi," Leaphorn said. "Be in Tuba City in maybe an hour." He flicked off the transmit button.

"What's this Boy Scout business?" Begay asked.

Leaphorn groaned. "Window Rock got the bright idea of inviting the Boy Scouts of America to have some sort of regional encampment at Canyon de Chelly. Kids swarming in from all over the West. And of course they tell Law and Order Division to make sure nobody gets lost or falls off a cliff or anything."

"Well," said Begay. "That's what we're paying you for."

Far to the left, perhaps ten miles up the dark Klethla Valley, a pinpoint of light was sliding along Route 1 toward them. Begay stopped admiring the sunset and watched the light. He whistled between his teeth. "Here comes a fast Indian."

"Yeah," Leaphorn said. He started the carryall rolling down the slope toward the highway and snapped off the headlights.

"That's sneaky," Begay said.

"Saves the battery," Leaphorn said.

"Pretty sneaky the way you got me, too," Begay said. There was no rancor in his words. "Parkin' over the hill and walkin' up to the hogan like that, so nobody figured you was a cop."

"Yeah," Leaphorn said.

"How'd you know I'd be there? You find out the Endischees was my people?"

"That's right," Leaphorn said.

"And you found out there was a Kinaalda for the Endischee girl?"

"Yeah," Leaphorn said. "So maybe you'd come to that."

Begay laughed. "And even if I didn't, it beat hell out of running all over looking for me." He glanced at Leaphorn. "You learn that in college?"

"Yeah," Leaphorn said. "We had a course on how to catch Begays."

The carryall jolted over a cattle guard and down the steep incline of the borrow ditch bank. Leaphorn parked on the shoulder and cut the ignition. It was almost night now—the afterglow dying on the western horizon and Venus hanging bright halfway up the sky. The heat had left with the light and now the thin high-altitude air was touched with coolness. A breeze stirred through the windows, carrying the faint sound of insects and the call of a hunting nighthawk. It died away, and when it came again it carried the high whine of engine and tires—still distant.

"Son-of-a-bitch is moving," Begay said. "Listen to that."

Leaphorn listened.

"Hundred miles an hour," Begay said. He chuckled. "He's going to tell you his speedometer needs fixing."

The headlights topped the hill, dipped downward and then raced up the slope behind them. Leaphorn started his engine and flicked on his headlights, and then the red warning blinker atop the car. For a moment there was no change in the accelerating whine. Then abruptly the pitch changed, a brief squealing sound of rubber on pavement, and the roar of a car gearing down. It pulled off on the shoulder and stopped some fifty feet behind the carryall. Leaphorn picked his clipboard off the dash and stepped out.

At first he could see nothing through the blinding glare of the headlights. Then he made out the circled Mercedes trademark on the hood, and behind the ornament, the windshield. Every two seconds, the beam of his revolving warning blinker flashed across it. Leaphorn walked down the gravel toward the car, irritated by the rudeness of the high-beam lights. In the flashing red illumination he saw the face of the driver, staring at him through round gold-rimmed glasses. And behind the man, in the back seat, another face, unusually large and oddly shaped.

The driver leaned out the window. "Officer," he shouted. "Your car's rolling backward."

The driver was grinning a broad, delighted,

anticipatory grin outlined in red by the blinker light. And behind the grinning man, the eyes in the narrow face still stared—dim but somehow avid—from the back seat.

Leaphorn spun and, blinded by glare, peered toward his carryall. His mind told him that he had set the handbrake and his eyes registered that the parked car was not rolling toward him. And then there was the voice of Begay screaming a warning. Leaphorn made a desperate, instinctive lunge for the ditch, hearing the squalling roar of the Mercedes accelerating, and then the thumping, oddly painless sound of the front fender striking his leg and spinning his already flying body into the roadside weeds.

A moment later he was trying to get up. The Mercedes had disappeared down the highway, trailing the diminishing scream of rapid acceleration, and Begay was beside him, helping him up.

"Watch the leg," Leaphorn said. "Let me see how it is."

It was numb, but it bore his weight. What pain he had was mostly in his hands, which had broken his fall on the weeds and dirt of the ditch bank, and his cheek—which somehow had picked up a long, but shallow, cut. It burned.

"Son-of-a-bitch tried to run you over," Begay said. "How about that?"

Leaphorn limped to the carryall, slid under the

wheel, and flicked on the radio with one bleeding hand and the ignition with the other. By the time he had arranged for a roadblock at Red Lake, the speedometer needle had passed 90.

"Always wanted a ride like this," Begay was shouting over the sound of the siren. "The tribe got a liability policy in case I get hurt?"

"Just burial insurance," Leaphorn said.

"You're never going to catch him," Begay said. "You get a look at that car? That was a rich man's car."

"You get a look at the license? Or at that guy in the back seat?"

"It was a dog," Begay said. "Great big rough-looking dog. I didn't think about the license."

The radio cleared its throat. It was Tomas Charley reporting he was set up in a half block at the Red Lake intersection. Charley asked, in precise Navajo, whether to figure the man in the gray car had a gun and how to handle it.

"Play it like he's dangerous," Leaphorn said. "The bastard tried to run over me. Use the shotgun and if he's not slowing for you, shoot for the tires. Don't get hurt."

Charley said he didn't intend to and signed off.

"He might have a gun, come to think of it," Begay said. He held his cuffed wrists in front of him. "You oughta take this off in case you need help."

Leaphorn glanced at him, fished in his pocket for a key ring and tossed it on the seat. "It's the little shiny one."

Begay unlocked the cuffs and put them in the glove compartment.

"Why the hell don't you stop stealing sheep?" Leaphorn asked. He didn't want to remember the Mercedes roaring toward him.

Begay rubbed his wrists. "They're just white man's sheep. They don't hardly miss 'em."

"And slipping off from jail. Do that again and it's your ass!"

Begay shrugged. "Stop to think about it, though," he said. "And about the worst they can do to you for getting out of jail is get you back in again."

"This is three times," Leaphorn said. The patrol car skidded around a flat turn, swayed, and straightened. Leaphorn jammed down on the accelerator.

"That bird sure didn't want a ticket," Begay said. He glanced at Leaphorn, grinning. "Either that, or he just likes running over cops. I believe a man could learn to enjoy that."

They covered the last twenty miles to the Red Lake intersection in just under thirteen minutes and slid to a gravel-spraying stop on the shoulder beside Charley's patrol car.

"What happened?" Leaphorn shouted. "Did he get past you?"

"Never got here," Charley said. He was a stocky man wearing a corporal's stripes on the sleeves of his uniform shirt. He raised his eyebrows. "Ain't no place to turn off," he said. "It's fifty-something miles back up there to the Kayenta turnoff—"

"He was past that when I started chasing him," Leaphorn interrupted. "He must have pulled it off somewhere."

Begay laughed. "That dog in the back. Maybe that was a Navajo Wolf."

Leaphorn didn't say anything. He was spinning the car across the highway in a pursuit turn.

"Them witches, they can fly, you know," Begay said. "Reckon they could carry along a big car like that?"

It took more than half an hour to find where the Mercedes had left the highway. It had pulled off the north shoulder on the upslope of a hill— leaving the roadbed and plowing through a thin growth of creosote bush. Leaphorn followed the track with his flashlight in one hand and his .38 in the other. Begay and Charley trotted along behind him—Begay carrying Leaphorn's 30-30. About fifty yards off the highway, the car had bottomed on an outcrop of sandstone. After that, its path was blotched with oil spurting from a broken pan.

"Hell of a way to treat a car," Begay said.

They found it thirty yards away, rolled into a

shallow arroyo out of sight from the highway. Leaphorn studied it a moment in the beam of his flashlight. He walked up to it cautiously. The driver's door was open. So was the trunk. The front seat was empty. So was the back seat. The front floorboards were littered with the odds and ends of a long trip—gum wrappers, paper cups, the wrapper from a Lotaburger. Leaphorn picked it up and sniffed it. It smelled of onions and fried meat. He dropped it. The nearest Lotaburger stand he could remember was at Farmington—about 175 miles east in New Mexico. The safety inspection sticker inside the windshield had been issued by the District of Columbia. It bore the name of Frederick Lynch, and a Silver Spring, Maryland, address. Leaphorn jotted it in his notebook. The car, he noticed, smelled of dog urine.

"He didn't leave nothing much back here," Charley said. "But here's a muzzle for a dog. A big one."

"I guess he went for a walk," Leaphorn said. "He's got a lot of room for that."

"Thirty miles to a drink of water," Charley said. "If you know where to find it."

"Begay," Leaphorn said. "Take a look in back and give me the license number."

As he said it, it occurred to Leaphorn that his bruised leg, no longer numb, was aching. It also occurred to him that he hadn't seen Begay since after they'd found the car. Leaphorn scrambled out of the front seat and made a rapid survey of the landscape with the flashlight. There was Corporal Charley, still inspecting the back seat, and there was Leaphorn's 30-30 leaning against the trunk of the Mercedes, with Leaphorn's key ring hung on the barrel.

Leaphorn cupped his hands and shouted into the darkness: "Begay, you dirty bastard!" Begay was out there, but he would be laughing too hard to answer.

THREE

THE FILE CLERK in the Tuba City subagency of the Navajo Tribal Police was slightly plump and extremely pretty. She deposited a yellow Manila folder and three brown accordion files on the captain's desk, flashed Leaphorn a smile and departed with a swish of skirt.

"You already owe me one favor," Captain Largo said. He picked up the yellow folder and peered into it.

"This will make two, then," Leaphorn said.

"If I do it, it will," Largo said. "I may not be that dumb."

"You'll do it," Leaphorn said.

Largo ignored him. "Here we have a little business that just came in today," Largo said from behind the folder. "A discreet inquiry is needed into the welfare of a woman named Theodora

Adams, who is believed to be at Short Mountain Trading Post. Somebody in the office of the Chairman of the Tribal Council would appreciate it if we'd do a little quiet checking so he can pass on the word that all is well."

Leaphorn frowned. "At Short Mountain? What would anyone—"

Largo interrupted him. "There's an anthropological dig out there. Maybe she's friendly with one of the diggers. Who knows? All I know is her daddy is a doctor in the Public Health Service and I guess he called somebody in the Bureau of Indian Affairs, and the BIA called somebody in . . ."

"Okay," Leaphorn said. "She's out in Indian country and daddy's worried and would we look out after her—right?"

"But discreetly," Largo said. "That would save me a little work, if you'd take care of that. But it won't look like much of an excuse to ask Window Rock to let you off guarding those Boy Scouts." Largo handed Leaphorn the Manila folder and pulled the accordion files in front of him. "Maybe there's an excuse in these," he said. "You can take your pick."

"I'll take an easy one," Leaphorn said.

"Here we have a little heroin stashed in the frame of a junk car over near the Keet Seel ruins," said Largo as he peered into one of the files. He closed the folder. "Had a tip on it and staked it out, but nobody ever showed up. That was last winter."

"Never any arrests?"

"Nope." Largo had pulled a bundle of papers and two tape cassettes out of another folder. "Here's the Tso-Atcitty killing," he said. "You remember that one? It was last spring."

"Yeah," Leaphorn said. "I meant to ask you about that one. Heard anything new?"

"Nada," Largo said. "Nothing. Not even any sensible gossip. Little bit of witch talk now and then. The kind of talk something like that stirs up. Not a damn thing to go on."

They sat and thought about it.

"You got any ideas?" Leaphorn asked.

Largo thought about it some more. "No sense to it," he said finally.

Leaphorn said nothing. There had to be sense to it. A reason. It had to fit some pattern of cause and effect. Leaphorn's sense of order insisted on this. And if the cause happened to be insane by normal human terms, Leaphorn's intellect would then hunt for harmony in the kaleido-scopic reality of insanity.

"You think the FBI missed something?" Leaphorn asked. "They screw it up?"

"They usually do," Largo said. "Whether they did or not, it's been long enough so we really ought to be checking around on it again." He stared at Leaphorn. "You any better at that than at bringing in prisoners?"

Leaphorn ignored the jibe. "Okay," he said. "You tell Window Rock you want me to work on the Atcitty case, and I'll run over to Short Mountain and check on the Adams woman, too. And I'll owe *you* a favor."

"Two favors," Largo said.

"What's the other one?"

Largo had put on a pair of horn-rimmed bifocals and was thumbing his way owlishly through the Atcitty report. "I didn't hoorah you for letting that Begay boy get away. That's the first one." He glanced at Leaphorn. "But I'm not so damn sure this second one's any favor. Dreaming up reasons to borrow you from Window Rock so you can go chasing after that feller that tried to run you down. That's not so damned smart—getting mixed up in your own thing. We'll find that feller for you."

Leaphorn said nothing. Somewhere back in the subagency building there was a sudden metallic clamor—a jail inmate rattling something against the bars. Outside the west-facing windows of Largo's office an old green pickup rolled down the asphalt road into Tuba City, trailing a thin haze of blue smoke. Largo sighed and began sorting the Atcitty papers and tapes back into the file.

"Herding Boy Scouts is not so bad," Largo said. "Broken leg or so. Few snakebites. One or two of them lost." He glanced up at Leaphorn, frowning. "You got nothing much to go on, looking for that guy, anyway. You don't even know what he looks like. Gold-rim glasses. Hell, I'm about the only one in this building that doesn't wear 'em. And all you really know is that they were wire rims. Just seeing 'em with that red blinker reflecting off of 'em—that would distort the color."

"You're right," Leaphorn said.

"I'm right, but you're going to go ahead on with it," Largo said. "If I can find an excuse for you."

He tapped the remaining file with a blunt fingertip, changing the subject. "And here's one that's always popular—the vanishing helicopter," Largo said. "The feds love that one. Every month we need to turn in a report telling 'em we haven't found it but we haven't forgotten it. This time we've got a new sighting report to look into."

Leaphorn frowned. "A new one? Isn't it getting kinda late for that?"

Largo grinned. "Oh, I don't know," he said. "What's a few months? Let's see—it was December when we were running our asses off in the snow up and down the canyons, looking for it. So now it's August, and somebody gets around to coming into Short Mountain and mentioning he's seen the damn thing." Largo shrugged. "Nine months? That's about right for a Short Mountain Navajo."

Leaphorn laughed. Short Mountain Navajos had a long-standing reputation among their fellow Dinee for being uncooperative, slow, cantankerous, witch-ridden and generally backward.

"Three kinds of time." Largo was still grinning. "On time, and Navajo time, and Short Mountain Navajo time." The grin disappeared. "Mostly Bitter Water Dinee, and Salts, and Many Goats people live out there," he said.

It wasn't exactly an explanation. It was absolution from this criticism of the fifty-seven other Navajo clans, including the Slow Talking Dinee. The Slow Talking Dinee was Captain Howard Largo's "born-to" clan. Leaphorn was also a member of the Slow Talking People. That made him and Largo something akin to brothers in the Navajo Way, and explained why Leaphorn could ask Largo for a favor, and why Largo could hardly refuse to grant it.

"Funny people," Leaphorn agreed.

"Lots of Paiutes live back in there," Largo added. "Lots of marrying back and forth." Largo's face had resumed its usual glumness. "Even a lot of marrying with the Utes."

Through the dusty window of Largo's office Leaphorn had been watching a thunderhead building over Tuba Mesa. Now it produced a distant rumble of thunder, as if the Holy People themselves were protesting this mixing of the blood of the Dinee with their ancient enemies.

"Anyway, the one who says she saw it wasn't really nine months late," Largo said. "She told a veterinarian out there looking at her sheep about it in June." Largo paused and peered into the folder. ". . . And the vet told the feller then that drives the school bus out there, and he told Shorty McGinnis about it back in July. And about three days ago, Tomas Charley was out there and McGinnis told *him*." Largo paused, and looked up at Leaphorn through his bifocals. "You know McGinnis?"

Leaphorn laughed. "From way back when I was new and working out of here. He was sort of a one-man radar station/listening post/gossip collector. I remember I used to think it wouldn't be too hard to catch him doing something worth about ten years in stir. He still have that place up for sale?"

"That place has been for sale for forty years," Largo said. "If somebody offered to buy it, it'd scare McGinnis to death."

"That sighting report," Leaphorn said. "Anything helpful?"

"Naw," Largo said. "She was driving her sheep out of a gully, and just as she came out of it, the

copter came over just a few feet off the ground."
Largo waved his hand impatiently at the file. "It's
all in there. Scared the hell out of her. Her horse
threw her and ran off and it scattered the sheep.
Charley went to talk to her day before yesterday.
Said she was still pissed off about it."

"Was it the right copter?"

Largo shrugged. "Blue and yellow or black and
yellow. She remembered that. And pretty big.
And noisy. Maybe it was, and maybe it wasn't."

"Was it the right day?"

"Seemed to be," Largo said. "She was bringing
in the sheep because she was taking her husband
and the rest of the bunch to a Yeibachi over at
Spider Rock the next day. Charley checked on it
and the ceremonial was the day after the Santa
Fe robbery. So that's the right day."

"What time?"

"That's about right, too. Just getting dark, she
said."

They thought about it. Outside there was
thunder again.

"Think we could have missed it?" Largo asked.

"We could have," Leaphorn said. "You could
hide Kansas City out there. But I don't think we
did."

"I don't either," Largo said. "You'd have to land
it someplace where you can get someplace else
from. Like near a road."

"Exactly," Leaphorn said.

"And if they left it near a road, somebody would have come across it by now." Largo extracted a pack of Winstons from his shirt pocket, offered them to Leaphorn, and then lit one for himself. "It's funny, though," he said.

"Yes," Leaphorn said. The strangest part of it all, he thought, was how well the entire plan had stuck together, how well it had been coordinated, how well it had worked. You didn't expect such meticulous planning from a militant political group—and the Buffalo Society was as militant as they get. It had split off from the American Indian Movement after the AIM's seizure of Wounded Knee had fizzled away into nothing—accusing the movement's leaders of being gutless. It had mailed out a formal declaration of war against the whites. It had pulled a series of bombings, and two kidnappings that Leaphorn could remember, and finally this affair at Santa Fe. There, a Wells Fargo armored truck leaving the First National Bank of Santa Fe had been detoured down one of Santa Fe's narrow old streets by a man wearing a city policeman's uniform. Other Society members had simultaneously congealed downtown traffic to a motionless standstill by artfully placed detour signs. There had been a brief fight at the truck and a Society member had been critically wounded and left behind. But the gang had blasted off the truck door and escaped with almost $500,000. The copter had been reserved at the Santa Fe airport for a charter flight. It had taken off with a single passenger about the same moment the Wells Fargo truck had left the bank. It hadn't been missed, in the excitement, until the pilot's wife had called the charter company late that night worrying about her husband. Checking back the next day, police learned it had been seen taking off from the Sangre de Cristo Mountain foothills just east of Santa Fe about an hour after the robbery. It was seen, and definitely identified, a little later by a pilot approaching the Los Alamos airport. It had been headed almost due west, flying low. It had been seen—and almost definitely identified—about sundown by a Gas Company of New Mexico pipeline monitoring crew working northeast of Farmington. Again it was flying low and fast, and still heading west. A copter, this time identified only as black and yellow and flying low, had been reported by the driver of a Greyhound bus crossing U.S. 666 northwest of Shiprock. These reports had been coupled with the fact that the missing copter's full-tank range was only enough to fly it from Santa Fe to less than halfway across the Navajo Reservation and had caused the Navajo Police a full week of hard and fruitless searching.

The FBI report on this affair showed the copter had been reserved by telephone the previous day in the name of the local engineering company which often chartered it, that a passenger had emerged from a blue Ford sedan and boarded the copter without anyone getting much of a look at him, and that the Ford had thereupon driven away. A check disclosed that the engineering company had not reserved the copter and there was absolutely nothing else to go on. The FBI noted that while it had no doubt the copter had been used to fly away seven large sacks of bulky cash, the connection was purely circumstantial. Again, the planning had been perfect.

"Oh, well," Largo said. He removed his glasses, frowned at them, ran his tongue over the lenses, polished them quickly with his handkerchief, and put them on again. He lowered his chin and peered at Leaphorn through the upper half of the bifocals. "Here they are," he said, sliding the accordion files and the folder across the desktop. "Old heroin case, old homicide, old missing aircraft, and new 'herd the tourist' job."

"Thanks," Leaphorn said.

"For what?" Largo asked. "Getting you into trouble? *You* know what I think, Joe? This isn't smart at all, this getting personal about this guy. That ain't good business in our line of work. Whyn't you forget it and go on over to Window Rock and help take care of the Boy Scouts? We'll catch this fellow for you."

"You're right," Leaphorn said. He tried to think of a way to explain to Largo what he felt. Would Largo understand if Leaphorn described how the man had grinned as he tried to kill him? Probably not, Leaphorn thought, because he didn't understand it himself.

"I'm right," Largo said, "but you're going after him anyway?"

Leaphorn got up and walked to the window. The thunderhead was drifting eastward, trailing rain which didn't quite reach the thirsty ground. The huge old cottonwoods that lined Tuba City's single paved street looked dusty and wilted.

"It's not just getting even with him," Leaphorn said to the window. "I think a guy that laughs when he tries to kill someone is dangerous. That's a lot of it."

Largo nodded. "And a lot of it is that it doesn't make sense to you. I know you, Joe. You've got to have everything sorted out so it's natural. You got to know how come that guy left his car there and headed north on foot." Largo smiled and made a huge gesture of dismissal. "Hell, man. He just got scared and ran for it. And he didn't show up today hitchhiking because he got lost out there. Another day he'll come wandering up to some hogan begging for water."

"Maybe," Leaphorn said. "But nobody's seen him. And his tracks didn't wander. They headed due north—like he knew where he was going."

"Maybe he did," Largo said. "Figure it this way. This tourist . . . What's the name of the Mercedes owner? This Frederick Lynch stops at a bar in Farmington, and one of those Short Mountain boys wanders out of the same bar, sees his car parked there, and drives it off. When you stopped him, he just dumped the car and headed home on foot."

"That's probably right," Leaphorn said.

On the way out, Leaphorn met the plump clerk coming in. She had two reports relayed by the Arizona State Police from Washington and Silver Spring, Maryland. Frederick Lynch lived at the address indicated on his car registration form, and was not known to Silver Spring police. The only item on the record was a complaint that he kept vicious dogs. He was not now at home and was last reported seen by a neighbor seven days earlier. The other report was a negative reply from the stolen-car register. If the Lynch Mercedes had been stolen in Maryland, New Mexico or anywhere else, the crime had not yet been reported.

FOUR

THERE IS NO way that one man, or one thousand
men, can search effectively the wilderness of stony
erosion which sprawls along the Utah-Arizona
border south of the Rainbow Plateau. Lieutenant
Joe Leaphorn didn't try. Instead he found Corporal Emerson Bisti. Corporal Bisti had been born
at Kaibito Wash and spent his boyhood with his
mother's herds in the same country. Since the
Korean War, he'd patrolled this same desert as a
Navajo policeman. He went over Leaphorn's map
carefully, marking in all the places where water
could be found. There weren't many. Then Bisti
went over the map again and checked off those
that dried up after the spring runoff, or that held
water only a few weeks after rainstorms. That
left only eleven. Two were at trading posts—
Navajo Springs and Short Mountain. One was at

Tsai Skizzi Rock and one was a well drilled by the Tribal Council to supply the Zilnez Chapter House. A stranger couldn't approach any of these places without being noticed, and Captain Largo's patrolmen had checked them all.

By late afternoon, Leaphorn had pared the remaining seven down to four. At the first three watering places he had found a maze of tracks—sheep, horses, humans, dogs, coyotes, and the prints of the menagerie of small mammals and reptiles that teem in the most barren deserts. The tracks of the man who had abandoned the Mercedes were not among them. Nor were any of the dog tracks large enough to match those Leaphorn had found at the abandoned Mercedes.

Even with Bisti's markings on his map, Leaphorn almost missed the next watering place. The first three had been easy enough to locate—marked either by the animal trails that radiated from them or by the cottonwoods they sustained in a landscape otherwise too arid for greenery. But Bisti's tiny "x" put the fourth one in a trackless world of red Chinle sandstone.

The long-abandoned wagon track that led toward this spring had been easy to find. Leaphorn had jolted down the seven point eight miles specified by Bisti's instructions and parked at a great outcropping of black shale as advised. Then he had walked two miles northeast by east toward the red butte which Bisti said overlooked the water hole. He found himself surrounded by carved rock without a trace of water or a hint of vegetation. He had searched in widening circles, climbing sandstone walls, skirting sandstone escarpments, engulfed in a landscape where the only colors were shades of pink and red. Finally he had scrambled to the top of a flat-topped pinnacle and perched there. He scanned the surroundings below him with his binoculars—looking for a trace of green, which would declare water, or for something that would suggest the geological fault that would produce a spring. Finding nothing helpful, he waited. Bisti had been a boy in this country. He would not be mistaken about water. Surface water in this desert would be a magnet for life. In time, nature would reveal itself. Leaphorn would wait and think. He was good at both.

The thunderhead that promised a shower to Tuba Mesa in the morning had drifted eastward over the Painted Desert and evaporated—the promise unfulfilled. Now another, taller thunderhead had climbed the sky to the north—over the slopes of Navajo Mountain in Utah. The color under it was blue-black, suggesting that on one small quadrant of mountainside the blessed rain was falling. Far to the southeast, blue and dim with distance, another towering cloud had risen over the Chuskas on the Arizona–New Mexico border. There were other promising clouds to the south, drifting over the Hopi Reservation. The Hopis had held a rain dance Sunday, calling on the clouds—their ancestors—to restore the water blessing to the land. Perhaps the kachinas had listened to their Hopi children. Perhaps not. It was not a Navajo concept, this idea of adjusting nature to human needs. The Navajo adjusted himself to remain in harmony with the universe. When nature withheld the rain, the Navajo sought the pattern of this phenomenon—as he sought the pattern of all things—to find its beauty and live in harmony with it.

Now Leaphorn sought some pattern in the conduct of the man who had tried to kill a policeman rather than accept a speeding ticket. Into what circumstances would such an action fit? Leaphorn sat, motionless as the stone beneath him, and considered a variation of Captain Largo's theory. The man with the gold-rimmed glasses was not Frederick Lynch. He was a Navajo who had killed Lynch, and had taken his car, and was running for cover in familiar country. A dead Lynch could not report his car stolen. And that would explain why Goldrims had headed so directly and confidently into the desert. As Largo had suggested, he was merely going home. He hadn't stopped for a drink at one of the nearer water holes because he had a bottle of water in the car, or because he had been willing to spend a hideously thirsty twenty-four hours rather than risk being tracked.

Leaphorn considered alternative theories, found none that made sense, and returned to Goldrims-is-Navajo. But what, then, about the dog? Why would a Navajo car thief take the victim's dog with him? Why would the dog—mean enough to require a muzzle—allow a stranger to steal his master's car? Why would the Navajo take the dog along with him at the risk of being bitten? Odder still, why had the dog followed this stranger?

Leaphorn sighed. None of the questions could be answered. Everything about this affair offended his innate sense of order. He began considering a Goldrims-is-Lynch theory and got nowhere with it. A pair of horned lark flicked past him and glided over a great hump of sandstone near the mesa wall. They did not reappear. A half hour earlier a small flight of doves had disappeared for at least five minutes in the same area. Leaphorn had been conscious of that point—among others—since seeing a young Cooper's hawk pause in its patrol of the mesa rim to circle over it. He climbed carefully from his perch. The birds had found the water for him.

The spring was at the bottom of a narrow declivity at a place where the sandstone met a harder formation of limestone. Thousands of years of wind had given this slot a floor of dust and sand, which supported a stunted juniper, a hummock of grama grass and a few tumbleweeds. Leaphorn had circled within a hundred yards of this hole without guessing its presence, and had missed a sheep trail leading into it through the tough luck of encountering the path at the place where it crossed track-resistant limestone. Now he squatted on the sand and considered what it had to tell him. There were tracks everywhere. Old and new. Among the new ones, the cloven hoofs of a small flock of sheep and goats, the pawprints of dogs, at least three, and the prints of the same boots in which Goldrims had walked away from his abandoned Mercedes. Leaphorn examined a rim of sand in a bootprint near the water, fingered it, tested its moisture content, considered the state of the weather, and weighed in cool humidity in this shadowed place. Goldrims had been here not many hours ago—probably not long before noon. The dog was still with him. Those tracks, almost grotesquely large for a dog, were everywhere. The other dogs had been here about the same time. Leaphorn studied the sandy floor. He examined an indentation, made by an oblong rectangle eighteen inches long and eight inches wide. It was either fairly heavy, or had been dropped on the damp sand. He examined another place, much more vague, where some sort of pressure had smoothed the sand. He studied this from several angles, with his face close to the earth. He concluded, finally, that Goldrims might have rested a canvas backpack here. Not far from where the backpack had been, Leaphorn picked up a bead-sized ball of sand. It flattened between thumb and forefinger into a sticky, gritty red. A droplet of drying blood. Leaphorn sniffed it, touched it with his tongue, cleaned his fingers with sand, and trotted partway up the sloping wall of the pocket. He stood looking down on the basin. Across the shallow pool a section of sand was smooth—its collection of tracks erased.

Leaphorn did not think about what he might find. He simply dug, scooping the damp sand out with his hands and piling it to the side. Less than a foot below the surface, his fingers encountered hair.

The hair was white. Leaphorn rocked back on his heels, giving himself a moment to absorb his surprise. Then he poked with an exploring finger. The hair was attached to a dog's ear, which, when pulled, produced from the engulfing sand the head of a large dog. Leaphorn pulled this body from its shallow grave. As he did so he saw the foreleg of a second dog. He stretched the two animals side by side near the water, dipped his hat into the pool to rinse the sand from the bodies, and began a careful examination. They were a large brown-and-white male mongrel and a slightly smaller, mostly black female. The female had teeth gashes across its back but had apparently died of a broken neck. The male had its throat torn out.

Leaphorn put on his wet hat, tipped it back and stood looking down at the animals. He stood long enough to feel the chill of evaporation on the back of his head, and to hear the call of a horned lark from somewhere back among the boulders, and the voice of an early owl from the mesa. And then he climbed out of the darkening basin and began walking rapidly back toward the place he had left his carryall.

The San Francisco Peaks made a dark blue bump against the yellow glare of the horizon. The cloud over Navajo Mountain was luminescent pink and the sandstone wilderness through which Leaphorn walked had become a universe of vermilion under this slanting light. Normally Leaphorn would have drunk in this dramatic beauty, and been touched by it. Now he hardly noticed it. He was thinking of other things.

He thought of a man named Frederick Lynch who had walked directly across thirty miles of ridges and canyons to a hidden spring. And when Leaphorn pushed this impossibility aside, his thoughts turned to sheepdogs and how they work, and fight, as a trained team. He thought of Lynch and his dog reaching the water hole, finding the flock there with the two dogs that had brought the sheep on guard. He tried to visualize the fight—the male dog staging a fighting retreat probably, while the female slashed at the flank. Then, with this diversion, the male going for the throat. Leaphorn had seen many such dogfights. But he'd never seen the single dog, no matter how fierce, manage better than a howling defeat. What would have happened had the shepherd—probably a child—come along with his dogs? And what would this shepherd think tomorrow when he came and found his dead helpers? Leaphorn shook his head. Incidents like this kept the tales of skinwalkers alive. No boy would be willing to believe his two dogs could be killed by a single animal. But he could believe, without loss of faith in his animals, that a witch had killed them. A werewolf was more than a match for a pack of dogs. Nothing could face a skinwalker.

Leaphorn turned away from this unproductive thought, to the fact that Goldrims seemed not to be running away from his affair with the Navajo police, but hurrying toward something. But what? And where? And why? Leaphorn drew an imaginary line on an imaginary map from the place where Lynch had abandoned the car to the water hole. And then he projected it northward. The line extended between Navajo Mountain and Short Mountain—into the Nokaito Bench and onward into the bottomless stone wilderness of the Glen Canyon country, and across Lake Powell Reservoir. It ran, Leaphorn thought, not far at all from the hogan on Nokaito Bench where an old man named Hosteen Tso and a girl named Anna Atcitty had been killed three months ago. Leaphorn wound his way through the sandstone landscape, his khaki-uniformed figure dwarfed by the immense outcroppings and turned red by the dying light. He was thinking now about why these two persons might have died. By the time he reached his vehicle, he decided he would get to the Short Mountain Trading Post tomorrow. Tonight he would read the Tso-Atcitty file and try to find an answer to that question.

That evening at Tuba City, Leaphorn read carefully through the three reports Largo had given him. The heroin affair provoked little thought. A small plastic package of heroin, uncut and worth perhaps five thousand dollars at wholesale, had been found taped behind the dashboard of an old stripped car which had been rusting away for years about seven miles from the Keet Seel ruins. The find had been made as a result of an anonymous call received at the Window Rock headquarters. The caller had been a female. The heroin had been removed and the package refilled with powdered white sugar and replaced. The cache had been watched, closely for a week and then loosely for a month. Finally it was merely checked periodically. No one had ever tampered with the plastic package. That could be easily explained. Probably the buyer or seller had scented the trap and the cache had been written off as a loss. And because it could be easily explained, it didn't interest Lieutenant Joe Leaphorn.

The affair of the missing helicopter was more challenging. The original sighting reports were familiar, as was the map on which a line had been penciled to connect them and recreate the copter's path, because Leaphorn had studied them while the search was under way. The map's line curved and jiggled erratically. Significantly, it tended to stick to empty country, avoiding Aztec, Farmington and Shiprock in New Mexico, and—as it entered the interior of the Big Reservation—skirting away from trading posts and water wells where people would be likely to see it.

There had been a definite, clear-cut sighting

fifteen miles north of Teec Nos Pos and after that the line became sketchy and doubtful. It zigzagged, with question marks beside most of the sighting points. Leaphorn flipped through more recent reports of sightings—those which had accumulated gradually in the months since the hunt had been called off. For the first two months, someone had kept the map current, revising the line to match the fresh reports. But this fruitless project had been abandoned. Leaphorn fished out his ballpoint pen and spent a few minutes bringing the job up to date, which confirmed the existing line without extending it. It still faded away about one hundred miles east of Short Mountain—perhaps because the copter had landed, or perhaps because there simply were no people in the empty landscape to see it pass. Leaphorn put down the pen and thought. Almost forty men had hunted the copter, crisscrossing the Navajo Mountain-Short Mountain wilderness, questioning everybody who could be found to question, and finding absolutely nothing.

The sightings had been sorted into three categories: "definite-probable," "possible-doubtful," and "unlikely." The ghost and witchcraft talk was in the "unlikely" grouping. Leaphorn examined it.

One sighting involved a twelve-year-old girl,

hurrying to get home before dark. A noise and a light in the evening sky. The sounds of ghosts crying in the wind. The sight of a black beast moving through the sky. The girl had run, crying, to her mother's hogan. No one else had heard anything. The investigating officer discounted it. Leaphorn checked the location. It was almost thirty miles south of the line.

The next sighting was from an old man, again hurrying back to his hogan to avoid the ghosts which would be coming out in the gathering darkness. He had heard a thumping in the sky and had seen a wolf flying—outlined black against the dim red afterglow on the stone face of a mesa wall. This, too, was south of the wildest zigzag of the line.

The others were similar. An old woman cutting wood, startled by a sound and a moving light overhead, and the noise returning four times from the four symbolic directions as she crouched in her hogan; a Dinne-hotso schoolboy on a visit to a relative, watching a coyote on a cliff near the south shore of Lake Powell. He reported that the coyote disappeared and moments later he'd heard a flapping of wings and had seen something like a dark bird diving toward the lake surface and disappearing like a duck diving for a fish. And finally, a young man seeing a great black bird flying over the highway north of Mexican Water and turning itself into a truck as it passed him, and then flying again as it disappeared to the west. This report, picked up by an Arizona highway patrolman, bore the notation: "Subject reportedly drunk at time."

Leaphorn marked each sighting location on the map with a tiny circle. The flying truck was close enough to the line to fit the pattern and the diving coyote/bird would fit if the line was extended about forty miles westward and jogged sharply northward.

Leaphorn yawned and slid the map back into the accordion file. Probably the helicopter had landed somewhere, refueled from a waiting truck, and flown through the covering night to a hiding place well away from the search area. He picked up the Atcitty-Tso homicide file, with a sense of anticipation. This one, as he remembered it, defied all applications of logic.

He read swiftly through the uncomplicated facts. A niece of Hosteen Tso had arranged for Mrs. Margaret Cigaret, a Listener of considerable reputation in the Rainbow Plateau country, to find out what was causing the old man to be ill. Mrs. Cigaret was blind. She had been driven to the Tso hogan by Anna Atcitty, a daughter of Mrs. Cigaret's sister. The usual examination had been conducted. Mrs. Cigaret had left the hogan to go into her trance and do her listening. While she was in her trance, someone had killed the Tso and Atcitty subjects by hitting them on the head with what might have been a metal pipe or a gun barrel. Mrs. Cigaret had heard nothing. As far as could be determined, nothing was taken from either of the victims or from the hogan. An FBI agent named Jim Feeney, out of Flagstaff, had worked the case with the help of a BIA agent and two of Largo's men. Leaphorn knew Feeney and considered him substantially brighter than the run-of-the-mill FBI man. He knew one of the men Largo had assigned. Also bright. The investigation had been conducted as Leaphorn would have run it—a thorough hunt for a motive. The four-man team had presumed, as Leaphorn would have presumed, that the killer had come to the Tso hogan not knowing that the two women were there, that the Atcitty girl had been killed simply to eliminate a witness, and that Mrs. Cigaret had lived because she hadn't been visible. And so the team had searched for someone with a reason to kill Hosteen Tso, interviewing, sifting rumors, learning everything about an old man except a motive for his death.

With all Tso leads exhausted, the team reversed the theory and hunted for a motive for the murder of Anna Atcitty. They laid bare the life of a fairly typical reservation teen-ager, with a circle of friends at Tuba City High School, a circle of cousins, two and possibly three nonserious boyfriends. No hint of any relationship intense enough to inspire either love or hate, or motive for murder.

The final report had included a rundown on witchcraft gossip. Three interviewees had speculated that Tso was the victim of a witch and there was a modest amount of speculation that the old man was himself a skinwalker. Considering that this corner of the reservation was notoriously backward and witch-ridden, it was about the level of witchcraft gossip that Leaphorn had expected.

Leaphorn closed the report and slipped it into its folder, fitting it beside the tape cassette that held what Margaret Cigaret had told the police. He slumped down in his chair, rubbed the back of his hand across his eyes, and sat—trying to recreate what had happened at the Tso hogan. Whoever had come there must have come to kill the old man—not the girl because it would have been simpler to kill her elsewhere. But what had caused the old man to be killed? There seemed to be no answer to that. Leaphorn decided that before he left for Short Mountain in the morning he would borrow a tape deck so that he could play back the Margaret Cigaret interview while he drove. Perhaps learning what Listening Woman thought had made Hosteen Tso sick might cast some light on what had made him die.

FIVE

LISTENING WOMAN'S VOICE accompanied Joe
Leaphorn eastward up Navajo Route 1 from Tuba
City to the Cow Springs turnoff and then, mile
after jolting mile, up the road to Short Mountain. The voice emerged from the tape player on
the seat beside him, hesitating, hurrying, sometimes stumbling, and sometimes repeating itself.
Leaphorn listened, his eyes intent on the stony
road but his thoughts focused on the words that
came from the speaker. Now and then he slowed
the carryall, stopped the tape, reversed it, and
repeated a passage. One section he replayed three
times—hearing the bored voice of Feeney asking:

"Did Tso tell you anything else? Did he say
anything about anyone being mad at him, having a grudge? Anything like that?"

And then the voice of Listening Woman: "He

thought maybe it could be the ghost of his great-grandfather. That's because . . ." Mrs. Cigaret's voice trailed off as she searched for English words to explain Navajo metaphysics. "That's because Hosteen Tso, he made a promise . . ."

"Made a promise to his great-grandfather? That would have been a long time ago." Feeney didn't sound interested.

"I think it was something they did with the oldest sons," Mrs. Cigaret said. "So Hosteen Tso would have made the promise to his own father, and Hosteen Tso's father made it to his father, and—"

"Okay," Feeney said. "What was the promise?"

"Taking care of some sort of secret," Mrs. Cigaret said. "Keeping something safe."

"Like what?"

"A secret," Mrs. Cigaret said. "He didn't tell me the secret." Her tone suggested that she wouldn't have been improper enough to ask.

"Did he say anything about getting any threats from anyone? Have any quarrels? Did he—"

Leaphorn grimaced, and pushed the fast forward button. Why hadn't Feeney pursued this line of questioning? Because, obviously, the FBI agent didn't want to waste time on the talk of great-grandfather ghosts during a murder investigation. But it was equally obvious, at least to Leaphorn, that Mrs. Cigaret considered it worth talking about. The tape rushed squawking through ten minutes of questions and answers probing into what Mrs. Cigaret had been told about Tso's relationship with neighbors and relatives. Leaphorn stopped it again at a point near the end of the interview. He pushed the play button.

". . . said it hurt him here in the chest a lot," Mrs. Cigaret was saying. "And sometimes it hurt him in the side. And his eyes, they hurt him, too. Back in the head behind the eyes. It started hurting him right after he found out that somebody had walked across some sand paintings and they stepped right on Corn Beetle, and Talking God, and Gila Monster, and Water Monster. And that same day, he was climbing and he knocked a bunch of rocks down and they killed a frog. And the frog was why his eyes—"

Feeney's voice cut in. "But you're sure he didn't say anything about anybody doing anything to hurt him? You're sure of that? He didn't blame it on any witch out there?"

"No," Mrs. Cigaret said. Was there a hesitation? Leaphorn ran it past again. Yes. A hesitation.

"Okay," Feeney said. "Now, did he say anything just before you left him and went over by the cliff?"

"I don't remember much," Mrs. Cigaret said. "I told him he ought to get somebody to take him to Gallup and get his chest x-rayed because maybe he had one of those sicknesses that white people cure. And he said he'd get somebody to write to his grandson to take care of everything, and then I said I'd go and listen and find out what was making his eyes hurt and what else was wrong with him and—"

Here the voice of Feeney cut in again, its tone tinged slightly with impatience. "Did he say anything about anyone stealing anything from him? Anything about fighting with relatives or—"

Leaphorn punched the off button, and guided the carryall around an outcrop of stone and over the edge of the steep switchback that dropped into Manki Canyon. He wished, as he had wished before, that Feeney hadn't been so quick to interrupt Mrs. Cigaret. What promise had Hosteen Tso made to his father? Taking care of a secret, Mrs. Cigaret had said. Keeping something safe. Tso hadn't told her the secret, but he might have told her much more than Feeney had let her report. And the sand paintings. Plural? More than one? Leaphorn had played that part over and over and she had clearly said "somebody had walked across some sand paintings." But there would be only a single sand painting existing at any one time at any curing ceremonial. The singer prepared the hogan floor with a background of fine sand, then produced his sacred painting with colored sands, and placed the patient properly upon it, conducted the chants and rituals, and then destroyed the painting, erased it, wiped away the magic. Yet she had said "some sand paintings." And the list of Holy People desecrated had been strange. Sand paintings recreated incidents from the mythic history of the Navajo People. Leaphorn could conceive of no incident which would have included both Gila Monster and Water Monster in its action. Water Monster had figured only once in the mythology of the Dinee—causing the flood that destroyed the Third World after his babies had been stolen by Coyote. Neither Gila Monster nor Talking God had a role in that episode. Leaphorn shook his head, wishing he had been there for the interrogation. But even as he thought it, he recognized he was being unfair to the FBI man. There would be no reason at all to connect incongruity in a curing sing with cold-blooded killing. And when he had talked to Listening Woman, Feeney had no way of knowing that all the more logical approaches to the case would dead-end. By the time Leaphorn pulled the carryall onto the bare packed earth that served as the yard of the Short Mountain Trading Post, he had decided that his own fascination with the oddities in Mrs. Cigaret's story was based more on his obsession with explaining the unexplained than with the murder investigation. Still, he would find Mrs. Cigaret and ask the questions

Feeney hadn't asked. He would find out what curing ceremonial Hosteen Tso had attended before his death, and who had desecrated its sand paintings, and what else had happened there.

He parked beside a rusty GMC stake truck and sat for a moment, looking. The FOR SALE sign which had been a permanent part of the front porch was still there. A midnight-blue Stingray, looking out of place, sat beside the sheep barn, its front end jacked up. Two pickups and an aging Plymouth sedan were parked in front. In the shade of the porch a white-haired matriarch was perched on a bale of sheep pelts, talking to a fat middle-aged man who sat, legs folded, on the stone floor beside her. Leaphorn knew exactly who they were talking about. They were talking about the Navajo policeman who had driven up, speculating on who Leaphorn was and what he was doing at Short Mountain. The old woman said something to the man, who laughed—a flash of white teeth in a dark shadowed face. A joke had just been made about Leaphorn. He smiled, and completed his quick survey. All was as he remembered it. The late-afternoon sun baked a collection of tired buildings clustered on a shadeless expanse of worn earth on the rim of Short Mountain Wash. Leaphorn wondered why this inhospitable spot had been chosen for a trading center. Legend had it that the Moab Mormon who founded the store about 1910 had picked the place because it was a long way from competition. It was also a long way from customers. Short Mountain Wash drained one of the most barren and empty landscapes in the Western Hemisphere. Legend also had it that after more than twenty hard years the Mormon became involved in a theological dispute concerning plural wives. He had picked up his own two and emigrated to a dissident colony in Mexico. McGinnis, then young and relatively foolish, had become the new owner. He had promptly realized his mistake. According to the legend, about thirty days after the purchase, he had hung out the THIS ESTABLISHMENT FOR SALE INQUIRE WITHIN sign that decorated his front porch for more than forty years. If anyone else had outsmarted John McGinnis, the event had not been recorded by reservation folklore.

Leaphorn climbed from the carryall, sorting out the questions he would ask McGinnis. The trader would know not only where Margaret Cigaret lived, but where she could be found this week—an important difference among people who follow sheep herds. And McGinnis would know if anything new had been heard about the mission helicopter, or about the reliability of those who brought in old reports, and everything about the lives and fortunes of the impoverished clans that occupied this empty end of the Rainbow Plateau. He would know why the Adams woman was here. Most important of all, he would know if a strange man wearing gold-rimmed glasses had been seen in the canyon country.

At this moment the screen door opened and John McGinnis emerged. He stood for a moment, blinking at Leaphorn through the fierce outside light, a stumpy, stooped, white-haired man swallowed up in new, and oversized, blue overalls. Then he squatted on the floor between the old woman and the man. Whatever he said produced a cackle of laughter from the woman and a chuckle from the man. Once again, Leaphorn guessed, he had been the subject of humor. He didn't mind. McGinnis would save him a lot of effort.

"I remember you," McGinnis said. "You're that Slow Talking Dinee boy who used to patrol out of Tuba City. Six, seven years ago." He had invited Leaphorn into his room at the rear of the store and gestured him to a chair. Now he poured a Coca-Cola glass half full from a bottle of Jack Daniel's, sloshed it around, and eyed Leaphorn. "The Dinee say you won't drink whiskey, so I ain't going to offer you any."

"That's right," Leaphorn said.

"Let me see, now. If I remember correct, your mama was Anna Gorman—ain't that right?—from way the hell over at Two Gray Hills? And you're a grandson of Hosteen Klee-Thlumie."

Leaphorn nodded. McGinnis scowled at him.

"I don't mean a goddam *clan* grandson," he said. "I mean a *real* grandson. He was the father of your mother? That right?"

Leaphorn nodded again.

"I knowed your granddaddy, then," McGinnis said. He toasted this fact with a long sip at the warm bourbon and then thought about it, his pale old man's eyes staring past Leaphorn at the wall. "Knowed him before he was Hosteen anything. Just a young buck Indian trying to learn how to be a singer. They called him Horse Kicker then."

"When I knew him he was called Hosteen Klee," Leaphorn said.

"We helped each other out, a time or two," McGinnis said, talking to his memories. "Can't say that about too many." He took another sip of bourbon and looked across the glass at Leaphorn—solidly back in the present. "You want to find that old Cigaret woman," he said. "Now, the only reason you'd want to do that is something must have come up on the Tso killing. That right?"

"Nothing much new," Leaphorn said. "But you know how it is. Time passes. Maybe somebody says something. Or sees something that helps us out."

McGinnis grinned. "And if anybody heard anything, it'd get to old John McGinnis. That right?" The grin vanished with a new thought. "Say, now, you know anything about a feller named Noni? Claims to be a Seminole Indian?" The tone of the question suggested that he doubted all claims made by Noni.

"Don't think so," Leaphorn said. "What about him?"

"He came in here a while back and looked the store over," McGinnis said. "Said he and a bunch of other goddam Indians had some sort of government loan and was interested in buying this hell hole. I figured to do that they'd have to deal with the Tribal Council for a license."

"They would," Leaphorn said. "But that wouldn't have anything to do with the police. They really going to buy it?" The idea of McGinnis actually selling the Short Mountain Post wasn't believable. It would be like the Tribal Council bricking up the hole in Window Rock, or Arizona selling the Grand Canyon.

"Probably didn't really have the money," McGinnis said. "Probably just come around looking to see if breaking in and stealing would be easy. I didn't like his looks." McGinnis scowled at his drink and at the memory. He put his rocking chair in motion, holding his elbow rigid on the chair arm and the glass rigid in his hand. In it, a brown tide of bourbon ebbed and flowed with the motion. "This Tso killing, now. You know what I hear about that?" He waited for Leaphorn to fill in the blank.

"What?" Leaphorn asked.

"Not a goddam thing," McGinnis said.

"Funny," Leaphorn said.

"It sure as hell is," McGinnis said. He stared at Leaphorn as if trying to find some sort of answer in his face. "You know what I think? I don't think a Navajo did it."

"Don't you?"

"Neither do you," McGinnis said. "Not if you've got as much sense as I hear you do. You Navajos will steal if you think you can get off with something, but I never heard of one going out to kill somebody." He flourished the glass to emphasize the point. "That's one kind of white man's meanness the Navajos never took to. Any killings you have, there's either getting drunk and doing it, or getting mad and fighting. You don't have this planning in advance and going out to kill somebody like white folks. That right?"

Leaphorn let his silence speak for him. McGinnis had been around Navajos long enough for that. What the trader had said was true. Among the traditional Dinee, the death of a fellow human being was the ultimate evil. He recognized no life after death. That which was natural in him, and therefore good, simply ceased. That which was unnatural, and therefore evil, wandered through the darkness as a ghost, disturbing nature and causing sickness. The Navajo didn't share the concept of his Hopi-Zuni-Pueblo Indian neighbors that the human spirit transcended death in the fulfillment of an eternal kachina, nor the Plains Indian belief in joining with a personal God. In the old tradition, death was unrelieved horror. Even the death of an enemy in battle was something the warrior cleansed himself of with an Enemy Way ritual. Unless, of course, a Navajo Wolf was involved. Witchcraft was a reversal of the Navajo Way.

"Except maybe if somebody thought he was a Navajo Wolf," McGinnis said. "They'd kill him if they thought he was a witch."

"You hear of anyone who thought that?"

"That's the trouble," McGinnis said cheerfully. "Nobody had nothing but good words to say about old Hosteen Tso." The cluttered room was silent again while McGinnis considered this oddity. He stirred his drink with a pencil from his shirt pocket.

"What do you know about his family?" Leaphorn asked.

"He had a boy, Tso did. Just one kid. That boy wasn't no good. They called him Ford. Married some girl over at Teec Nos Pos, a Salt Cedar I think she was, and moved over with her people and got to drinking and whoring around at Farmington until her folks run him off. Ford was always fighting and stealing and raising hell." McGinnis sipped at his bourbon, his face disapproving. "You could understand it if somebody hit *that* Navajo on the head," he said.

"He ever come back?" Leaphorn asked.

"Never did," McGinnis said. "Died years ago. In Gallup I heard it was. Probably too much booze and his liver got him." He toasted this frailty with a sip of bourbon.

"You know anything about a grandson?" Leaphorn asked.

McGinnis shrugged. "You know how it is with Navajos," he said. "The man moves in with his wife's outfit and if there's any kids they're born into their mother's clan. If you want to know anything about Tso's grandson, you're going to have to drive to Teec Nos Pos and start asking around among them Salt Cedar people. I never even heard Ford had any children until old Hosteen Tso come in here a while before he got killed and told me he wanted to write this letter to his grandson." McGinnis's face creased with remembered amusement. "I told him I didn't know he had a grandson, and he said that made two things I didn't know about him and of course I asked him what the other one was and he said it was which hand he used to wipe himself." McGinnis chuckled and sipped his bourbon. "Witty old fart," he said.

"What did he say in the letter?"

"I didn't write it," McGinnis said. "But let's see what I can remember about it. He come in one day. It was colder'n a wedge. Musta been early in March. He asked me what I charged to write a letter and I told him it was free for regular customers. And he started telling me what he wanted to tell this grandson and would I send the letter to him and of course I asked him where this boy lived and he said it was way off east somewhere with nothing but white people. And I told him he'd have to know more than that for me to know what to write on the front of the envelope."

"Yeah," Leaphorn said. When a marriage broke up in the matriarchal Navajo system, it wouldn't be unusual for paternal grandparents to lose track of children. They would be members of their mother's family. "Ever hear anything about Ford's wife?"

McGinnis rubbed his bushy white eyebrow

with a thumb, stimulating his memory. "I think I heard she was a drunk, too. Another no-good. Works that way a lot. Birds of a feather." McGinnis interrupted himself suddenly by slapping the arm of the rocker. "By God," he said. "I just thought of something. Way back, must have been almost twenty years ago, there was a kid staying with Hosteen Tso. Stayed there a year or so. Helped with the sheep and all. I bet that was the grandbaby."

"Maybe," Leaphorn said. "If his mother really was a drunk."

"Hard to keep track of Navajo kids," McGinnis said. "But I remember hearing that one went off to boarding school at St. Anthony's. Maybe that'd explain what Hosteen Tso said about him going on the Jesus Road. Maybe them Franciscan priests there turned him Catholic."

"There's something else I want to know about," Leaphorn said. "Tso went to a sing not very long before he was killed. You know about that?"

McGinnis frowned. "There wasn't no sing. About last March or so? We had all that sorry weather then. Remember? Blowing snow. Wasn't no sings anywhere on the plateau."

"How about a little earlier?" Leaphorn asked. "January or February?"

McGinnis frowned again. "There was one a

little after Christmas. Girl got sick at Yazzie Springs. Nakai girl. Would have been early in January."

"What was it?"

"They did the Wind Way," McGinnis said. "Had to get a singer from all the way over at Many Farms. Expensive as hell."

"Any others?" Leaphorn asked. The Wind Way was the wrong ritual. The sand painting made for it would include the Corn Beetle, but none of the other Holy People mentioned by Hosteen Tso.

"Bad spring for sings," McGinnis said. "Everybody's either getting healthy, or they're too damn poor to pay for 'em."

Leaphorn grunted. There was something he needed to connect. They sat. McGinnis moved the glass in small, slow circles which spun the bourbon to within a centimeter of its rim. Leaphorn let his eyes drift. It was a big room, two high windows facing east and two facing west. Someone, years ago, had curtained them with a cotton print of roses on a blue background. Big as the room was, its furniture crowded it. In the corner, a double bed covered with quilts; beside it a worn 1940-modern sofa; beyond that, a recliner upholstered in shiny blue vinyl; two other nondescript overstuffed chairs; and three assorted chests and cabinets. Every flat surface was cluttered with the odds and ends accumulated in a long lifetime—

Indian pottery, kachina dolls, a plastic radio, a shelf of books, and even—on one of the window sills—an assortment of flint lance points, artifacts which had interested Leaphorn since his days as an anthropology student at Arizona State. Outside, through the dusty glass window, he saw two young men talking beside one of the trading post's outbuildings. The building was of stone, originally erected, Leaphorn had been told, by a Church of Christ missionary early in McGinnis's tenure as trader and postmaster. It had been abandoned after the preacher's optimism had been eroded by his inability to cause the Dinee to accept the idea that God had a personal and special interest in humans. McGinnis then had partitioned the chapel into three tourist cabins. But, as one of his customers had put it, "it was as hard to get white-man tourists to go over that Short Mountain road as it was to get Navajos to go to heaven." The cabins, like the church, had been mostly empty.

Leaphorn glanced at McGinnis. The trader sat swirling his drink, his face lined and compressed by age. Leaphorn understood the old man's distaste for Noni. McGinnis didn't want a buyer. Short Mountain had trapped him in his own stubbornness, and held him here all his life, and the FOR SALE sign had been no more than a gesture—a declaration that he was smart enough to know he'd been screwed. And the asking price, Leaphorn had always heard, had been grotesquely high.

"No," McGinnis said finally. "There just wasn't any sings close around here at all."

"Okay," Leaphorn said. "So if there wasn't any sings, and Hosteen Tso told you he'd seen somebody step on two or three sand paintings last March, where would you figure that could have happened?"

McGinnis shifted his gaze from the bourbon to Leaphorn, peering at him quizzically. "No place," he said. "Shit. What kind of a question is that?"

"Hosteen Tso was there when it happened."

"No damned place," McGinnis said. He looked puzzled. "What the hell you going to have two or three sand paintings for at once?"

"It wouldn't be that Wind Way Chant," Leaphorn said. "Wrong painting."

"And the wrong clan. The Nakais are Red Foreheads. Wouldn't be no reason for Old Man Tso to go down there for the Wind Way." He took another sip of his bourbon. "Where'd you hear that crap?"

"Margaret Cigaret passed it on to the FBI when they were questioning her. When I leave here I'm going to go out to her place and find out more about it."

"She probably ain't home," McGinnis said.

"Somebody said she was off somewhere. Visiting kin, I think. Somewhere up east of Mexican Water."

"Maybe she's back by now."

"Maybe," McGinnis said. His tone said he doubted it.

"I guess I'll go find out," Leaphorn said. He probably wouldn't find her at home, but "up east of Mexican Water" meant just about anywhere in a thousand square miles along the Arizona-Utah border. Leaphorn decided it was time to move the conversation toward what had really brought him here—the man in the gold-rimmed glasses. He moved obliquely.

"Those your lance points?" Leaphorn asked, nodding toward the window sill.

McGinnis pushed himself laboriously out of the chair and waddled to the window, brought back three of the flint points. He handed them to Leaphorn and lowered himself into the rocker again.

"Came out of that dig up Short Mountain Wash," he said. "Anthropologists say they're early Anasazi but they look kind of big to me for that. They musta found a hundred of 'em."

The points had been chipped out of a shiny black basaltic schist. They were thick, and crude, with only slight fluting where the butt of the point would be fastened into the lance shaft. Leaphorn wondered how McGinnis had got his hands on them. But he didn't ask. Obviously the anthropologists would guard such artifacts zealously, and obviously the way McGinnis had got them wouldn't stand scrutiny. Leaphorn changed the subject, angling toward his main interest.

"Anybody come in and tell you they found an old helicopter?"

McGinnis laughed. "That son-of-a-bitch is long gone," he said. "If it ever flew into this country in the first place." He sipped again. "Maybe it did come in here. The feds seemed to have that pinned down pretty good. But if it crashed, I'da had some of those Begay boys, or the Tsossies, or somebody in here long ago nosing around to see if there was a reward, or trying to pawn it to me, or selling spare parts, or something."

"Another thing," Leaphorn said. "Mrs. Cigaret said Tso was worried about getting a sickness from his great-grandfather's ghost. That mean anything to you?"

"Well, now," McGinnis said. "Now, that's interesting. You know who his great-grandfather was? He came from quite a line, Tso did."

"Who was it?"

"Course he had four great-grandfathers," McGinnis said. "But the one they talk about around here was a big man before the Long Walk. Lots of stories about him. They called him Standing Medicine. He was one of them that wouldn't surrender when Kit Carson came through. One of that bunch with Chief Narbona and Ganado Mucho who fought it out with the army. Supposed to been a big medicine man. They claim he knew the whole Blessing Way, all seven days of it, and the Mountain Way, and several other sings."

McGinnis poured another dollop of bourbon into his glass—raising the level carefully to the bottom of the Coca-Cola trademark. "But I never heard anything about his ghost being any particular place—or bothering people." He sampled the freshened drink, grimaced. "God knows, though, he might be causing ghost sickness all over that country out there." It was time now, Leaphorn thought, for the crucial question.

"Last day or two you hear anything about a stranger with a big dog? A great big dog?"

"A stranger?"

"Or a Navajo, either."

McGinnis shook his head. "No." He laughed. "Heard a Navajo Wolf story this morning, though. Feller from back on the plateau said a skinwalker killed his nephew's sheepdogs at the Falling Rock water hole way out there on the plateau. But you're talking about a real dog, ain't you?"

"A real one," Leaphorn said. "But did this nephew see the witch?"

"Not the way I heard it," McGinnis said. "The dogs didn't come back with the sheep. So the next day the boy went to see about it. He found 'em dead and the werewolf tracks where they'd been killed." McGinnis shrugged. "You know how it goes. Pretty much the same old skinwalker story."

"Nothing about a stranger, then," Leaphorn said.

McGinnis eyed Leaphorn carefully, watching his reaction. "Well, now. We got us a stranger right here at Short Mountain. Got in early this morning." He paused with the storyteller man's talent for increasing the impact. "A woman," he said.

Leaphorn said nothing.

"Pretty young woman," McGinnis said, still watching Leaphorn. "Big sports car. From Washington."

"You mean Theodora Adams?" Leaphorn asked.

McGinnis didn't show his disappointment.

"You know all about her, then?"

"A little bit," Leaphorn said. "She's the daughter of a doctor in the Public Health Service. I don't know what the hell she's doing here. Or care, for that matter. What's she after? One of those anthropologists up the wash?"

McGinnis examined the level of bourbon in his glass, sloshed it gently, and examined Leaphorn out of the corner of his eye.

"She's trying to find someone who can take her up to Hosteen Tso's hogan," McGinnis said. He grinned then. He'd finally gotten a reaction out of Lieutenant Joe Leaphorn.

SIX

LOOKING FOR THEODORA Adams proved to be unnecessary. Joe Leaphorn emerged from the front door of the Short Mountain Trading Post and found Theodora Adams hurrying up, looking for him.

"You're the policeman who drives that car," she told him. The smile was brilliant, a flashing white arch of perfect teeth in a very tanned perfect face. "There's something you could do for me"—again the smile—"if you would."

"Like what?" Leaphorn asked.

"I have to get to the hogan of a man named Hosteen Tso," Theodora Adams said. "I've found a man who knows how to get there, but my car won't go over that road." She glanced ruefully at the Corvette Stingray parked in the shade of the barn. Two young men were tinkering with it now. And then the full force of her eyes was again on Leaphorn. "It's too low," she explained. "The rocks hit the bottom."

"You want me to take you to the Tso hogan?"

"Yes," she said. Her smile said "please" for her.

"Why do you want to go?"

The smile faded slightly. "I have some business there."

"With Hosteen Tso?"

The smile left. "Hosteen Tso is dead," she said. "You know that. You're a policeman." Her eyes studied Leaphorn's face, slightly hostile but mostly with frank, unabashed curiosity. Leaphorn remembered suddenly when he had first seen blue eyes like that. He had gone to the boarding school at Kayenta with his uncle and cousin and there had been a white woman there with blue eyes who had stared at him. He had thought, at first, that eyes as odd as that must be blind. That woman, too, had stared at him as if he were an interesting object. On that same day, he remembered, he had seen his first bearded man—something to a Navajo boy as curious as a winged snake—but somehow the unaccustomed rudeness of those pale eyes had affected him more. He had always remembered it. And the memory, now, affected his response.

"Who's your business with?"

"That's none of *your* business," Theodora Adams

said. She took a half step away from him, stopped, turned back. "I'm sorry," she said. "Of course it's your business. You're a policeman." She made a deprecating face, and shrugged. "It's just that it's something very private. Nothing to do with the law and I simply can't talk about it." She smiled again, plaintively. "I'm sorry," she said.

Her expression told Leaphorn that the regret was genuine. She was a remarkably handsome girl, high-breasted, slender, dressed in white pants and a blue shirt which exactly matched the color of her eyes. She looked expensive, Leaphorn thought, and competent and assured. She also looked utterly out of place at Short Mountain Trading Post.

"Do you know how to get to Tso's place?"

"That man was going to show me." She pointed to the two young men at her car, one under it now—apparently inspecting front-end damage— and the other squatted beside him. "But we couldn't get that damned Stingray over the rocks." She paused, her eyes intent on Leaphorn's. "I was going to pay him twenty-five dollars," she said. The statement hung there, not an offer, not a bribe, simply a statement for Leaphorn to consider and make what he wanted of. He considered it, and found it neatly done. The girl was smart.

"One thing I've got. Plenty of money," she said.

"The Navajo Tribal Police have a regulation against picking up hitchhikers," Leaphorn said.

He turned it over in his mind. He would tell Largo his Theodora Adams was here and healthy. He would tell Largo where she wanted to go. He was almost sure Largo would tell him to take her to the Tso place, simply to find out what she wanted there. But maybe not. By asking Largo to find out about the welfare of Theodora Adams, Window Rock had, in an unofficial, unspoken way, made him responsible for it. Under the circumstances, Largo might not want her taken into that back country.

"Look," he said. "How much do you know about Hosteen Tso?"

"I know somebody killed him, if that's what you mean. Last spring."

"And we don't know who did it," Leaphorn said. "So we're interested in anybody who has business out there."

"My business doesn't have anything to do with crime," Theodora Adams said. She looked amused. "It doesn't have anything to do with the law, or with the police. It's just personal business. And if you're not willing to help me, I'll find somebody who will." And with that, she walked across the yard and disappeared into the trading post.

One of the disadvantages of the Short Mountain Trading Post location was that it was impossible for shortwave radio communication. To contact

Tuba City, Leaphorn had to drive out of the declivity made by the wash, going high enough up the mesa so that his reception wasn't blanked out by the terrain. He found Captain Largo suitably surprised at the Adams woman's aim of visiting the Tso hogan.

"You want me to take her?" Leaphorn asked. "I'm going out to see the Cigaret woman and it's sort of on the way. Same direction anyway."

"No," Largo said. "Just find out what the hell she's doing."

"I'm pretty sure she's not going to tell me," Leaphorn said. "She already told me it was none of our business."

"You could bring her in here for questioning."

"Could I? You recommending that?"

The pause was brief—Largo remembering the reason for his original interest in Theodora Adams. "I guess not," he said. "Not unless we have to. Handle it your own way. But don't let anything happen to her."

The way Leaphorn had already decided to handle it would be to offer to drive Theodora Adams to the Tso hogan. If he did that there would be no conceivable way she could prevent him from learning why she had gone there. He would find the Adams woman and get on the road.

But when he got back to the trading post, it

was after 10 P.M. and Theodora Adams was gone. So was a GMC pickup truck owned by a woman named Naomi Many Goats.

"I saw her talking to Naomi Many Goats," McGinnis said. "She came in here and got me to draw her a little map of how to get to the Tso place. And then she asked if you were headed back to Tuba City, and I told her you'd probably just gone off to do some radio talking because you was fixing to go out and talk to the Cigaret woman. So she got me to show her where the Cigaret hogan was on the map. Then she asked who she could hire to take her to the Tso place, and I said you never could tell with you Navajos, and the last thing I saw her doing was talking to Naomi."

"She get the Many Goats woman to drive her?"

"Hell, I don't know," McGinnis said. "I didn't see 'em leave."

"I'll guess she did," Leaphorn said.

"It occurs to me that I've been telling you a hell of a lot and you ain't been telling me nothing," McGinnis said. "Why does that girl want to go to the Tso hogan?"

"Tell you what," Leaphorn said. "When I find out, I'll tell you."

SEVEN

BY THE RELAXED standards of the Navajo Reservation, the first three miles of the road to the hogan of Hosteen Tso were officially listed as "unimproved—passable in dry weather." They led up Short Mountain Wash to the site where the anthropological team was excavating cliff ruins. The road followed the mostly hard-packed sand of the wash bottom, and if one was careful to avoid soft places, offered no particular hazard or discomfort. Leaphorn drove past the ruins a little after midnight. Except for a pickup and a small camping trailer parked in the shade of a cottonwood, there was no sign of life. From there, the road quickly deteriorated from fair, to poor, to bad, to terrible, until it was, in fact, no road at all, merely a track. It left the narrowing wash via a subsidiary arroyo, snaked its way through a half mile of broken shale and emerged on the top of Rainbow Plateau. The landscape became a roadbuilder's nightmare and a geologist's dream. Here, eons ago, the earth's crust had writhed and twisted. Nothing was level. Limestone sediments, great masses of gaudy sandstone, granite outcroppings, and even thick veins of marble had been churned together by some unimaginable paroxysm—then cut and carved and washed away by ten million years of wind, rain, freeze and thaws. Driving here was a matter of following a faintly marked pathway through a stone obstacle course. It required care, patience and concentration. Leaphorn found concentration difficult. His head was full of questions. Where was Frederick Lynch? Where was he going? His course northward from his abandoned car would take him near the Tso hogan. Was Theodora Adams's business at the hogan business with Frederick Lynch? That seemed logical—if anything about this odd business made any logic at all. If two white strangers appeared at about the same time in this out-of-the-way corner, one headed for the Tso hogan and the other aimed in that direction, logic insisted that more than coincidence was involved. But why in the name of God would they cross half a continent to meet at one of the most remote and inaccessible spots in the hemisphere? Leaphorn could think of no possible reason. Common sense insisted that their coming must have something to do with the murder of Hosteen Tso, but Leaphorn could conceive no link. He felt the irritation and uneasiness that he always felt when the world around him seemed out of its logical order. There was also a growing sense of anxiety. Largo had told him not to let anything happen to Theodora Adams. Most likely, Theodora Adams was somewhere ahead of him on this road, riding with a woman familiar with its hazards, who could drive it faster than could Leaphorn. Leaphorn remembered once again the face of Lynch grinning as he set Leaphorn up for the kill. He thought of the shepherd's dogs savaged by the animal Lynch had with him. This was what Theodora Adams was going to meet. Leaphorn jolted the carryall over a boulder faster than he should have, heard the bottom grate against stone, and cursed aloud in Navajo.

As he braked the carryall to a halt, he became aware that something was in the vehicle with him. Some sense of motion, or unexplained sound, reached him. He unsnapped the holding strap over his pistol, drew the hammer quietly back to the half-cocked position, palmed it, and spun in the seat. Nothing. He peered over the back of the seat, the pistol ready. On the floor, cushioned by his sleeping bag, lay Theodora Adams.

"I hope you didn't get stuck," she said. "That's what happened to me—banging over the rocks like that."

Leaphorn flicked on the dome light and stared down at her, saying nothing. Surprise was replaced by anger, and this was quickly diluted by relief. Theodora Adams was safe enough.

"I told you we had a rule against riders," Leaphorn said.

She pulled herself from the floor to the back seat, shook her head to untangle the mass of blond hair. "I didn't have any choice. That woman wouldn't take me. And that old man told me you were going out here anyway."

"McGinnis?"

Theodora Adams shrugged. "McGinnis. Whatever his name is. So there wasn't any reason for me not to come along."

It was a statement that could be argued, but not answered. Leaphorn rarely argued. He considered his impulse to order her out of the carry-all, to be picked up on his way back. The impulse died quickly, anger overcome by the need to know why she was going to the Tso hogan. Her eyes were an unusually deep blue, or perhaps the color was accentuated by the unusual clarity of the whiteness that surrounded the iris. They were eyes that would not be stared down, which fixed on Leaphorn's eyes—unabashed, arrogant, slightly amused.

"Get in the front seat," Leaphorn said. He didn't want her behind him.

They jolted through the boulder field in silence and onto the smoother going of a long sandstone slope. Theodora Adams dug into her purse, extracted a folded square of notepaper and smoothed it on the leg of her pants. It was a pencil-drawn map. "About where are we?"

Leaphorn turned up the dash light and peered at it. "About here," he said. He was conscious of her thigh under his fingertip. Exactly, he knew, as she knew he would be.

"About ten miles?"

"About twenty."

"So we'll be there pretty soon?"

"No," Leaphorn said, "we won't." He downgeared the carryall over a hump of stone. The carryall rolled into the shadow of an outcrop, making her reflection suddenly visible on the inside of the windshield. She was watching him, waiting for the answer to be expanded.

"Why not?"

"Because first we're going to the Cigaret hogan. I'll talk to Margaret Cigaret. *Then* we'll decide whether to go to the Tso hogan." In fact, there was no reason to reach the Cigaret place before dawn.

He had intended to find it and then park for some sleep.

"Decide?"

"You'll tell me what your business is. I'll decide whether we go on from there."

"Look," she said. "I'm sorry if I was rude back there. But you were rude, too. Why don't we . . ." She paused. "What's your name?"

"Joe Leaphorn."

"Joe," she said, "my name is Judy Simons, and my friends all call me Judy, and I don't see why we can't be friends."

"Reach into your purse, Miss Simons, and let me see your driver's license," Leaphorn said. He pushed the handbag toward her.

"I don't have it with me," she said.

Leaphorn's right hand fished deftly into the handbag, extracted a fat blue leather wallet.

"Put that back." Her voice was icy. "You don't have any right to do that."

The driver's license was in the first plastic cardholder. The face that stared from the square was the face of the woman beside him, the smile appealing even when directed at the license bureau camera. The name was Theodora Adams. Leaphorn flipped the wallet shut and pushed it back into the handbag.

"Okay," she said. "It's none of your business, but I'll tell you why I'm going to the Tso place."

The carryall tilted over the sloping stone. She clutched the door to keep from sliding down the seat against him. "But you'll have to promise to take me there."

She waited for an answer, staring at him expectantly. Leaphorn said nothing.

"I have a friend. A Navajo. He's been having a lot of trouble." Leaphorn glanced at her. Her smile disparaged her good Samaritan role. "You know. Getting his head together. So he decided to come home. And I decided I would come out and help him."

The voice stopped, the silence inviting comment. Leaphorn shifted again to cope with another steep slope.

"What's his name?"

"Tso. He's Hosteen Tso's grandson. The old man wanted him to come to see him."

"Ah," Leaphorn said. But was this grandson also Frederick Lynch? Was he Goldrims? Leaphorn was almost certain he was.

"Joe," she said. Her fingertip touched his leg. "You could drop me off at the Tso place and talk to Mrs. Cigaret on the way home. It won't take any longer."

"I'll think about it," Leaphorn said. Mrs. Cigaret probably wasn't home. And whatever Margaret Cigaret could tell him seemed trivial against the thought of confronting Goldrims—of taking the man who had tried, so gleefully, to kill him. "Is he expecting you?"

"Look," she said. "You're not going to take me there first. You're not going to do anything for me. Why should I tell you anything about my business?"

"We'll go there first," Leaphorn said. "But what's the hurry? Does he know you're coming?"

She laughed. There was genuine merriment in the sound, causing Leaphorn to take his eyes off the track he was following to look at her. It was a hearty laugh, a sound full of happy memories. "Yes and no," she said. "Or just yes. He knows." She glanced at Leaphorn, her eyes still amused. "That's like asking somebody if they know the sun's going to come up. Of course it's going to come up. If it doesn't, the world ends."

She is a formidable young woman, Leaphorn thought. He didn't want her with him when he first approached Hosteen Tso's place. Whether she liked it or not, she'd wait in the carryall while he determined who, or what, waited at the hogan.

EIGHT

HAD LEAPHORN'S TIMING been perfect, he would have arrived on the mesa rim overlooking the Tso hogan at dawn. In fact, he arrived perhaps an hour early, the moon almost down on the western horizon and the starlight just bright enough to confirm the dim shape of the buildings below. Leaphorn sat and waited. He sat far enough back from the mesa edge so that the downdrift of cooling air would not carry his scent. If the dog was there, Leaphorn didn't want it alerted. The dog had been very much on his mind as he found his way down the dark wagon track toward the hogan and up the back slope of this small mesa. Leaphorn doubted that it would be out hunting, but anything seemed possible in this peculiar affair. The thought of the dog had increased his caution and tightened his nerves. Now, sitting motion-less with his back protected by a slab of stone, he relaxed. If the animal was prowling, he would hear it in time to react to an attack. The dan-ger—if indeed there had been danger—was gone now.

Silence. In the dim, still, predawn universe, scent dominated sight and hearing. Leaphorn could smell the acrid perfume of the junipers just behind him, the aroma of dust and other scents so faint they defied identification. From some-where far behind him there came a single, al-most inaudible snapping sound. Perhaps a stone cooling and contracting from yesterday's heat, perhaps a predator moving suddenly and break-ing a stick, perhaps the earth growing one tick older. The sound turned Leaphorn's thoughts back to the dog, to the eyes staring at him out of the car, to what had happened to the sheepdogs at the water hole, and to witch dogs, the Navajo Wolves, of his people's ancient traditions. The Navajo Wolves were men and women who turned from harmony to chaos and gained the power to change themselves into coyotes, dogs, wolves or even bears, and to fly through the air, and to spread sickness among the Dinee. As a boy he had believed, fervently and fearfully, in this con-cept of evil. Two miles from his grandmother's hogan was a weathered volcanic upthrust which the People avoided. In a cave there the witches supposedly gathered to initiate new members into their Clan of Wolves. As a sophomore at Arizona State, he had come just as fervently to disbelieve in the ancient ways. He had visited his grandmother, and gone alone to the old volcano core. Climbing the crumbling basalt crags, feeling brave and liberated, he had found two caves—one of which seemed to lead downward into the black heart of the earth. There had been no witches, nor any sign that anything used these caves except, perhaps, a den of coyotes. But he hadn't climbed down into the darkness.

Now for many minutes, Leaphorn's imagination had been suggesting a dim opalescence along the eastern horizon, and presently his eyes confirmed it. A ragged division between dark sky and darker earth, the shape of the Chuska Mountains on the New Mexico border. At this still point, another sound reached Leaphorn. He realized he had been aware of it earlier somewhere below the threshold of hearing. Now it became a murmuring which came and died and came again. It seemed to come from the north. Leaphorn frowned, puzzled. And then he realized what it must be. It was the sound of running water, the San Juan River moving over its rapids, sliding down its canyon toward Lake Powell. At this season the river would be low, the snow melt of the Rockies long since drained away. Even in this stillness Leaphorn doubted if the sound muffled by the depth of its canyon would carry far. One of the river bends must bring it to within a couple of miles of Tso's hogan.

Leaphorn's eye caught a flick of movement in the gray light below—an owl on the hunt. Or, he thought, sardonically, the ghost of Hosteen Tso haunting the old man's hogan. The east was brightening. Leaphorn eased himself silently from the stone and moved nearer the rim. The buildings were clearly visible. He examined the setting. Directly below him, drainage had eroded a cul-de-sac from the sandstone face of the mesa. This must be where Listening Woman had communed with the earth while her patient and her assistant were being murdered. He studied the topography. It was light enough now to make out the wagon track that connected the Tso hogan tenuously with the world of men. Down this track the killer must have come. The investigators had found only the tracks of Mrs. Cigaret's pickup, and no hoofprints. So, the killer had come on foot, visible from the hogan for more than three hundred yards. Tso and the girl must have watched death walking toward them. They had recognized no threat, apparently. Had they seen a friend? A stranger? Below Leaphorn's feet the track swerved toward the cliff, passing within a dozen yards of where Mrs. Cigaret had sat invisible behind a curtain of stone while the killer had walked past. What had he done then? He would have seen the ritual design painted on the old man's chest. That should have told him that Tso was undergoing a ceremonial diagnosis, that a Listener, or Hand Trembler, must be somewhere nearby. He might have believed the teenage girl was the diagnostician. But not if he was a local Navajo. Then he would have known the truck belonged to Listening Woman. Leaphorn studied the grounds below him, trying to recreate the scene. The killer apparently had left immediately after the killing. At least, nothing was known to be missing from Tso's belongings. He had simply walked away as he had come—down the track forty feet below Leaphorn's boot tips. Leaphorn retraced this line of retreat with his eyes, then stopped. He frowned, puzzled. At that same moment, he smelled smoke.

The east was streaked with red and yellow now, providing enough light to illuminate a wavering thin blue line emerging from the smoke hole in the Tso hogan. The man was there. Leaphorn felt a fierce excitement. He took out his binoculars, adjusted them quickly, and studied the ground around the hogan. If the dog was to be part of this contest he needed to know it. He could detect no sign of the animal. The few places where tracks might show bore only boot prints. There was no sign of droppings. Leaphorn studied places where a dog would be likely to urinate, where it might sprawl in the afternoon shade. He found nothing. He lowered the glasses and rubbed his eyes. As he did, the door of the hogan swung open and a man emerged.

He stood, one hand resting on the plank door, and stared out at the dawn. A largish man, young, wearing an unbuttoned blue shirt, white boxer shorts, and short boots not yet laced. Leaphorn studied him through the binoculars, trying to connect this man enjoying the beauty of the dawn with the grinning face seen through the windshield of the Mercedes. The hair was black, which was as he had remembered it. The man was tall, his figure foreshortened by the magnification of Leaphorn's binoculars and the viewing angle. Perhaps six feet, with narrow hips and a heavy muscular torso. The man examined the morning, showing more of his face now. It was a Navajo face, longish, rather bony. A shrewd, intelligent face reflecting only calm enjoyment of the morning. Discomfort in his chest made Leaphorn realize that he had been holding his breath. He breathed again. Some of the tension of the night had left him. He had hunted a sort of epitome of evil, something that would kill with reckless enjoyment. He had found a mere mortal. And yet this Navajo who stood below him inspecting the rosy dawn sky must be the same man who, just three nights ago, had run him down with a laugh. Nothing else made sense.

The man turned abruptly and ducked back into the hogan. Leaphorn lowered the binoculars and thought about it. No glasses. No goldrims. That might simply mean that the man had them in his pocket. Leaphorn studied the layout of the buildings below him. He located a place where he could climb down the mesa without being seen and approach the hogan away from its east-facing entrance. Before he could move, the man emerged again. He was dressed now, wearing black trousers, with what looked like a purple scarf over his shoulders. He was carrying something. Through the binoculars Leaphorn identified two bottles and a small black case. What appeared to be a white towel hung over his wrist. The man walked rapidly to the brush arbor and put the bottles, the case and the towel on the plank table there.

Shaving, Leaphorn thought. But what the man was doing had nothing to do with shaving. He had taken several objects from the case and arranged them on the table. And then he stood motionless, apparently simply staring down at them. He dropped suddenly to one knee, then rose again almost immediately. Leaphorn frowned. He examined the bottles. One seemed to be half filled with a red liquid. The other held something as clear as water. Now the man had taken an object small and white and held it up to the light, staring at it. He held it in the fingers of both hands, as if it were heavy, or extremely fragile. Through the binoculars it appeared to be a broken piece of bread. The man was pouring the red liquid into a cup, adding a few drops of the clear, raising the cup in both hands to above eye level. His face was rapt and his lips moved slightly, as if he spoke to the cup. Abruptly Leaphorn's memory served him—something he had witnessed years ago and which had then dominated his thoughts for weeks. Leaphorn knew what the man was doing and even the words he was speaking: ". . . this is the cup of my blood, the blood of the new and everlasting covenant. It will be shed for you and for all men so that sins may be forgiven . . ."

Leaphorn lowered the binoculars. The man at the Tso hogan was a Roman Catholic priest. As the rules of his priesthood required of him each day, he was celebrating the Mass.

Back at the carryall, Leaphorn found the girl asleep. She lay curled on the front seat, her head cushioned on her purse, her mouth slightly open. Leaphorn examined her a moment, then unlocked the driver-side door, moved her bare feet and slid under the steering wheel.

"You were gone long enough," Theodora Adams said. She sat up, pushed the hair away from her face. "Did you find the place?"

"We're going to make this simple and easy to understand," Leaphorn said. He started the engine. "If you'll answer my questions about this man, I'll take you there. If you start lying, I'll take you back to Short Mountain. And I know enough to tell when the lying starts."

"He was there, then," she said. It wasn't really a question. The girl hadn't doubted he'd be there. But there was a new expectancy in her face—something avid.

"He was there," Leaphorn said. "About six foot, black hair. That sound like the man you expected?"

"Yes," she said.

"Who is he?"

"I'm going to raise hell about this," the girl said. "You don't have any right."

"Okay," Leaphorn said. "Do that. Who is he?"

"I told you who he is. Benjamin Tso."

"What does he do?"

"Do?" She laughed. "You mean for a living? I don't know."

"You're lying," Leaphorn said. "Tell me, or we go back to Short Mountain."

"He's a priest," the girl said. "A member of the Order of Friars Minor . . . a Franciscan." Her voice was resentful, perhaps at the information, perhaps at having been forced to reveal it.

"What's he doing here?"

"Resting. He was tired. He had a long trip."

"From where?"

"From Rome."

"Italy?"

"Italy." She laughed. "That's where Rome is."

Leaphorn turned off the ignition. "We stop playing these games," he said. "If you want to see this man, you're going to tell me about it."

"Oh, well," she said. "What the hell?" And having decided to talk, she talked freely, enjoying the narration.

She had met Tso in Rome. He had been sent there to complete his studies at the Vatican's American College and at the Franciscan seminary outside the city. She had gone with her father and had met Tso through the brother of her college roommate, who was also about to be ordained. Having met him, she stayed behind when her father returned to Washington.

"The bottom line is we're going to get married. To skip a little, he came out here to see about his grandfather and I came out to join him."

You've skipped a lot, Leaphorn thought. You've skipped the part about seeing something you can't have, and wanting it, and going after it. And the Navajo, a product of the hogan life, of the mission boarding school, and then of the seminary, seeing something he had never seen before, and not knowing how to handle it. It would have been strictly no contest, Leaphorn guessed. He remembered Tso's rapt face staring up at the elevated bread, and felt unreasonably angry. He wanted to ask the girl how she had let Tso struggle this far off the hook.

Instead he said, "He giving up being a priest?"

"Yes," she said. "Priests can't marry."

"What brought him here?"

"Oh, he got a letter from his grandfather, and then, as you know, his grandfather got killed. So he said he had to come and see about it."

"And what brings you here?"

She glanced at him, eyes hostile. "He said to join him here."

Like hell he did, Leaphorn thought. He ran and you tracked him down. He started the carryall again and concentrated for a moment on steering. He doubted if he would learn anything more from Theodora Adams. Probably she and Tso were simply what they seemed to be. Rabbit and coyote. Probably Tso was simply a priest who had been inspired to escape from this woman by some instinct for self-preservation. To save what? Himself? His honor? His soul? And probably Theodora Adams was the woman who has everything pursuing the man made desirable because he is taboo.

Or perhaps Father Tso *was* Goldrims. If he was, Theodora Adams's role would be something more complex than sexual infatuation. But whatever her role, Leaphorn felt she was too tough and too shrewd to reveal more than she wanted to reveal.

The carryall jolted and groaned over the sloping track beneath the mesa and rolled across the expanse of packed earth that served as the yard of Hosteen Tso. The girl was out of the vehicle before it stopped rolling, running toward the hogan shouting, "Bennie, Bennie." She pulled open the plank door and disappeared inside. Leaphorn waited a moment, watching for the dog. There was no trace of it. He stepped out of the carryall as the girl emerged from the hogan.

"You said he was here," she said. She looked angry and disappointed.

"He was," Leaphorn said. "In fact, he is."

Tso had emerged from the screen of junipers west of the hogan and was walking slowly toward them, looking puzzled. The morning sun was in his eyes and he had not yet identified the girl. Then he did. He stopped, stunned. Theodora Adams noticed it, too.

"Bennie," she said. "I tried to stay away." Her voice broke. "I just couldn't."

"I see," Tso said. His eyes were on her face. "Was it a good trip?"

Theodora Adams laughed a shaky laugh. "Of course not," she said. She took his hand. "It was awful. But it's all right now."

Tso glanced over her shoulder at Leaphorn. "The policeman brought you," he said. "You shouldn't have come."

"I had to come," she said. "Of course I'd come. You knew that."

Leaphorn was suddenly acutely embarrassed.

"Father Tso," he said. "I'm sorry. But I need to ask some questions. About your grandfather."

"Sure," Tso said. "Not that I know much. I hadn't seen him for years."

"I understand you got a letter from him. What did he say?"

"Not much," Tso said. "He just said he was sick. And wanted me to come and arrange a sing and take care of things when he died." Tso frowned. "Why would anyone want to kill an old man like that?"

"That's the problem," Leaphorn said. "We don't know. Did he say anything that would help? Do you have the letter?"

"It's with my stuff," Tso said. "I'll get it." He disappeared into the hogan.

Leaphorn looked at Theodora Adams. She stared back.

"Congratulations," Leaphorn said.

"Screw you," she said. "You—" She stopped. Tso was coming through the hogan doorway.

"It really doesn't say much, but you can read it," he said.

The letter was handwritten in black ink on inexpensive typing paper.

"My Grandson," it began. "I have the ghost sickness. There is no one here to talk to the singer and do all the things that have to be done so that I can go again in beauty. I want you to come and get the right singer and see about the sing. If you don't come I will die very soon. Come. There are valuable things I must give you before I die."

"I'm afraid it doesn't help much," Tso said.

"Your grandfather couldn't write, could he? Do you know who he would get to write it for him?"

"I don't know," Tso said. "Some friend, probably."

"How did he get your address?"

"It was just addressed care of the Franciscan abbot at the American College. I guess they asked the Franciscans over at St. Anthony's how to send it."

"When was it mailed?"

"I got it about the middle of April. So I guess it was mailed just before he got killed." Tso glanced down at his hands. He had obviously thought a lot about this. "I was busy with a lot of things then," he said. He glanced up at Leaphorn, looking for some sort of understanding of this failure. "And it was already too late, anyway."

"Bennie thought it could wait a little while," Theodora Adams said.

"I suppose I operated on Navajo time," Tso said. But he didn't smile at the old joke. "I hadn't seen the old man since I was eleven or twelve. I guess I thought it could wait."

Leaphorn said nothing. He was remembering Mrs. Cigaret's voice on the tape recording, recalling for Feeney what Hosteen Tso had told her. ". . . And he said he'd get somebody to write to his grandson." That's what Mrs. Cigaret had said. Get somebody to write. Hosteen Tso hadn't lived more than an hour after that. And yet the letter had been written. Who the hell could have done it? Leaphorn decided he'd go back to Short Mountain and talk to McGinnis again.

"You have any idea what those 'valuable things' he wanted to give you could be?" Leaphorn asked.

"No," Tso said. "I have no idea. Everything I found in the hogan wouldn't be worth a hundred dollars." Tso looked thoughtful. "But maybe he didn't mean money value."

"Maybe not," Leaphorn said. He was still thinking of the letter. If McGinnis hadn't written it, who the hell had?

NINE

MCGINNIS POURED THE bourbon carefully, stopping exactly at the copyright symbol under the Coca-Cola trademark on the glass. That done, he glanced up at Leaphorn.

"Had a doctor tell me I ought to quit this stuff because it was affecting my eardrums and I told him I liked what I was drinking better'n what I was hearing."

He held the glass to the light, enjoying the amber as a wine-lover enjoys the red.

"Two things I can't even guess at," McGinnis said. "The first is who he got to write that letter for him, and the other is how come he didn't come back to me to write it for him after he found out the address." McGinnis considered this, his expression sour. "You might think it's because I'm a man who's known for knowing everybody's business. A gossip. But then all those people out here know I don't talk what I write in their letters for them. They've had many a year to learn that."

"I'm going to tell you exactly what was in that letter," Leaphorn said. He leaned forward in his chair, eyes intent on McGinnis's face. "I want you to listen. It said, 'My Grandson. I have ghost sickness. Nobody is here to get me a singer and do the things necessary so I can go again in beauty. I need you to come here and hire the right singer and see about things. If you don't come I will die soon. Come. There are valuable things I must give you before I die."

McGinnis stared into the bourbon, full of thought. "Go on," he said. "I'm listening."

"That's it," Leaphorn said. "I memorized it."

"Funny," McGinnis said.

"I'm going to ask you if that's about the same as the letter he was telling you he wanted written."

"I figured that's what you were going to ask," McGinnis said. "Let me see the letter."

"I don't have it," Leaphorn said. "This Benjamin Tso let me read it."

"You got a hell of a memory, then," McGinnis said.

"Nothing much wrong with it," Leaphorn said. "How about yours? You remember what he wanted you to write?"

McGinnis pursed his lips. "Well, now," he said. "It's kind of like I told you. I got a reputation around here for not gossiping about what people want put in their letters."

"I want you to hear something else, then," Leaphorn said. "This is a tape of an FBI agent named Feeney talking to Margaret Cigaret about what Hosteen Tso told her that afternoon just before he got killed." Leaphorn picked up the recorder and pushed the play button.

". . . say anything just before you left him and went over by the cliff?" the voice of Feeney asked.

And then the voice of the Listening Woman. "I don't remember much. I told him he ought to get somebody to take him to Gallup and get his chest x-rayed because maybe he had one of those sicknesses that white people cure. And he said he'd get somebody to write to his grandson to take care of everything, and then I said I'd go and listen—"

Leaphorn stopped the tape, his eyes still on McGinnis's.

"Well, well," McGinnis said. He started the rocking chair in motion. "Well, now," he said. "If I heard what I think I heard . . ." He paused. "That was her talking about just before old Tso got hit on the head?"

"Right," Leaphorn said.

"And he was saying he still hadn't got the letter

written. So nobody could have written it—except Anna Atcitty, and that's damned unlikely. And even if she wrote it, which I bet my ass she didn't, the guy that hit 'em on the head would've had to gone and mailed it." He glanced at Leaphorn. "You believe that?"

"No," Leaphorn said.

McGinnis abruptly stopped the rocking chair. In the Coca-Cola glass the oscillation of the bourbon turned abruptly into splashing waves.

"By God," McGinnis said, his voice enthusiastic. "This gets mysterious."

"Yeah," Leaphorn said.

"That was a short letter," McGinnis said. "What he told me would make a long one. Maybe a page and a half. And I write small."

McGinnis pushed himself out of the rocker and reached for the bourbon. "You know," he said, uncapping the bottle, "I'm known for keeping secrets as well as for talking. And I'm known as an Indian trader. By profession, in fact, that's what I am. And you're an Indian. So let's trade."

"For what?" Leaphorn asked.

"Tit for tat," McGinnis said. "I tell you what I know. You tell me what you know."

"Fair enough," Leaphorn said. "Except right now there's damned little I know."

"Then you'll owe me," McGinnis said. "When you get this thing figured out you tell me. That means I gotta trust you. Got any problems with that?"

"No," Leaphorn said.

"Well, then," McGinnis said. "You know anything about somebody named Jimmy?" Leaphorn shook his head.

"Old Man Tso come in here and he sat down over there." McGinnis waved the glass in the direction of an overstuffed chair. "He said to write a letter telling his grandson that he was sick, and to tell the grandson to come right away and get a singer to cure him. And to tell him that Jimmy was acting bad, acting like he didn't have any relatives."

McGinnis paused, sipped, and thought. "Let's see now," he said. "He said to tell the grandson that Jimmy was acting like a damned white man. That maybe Jimmy had become a witch. Jimmy had stirred up the ghost. He said to tell his grandson to hurry up and come right away because there was something that he had to tell him. He said he couldn't die until he told him." McGinnis had been staring into the glass as he spoke. Now he looked up at Leaphorn, his shrunken old face expressionless but his eyes searching for an answer. "Hosteen Tso told me he wanted to put that down twice. That he couldn't die until he told that grandson something. And that after he told him, then it would be time to die. Looks like somebody hurried it up." He was motionless in the chair a long moment. "I'd like to know who did that," he said.

"I'd like to know who Jimmy is," Leaphorn said.

"I don't know," McGinnis said. "I asked the old fart, and all he'd say was that Jimmy was a son-of-a-bitch, and maybe a skin-walking witch. But he wouldn't say who he was. Sounds like he figured the grandson would know."

"He say anything about wanting to give the grandson something valuable?"

McGinnis shook his head. "Hell," he said. "What'd he have? A few sheep. Forty, fifty dollars' worth of jewelry in pawn here. Change of clothes. He didn't have nothing valuable." McGinnis pondered this, the only sound in the room the slow, rhythmic creaking of his rocker.

"That girl," he said finally. "Let me see if I guessed right about the way that is. She's after that priest. He's running and she's chasing and now she's got him." He glanced at Leaphorn for confirmation. "That about it? You left her out there with him?"

"Yeah," Leaphorn said. "You got it figured right."

They thought about it awhile. The old mantel clock on the shelf behind Leaphorn's chair became suddenly noisy in the silence. McGinnis smiled faintly over his Coca-Cola glass. But Mc-Ginnis hadn't seen it happen, hadn't seen the defeat of Father Benjamin Tso as Leaphorn had. Leaphorn had asked the priest a few more questions about the letter, and had established that Father Tso had seen nothing of Goldrims, and no sign of the dog. And then Theodora Adams had opened the back door of the carryall, and taken out her small duffel bag, and put it on the ground beside the vehicle. Benjamin Tso had looked at it, and at her, and had taken a long, deep breath and said, "Theodora, you can't stay." And Theodora had stood silently, looking first at him and then down at her hands, and her shoulders had slumped just a fraction, and Leaphorn had become aware from the tortured expression on the face of Father Tso that Theodora Adams must be crying, and Leaphorn had said he would "look around a little" and had walked away from this struggle of two souls, which was, as Miss Adams had told him, not the business of the Navajo Tribal Police. The struggle had been brief. When Leaphorn had completed his idle, fruitless examination of the ground behind the hogan, Father Tso was holding the girl against him, saying something into her hair.

"That's some woman," McGinnis said, mostly to himself. His watery old eyes were almost closed. Leaphorn had nothing to add to that. He was thinking of the expression on Father Tso's face when Tso had told him to leave the girl. The God Tso had worshipped was no more than a distant abstraction then. The girl stood against his side, warm and alive, though at this stage of the Fall of Father Tso lust hadn't been the enemy. Tso's enemy, Leaphorn thought, would be a complicated mixture. It would include pity, however sadly misplaced, and affection, and loneliness and vanity. Lust would come later, when Theodora Adams wanted it to come—and Tso would learn then how he had overestimated himself.

"Certain kind of woman likes what she can't have," McGinnis said. "They hate to see a man keep a promise. Some of 'em go after married men. But you take a real tiger like that Adams— she goes gets herself a priest." He sipped the bourbon, glanced sidewise at Leaphorn. "You know how that works with a Catholic priest?" he asked. "Before they're ordained, they get some time to think about the promises they're going to make— giving up the world, and women, and all that. And then when the time comes, they go up to the altar, and they stretch out on the floor, flat on their face, and they make the promise in front of the bishop. Psychologically it makes it mean as hell to change your mind. Just one step short of getting your balls cut off if you break a promise like that." McGinnis sipped again. "Makes it a hell of a challenge for a woman," he added.

Leaphorn was thinking of another challenge. It was obsessing him. Somewhere in this jumble of contradictions, oddities, coincidences and unlikely events there must be a pattern, a reason, something that linked a cause and an effect, which the laws of natural harmony and reason would dictate. It had to be there.

"McGinnis," he said. He tried to keep his voice from sounding plaintive. "Is there anything you're not telling me that would help make sense out of this? This secret the old man was keeping—what could it have been? Could it have been worth killing for?"

McGinnis snorted. "There ain't nothing around here worth killing for," he said. "Put it all together and this whole Short Mountain country ain't worth hitting a man with a stick for."

"What do you think, then?" Leaphorn asked. "Anything that would help."

The old man communed with the inch of amber left in the Coca-Cola glass. "I can tell you a story," he said finally. "If you don't mind having your time wasted."

"I'd like to hear it," Leaphorn said.

"Part of it's true," McGinnis said. "And some of it's probably Navajo bullshit. It starts off about a hundred twenty years ago when Standing Medicine was headman of the Bitter Water Dinee and a man noted for his wisdom." McGinnis rocked back in his chair, slowly telling how, in 1863, the territorial governor of New Mexico decided to destroy the Navajos, how Standing Medicine had joined Narbona and fought Kit Carson's army until, after the bitter starvation winter of 1864, what was left of the group surrendered and was taken to join other Navajos being held at Bosque Redondo.

"That much is the true part," McGinnis said. "Anyhow, Standing Medicine shows up on the army records as being brought in in 1864, and he died at Bosque Redondo in 1865. And that gets us to the funny story." McGinnis tipped his head back and drained the last trickle of bourbon onto his tongue. He put the glass down, carefully refilled it to the copyright symbol, capped the bottle, and raised the glass to Leaphorn. "Way they told it when I was a young man, this Standing Medicine was known all around this part of the reservation for his curing. Maybe I told you about that already. But he knew every bit of the Blessing Way, and he could do the Wind Way, and the Mountain Way Chant and parts of some of the others. But they say he also knew a ceremonial that nobody at all knows anymore. I heard it called the Sun Way, and the Calling Back Chant.

Anyway, it's supposed to be the ceremonial that Changing Woman and the Talking God taught the people to use when the Fourth World ends."

McGinnis paused to tap the Coca-Cola glass— just a few drops on the tongue. "Now, you may have another version in your clan," he said. "The way we have it around Short Mountain, the Fourth World isn't supposed to end like the Third World did, with Water Monster making a flood. This time the evil is supposed to cause the Sun Father to make it cold, and the Dinee are supposed to hole up somewhere over in the Chuska range. I think Beautiful Mountain opens up for them. Then when the time is just right, they do this Sun Way and call back the light and warmth, and they start the Fifth World."

"I never heard a version quite like that," Leaphorn said.

"Like I said, maybe it's bullshit. But there's a point. There is a point. The way the old story goes, Standing Medicine figured this Way was the most important ceremonial of all. And he figured Kit Carson and the soldiers were going to catch him, and he was afraid the ritual would be forgotten, so . . ." McGinnis sipped again, watching Leaphorn, timing his account. "So he found a place and somehow or other in some magic way he preserved it all. And he just told his oldest son, so that Kit Carson and the Belacani soldiers wouldn't find it and so the Utes wouldn't find it and spoil it."

"Interesting," Leaphorn said.

"Hold on. We ain't got to the interesting part yet," McGinnis said. "What's interesting is that Standing Medicine's son came back from the Long Walk, and married a woman in the Mud clan, and this feller's oldest son was a man named Mustache Tsossie, and he married back into the Salt Cedar clan, and his oldest boy turned out to be the one we called Hosteen Tso."

"So maybe that's the secret," Leaphorn said.

"Maybe so. Or like I said, maybe it's all Navajo bullshit." McGinnis's expression was carefully neutral.

"And part of the secret would be where this place was where Standing Medicine preserved the Sun Way," Leaphorn said. "Any guesses?"

"My God," McGinnis said. "It's magic. And magic could be up in the sky, or under the earth. Out in that canyon country it could be anywhere."

"It's been my experience," Leaphorn said, "that secrets are hard to keep. If fathers know and sons know, pretty soon other people know."

"You're forgetting something," McGinnis said. "Lot of these people around here are Utes, or half Utes. Lot of intermarrying. You got to think about how a die-hard old-timer like Hosteen Tso, and his folks before him, would feel about that.

That sort of makes people close-mouthed about secrets."

Leaphorn thought about it. "Yeah," he said. "I see what you mean." The Utes had always raided this corner of the reservation. And when Kit Carson and the army had come, Ute scouts had led them—betraying hiding places, revealing food caches, helping hunt down the starving Dinee. Standing Medicine would have been guarding his secret as much from the Utes as from the whites—and now the Utes had married into the clans.

"Even if we knew what it was and where it is, it wouldn't help anyway," McGinnis said. "You probably got an old medicine bundle and some Yei masks and amulets hidden away somewhere. It's not the kind of stuff anybody kills you for."

"Not even if it's the way to stop the world from ending?" Leaphorn asked.

McGinnis looked at him, saw he was smiling. "That's what you birds got to do, you know," McGinnis said. "If you're going to solve that Tso killing, you got to figure the reason for it." McGinnis stared into the glass. "It's a damn funny thing to think about," he said. "You can just see it. Somebody walking up that wagon track, and the old man and that Atcitty girl standing there watching him coming, and probably saying 'Ya-ta-hey' whether it was friend or stranger, and then this feller taking a gun barrel or something, and clouting the old man with it and then running the girl down and clubbing her, and then . . ." McGinnis shook his head in disbelief. "And then just turning right around and walking right up that wagon track away from there." McGinnis stared over the glass at Leaphorn. "You just plain *know* a feller would have to have a real reason to do something like that. Just think about it."

Joe Leaphorn thought about it.

Outside there was the sound of hammering, of laughter, of a pickup engine starting. Leaphorn was oblivious to it. He was thinking. He was again recreating the crime in his mind. The reason for what had happened at the Tso hogan must have been real—desperate and urgent—even if it had been done by the sort of person who laughed as he ran over a strange policeman beside a lonely road. Leaphorn sighed. He would have to find out about that reason. And that meant he would *have* to speak with Margaret Cigaret.

"You were right about Mrs. Cigaret not being home," Leaphorn said. "I went by there to check. Nobody there and the truck's gone. You got any ideas where she is?"

"No telling," McGinnis said. "She could be anyplace. I'd guess visiting kin, like I told you."

"How did you know she wasn't home?"

McGinnis frowned at him. "That don't take

any great brains," he said. "She come through here three or four days ago. Had one of Old Lady Nakai's girls driving her truck. And she ain't been back." He stared belligerently at Leaphorn. "And I *knew* she didn't come home because the only way to get to her place from the outside is right past my place here."

"Three or four days ago? Can you remember which day?"

McGinnis thought about it. It took only a moment. "Wednesday. Little after I ate. About 2 P.M."

Wednesday. The Kinaalda where Leaphorn had arrested young Emerson Begay would have been starting about then. Begay was a member of the Mud clan. His niece was being initiated into womanhood at the ceremony.

"What's Mrs. Cigaret's clan?" Leaphorn asked. "Is she a Mud Dinee?"

"She's a born-to Mud," McGinnis said.

So Leaphorn knew where he could find Mrs. Cigaret. For a hundred miles around, every member of the Mud People healthy enough to stir would be drawn to the ritual reunion to share its blessing and reinforce its power.

"There's not many Mud Dinee around Short Mountain," McGinnis said. "Mrs. Cigaret's bunch, and the Nakai family, and the Endischee outfit, and Alice Frank Pino, and a few Begays, and I think that's all of them."

Leaphorn got up and stretched. He thanked McGinnis for the hospitality and said he would go to the sing. He used the Navajo verb *hodeeshtal,* which means "to take part in a ritual chant." By slightly changing the guttural inflection, the word becomes the verb "to be kicked." As Leaphorn pronounced it, a listener with an ear alert to the endless Navajo punning could have understood Leaphorn to mean either that he was going to get himself cured or get himself kicked. It was among the oldest of old Navajo word plays, and McGinnis—grinning slightly—replied with the expected pun response.

"Good for a sore butt," he said.

TEN

THE WIND FOLLOWED Leaphorn's carryall half the way across the Nokaito Bench, enveloping the jolting vehicle in its own gritty dust and filling the policeman's nostrils with exhaust fumes. It was hot. The promise of rain had faded as the west wind raveled away the thunderheads. Now the sky was blank blue. The road angled toward the crest of the ridge, growing rockier as it neared the top. Leaphorn down-shifted to ease the vehicle over a corrugation of stone and the following wind gusted past him. He drove across the ridge line, blind for a moment. Then, with a shift in the wind, the dust cleared and he saw the place of Alice Endischee.

The land sloped northward now into Utah, vast, empty and treeless. In Leaphorn the Navajo sensitivity to land and landscape was fine-tuned.

Normally he saw beauty in such blue-haze distances, but today he saw only poverty, a sparse stony grassland ruined by overgrazing and now gray with drought.

He shifted the carryall back into third gear as the track tilted slightly downward, and inspected the place of Alice Endischee far down the slope. There was the square plank "summer hogan" with its tar-paper roof, providing a spot of red in the landscape, and beyond it a "winter hogan" of stone, and a pole arbor roofed with sage and creosote brush, and two corrals, and an older hogan built carefully to the prescription of the Holy People and used for all things sacred and ceremonial. Scattered among the buildings Leaphorn counted seven pickups, a battered green Mustang, a flatbed truck and two wagons. The scene hadn't changed since he had come there to find Emerson Begay, when the Kinaalda had only started and the Endischee girl had been having her hair washed in yucca suds by her aunts as the first step of the great ritual blessing. Now the ceremonial would be in the climactic day.

People were coming out of the medicine hogan, some of them watching his approaching vehicle, but most standing in a milling cluster around the doorway. Then, from the cluster, a girl abruptly emerged—running.

She ran, pursued by the wind and a half-dozen

younger children, across an expanse of sagebrush. She set the easy pace of those who know that they have a great distance to go. She wore the long skirt, the long-sleeved blouse and the heavy silver jewelry of a traditional Navajo woman—but she ran with the easy grace of a child who has not yet forgotten how to race her shadow.

Leaphorn stopped the carryall and watched, remembering his own initiation out of childhood, until the racers disappeared down the slope. For the Endischee girl, this would be the third race of the day, and the third day of such racing. Changing Woman taught that the longer a girl runs at her Kinaalda, the longer she lives a healthy life. But by the third day, muscles would be sore and the return would be early. Leaphorn shifted back into gear. While the girl was gone, the family would re-enter the hogan to sing the Racing Songs, the same prayers the Holy People had chanted at the menstruation ceremony when White Shell Girl became Changing Woman. Then there would be a pause, while the women baked the great ceremonial cake to be eaten tonight. The pause would give Leaphorn his chance to approach and cross-examine Listening Woman.

He touched the woman's sleeve as she emerged from the hogan, and told her who he was, and why he wanted to talk to her.

"It's like I told that white policeman," Margaret Cigaret said. "The old man who was to die told me some dry paintings had been spoiled, and the man who was to die had been there. And maybe that was why he was sick."

"I listened to the tape recording of you talking to the white policeman," Leaphorn said. "But I noticed, my mother, that the white man didn't really let you tell about it. He interrupted you."

Margaret Cigaret thought about that. She stood, arms folded across the purple velvet of her blouse, her blind eyes looking through Leaphorn.

"Yes," she said. "That's the way it was."

"I came to find you because I thought that if we would talk about it again, you could tell me what the white man was too impatient to hear." Leaphorn suspected she would remember he was the man who had come to this ceremonial three days before and arrested Emerson Begay. While Begay was not a member of the Cigaret family as far as Leaphorn knew, he was Mud clan and he was probably some sort of extended-family nephew. So Leaphorn was guilty of arresting a relative. In the traditional Navajo system, even distant nephews who stole sheep were high on the value scale. "I wonder what you are thinking about me, my mother," Leaphorn said. "I wonder if you are thinking that it's no use talking to a policeman who is too stupid to keep the Begay boy from escaping because he would be too stu-pid to catch the one who killed those who were killed." Like Mrs. Cigaret, Leaphorn refrained from speaking the name of the dead. To do so was to risk attracting the attention of the ghost, and even if you didn't believe this, it was bad manners to risk ghost sickness for those who did believe. "But if you think about it fairly, you will remember that your nephew is a very smart young man. His handcuffs were uncomfortable, so I took them off. He offered to help me, and I accepted the offer. It was night, and he slipped away. Remember, your nephew has escaped be-fore."

Margaret Cigaret acknowledged this with a nod, then she tilted her head toward the place near the hogan door. There three women were pouring buckets of batter into the fire pit, mak-ing the ritual cake of the menstruation ceremony. Steam now joined the smoke. She turned toward them and away from Leaphorn.

"Put corn shucks over all of it," Mrs. Cigaret instructed them in a loud, clear voice. "You work around in a circle. East, south, west, north."

The women stopped their work for a moment. "We haven't got it poured in yet," one of them said. "Did you say we could put the raisins in?"

"Sprinkle them across the top," Mrs. Cigaret said. "Then arrange the corn-shuck crosses all across it. Start from the east side and work around like I said." She swiveled her face back toward Leaphorn. "That's the way it was done when First Man and First Woman and the Holy People gave White Shell Girl her Kinaalda when she menstruated," Mrs. Cigaret said. "And that's the way Changing Woman taught us to do."

"Yes," Leaphorn said. "I remember."

"What the white man was too impatient to hear was all about what was making the one who was killed sick," Mrs. Cigaret said.

"*I* would like to hear that when there is time for you to tell me, my mother."

Mrs. Cigaret frowned. "The white man didn't think it had anything to do with the killing."

"I am not a white man," Leaphorn said. "I am one of the Dinee. I know that the same thing that makes a man sick sometimes makes him die."

"But this time the man was hit by a gun barrel."

"I know that, my mother," Leaphorn said. "But can you tell me why he was hit with the gun barrel?"

Mrs. Cigaret thought about it.

The wind kicked up again, whipping her skirts around her legs and sending a flurry of dust across the hogan yard. At the fire pit, the women were carefully pouring a thin layer of dirt over newspapers, which covered the corn shucks, which covered the batter.

"Yes," Mrs. Cigaret said. "I hear what you are saying."

"You told the white policeman that you planned to tell the old man he should have a Mountain Way sing and a Black Rain ceremony," Leaphorn said. "Why those?"

Mrs. Cigaret was silent. The wind gusted again, moving a loose strand of gray hair against her face. She had been beautiful once, Leaphorn saw. Now she was weathered, and her face was troubled. Behind Leaphorn there came a shout of laughter. The kindling of split piñon and cedar arranged atop the cake batter in the fire pit was flaming.

"It was what I heard when I listened to the Earth," Mrs. Cigaret said, when the laughter died out.

"Can you tell me?"

Mrs. Cigaret sighed. "Only that I knew it was more than one thing. Some of the sickness came from stirring up old ghosts. But the voices told me that the old man hadn't told me everything." She paused, her eyes blank with the glaze of glaucoma, and her face grim and sad. "The voices told me that what had happened had cut into his heart. There was no way to cure it. The Mountain Way sing was the right one because the sickness came from the spoiling of holy things, and the Black Rain because a taboo had been broken.

But the old man's heart was cut in half. And there was no sing anymore that would restore him to beauty."

"Something very bad had happened," Leaphorn said, urging her on.

"I don't think he wanted to live anymore," Margaret Cigaret said. "I think he wanted his grandson to come, and then he wanted to die."

The fire was blazing all across the fire pit now and there was a sudden outburst of shouting and more laughter from those waiting around the hogan. The girl was coming—running across the sagebrush flat at the head of a straggling line. One of the Endischees was hanging a blanket across the hogan doorway, signifying that the ceremonial would be resumed inside.

"I have to go inside now," Mrs. Cigaret said. "There's no more to say. When someone wants to die, they die."

Inside, a big man sat against the hogan wall and sang with his eyes closed, the voice rising, falling and changing cadence in a pattern as old as the People.

"She is preparing her child," the big man sang. "She is preparing her child."

White Shell Girl, she is preparing her,
With white shell moccasins, she is preparing her,

With white shell leggings, she is preparing her,
With jewelry of white shells, she is preparing
  her."

The big man sat to Leaphorn's left, his legs
folded in front of him, among the men who lined
the south side of the hogan. Across from them, the
women sat. The hogan floor had been cleared. A
small pile of earth covered the fire pit under the
smoke hole in the center. A blanket was spread
against the west wall and on it were arranged the
hard goods brought to this affair to be blessed by
the beauty it would generate. Beside the blanket,
one of the aunts of Eileen Endischee was giving
the girl's hair its ceremonial brushing. She was a
pretty girl, her face pale and fatigued now, but
also somehow serene.

"White Shell Girl with pollen is preparing her,"
the big man sang.

"With the pollen of soft goods placed in her
mouth, she will speak.

With the pollen of soft goods she is preparing her.
With the pollen of soft goods she is blessing her.
She is preparing her.
She is preparing her.
She is preparing her child to live in beauty.
She is preparing her for a long life in beauty.

> *With beauty before her, White Shell Girl prepares*
> *her.*
> *With beauty behind her, White Shell Girl prepares*
> *her.*
> *With beauty above her, White Shell Girl prepares*
> *her."*

Leaphorn found himself, as he had since child-hood, caught up in the hypnotic repetition of pat-tern which blended meaning, rhythm and sound in something more than the total of all of them. By the blanket, the aunt of the Endischee girl was tying up the child's hair. Other voices around the hogan wall joined the big man in the singing.

"With beauty all around her, she prepares her."

A girl becoming a woman, and her people celebrating this addition to the Dinee with joy and reverence. Leaphorn found himself singing, too. The anger he had brought—despite all the taboos—to this ceremonial had been overcome. Leaphorn felt restored in harmony.

He had a loud, clear voice, and he used it. "With beauty before her, White Shell Girl pre-pares her."

The big man glanced at him, a friendly look. Across the hogan, Leaphorn noticed, two of the women were smiling at him. He was a stranger, a policeman who had arrested one of them, a man from another clan, perhaps even a witch, but he was accepted with the natural hospitality of the Dinee. He felt a fierce pride in his people, and in this celebration of womanhood. The Dinee had always respected the female equally with the male—giving her equality in property, in metaphysics and in clan—recognizing the mother's role in the footsteps of Changing Woman as the preserver of the Navajo Way. Leaphorn remembered what his mother had told him when he had asked how Changing Woman could have prescribed a Kinaalda cake "a shovel handle wide" and garnished with raisins when the Dinee had neither shovels nor grapes. "When you are a man," she had said, "you will understand that she was teaching us to stay in harmony with time." Thus, while the Kiowas were crushed, the Utes reduced to hopeless poverty, and the Hopis withdrawn into the secret of their kivas, the eternal Navajo adapted and endured.

The Endischee girl, her hair arranged as the hair of White Shell Girl had been arranged by the Holy People, collected her jewelry from the blanket, put it on, and left the hogan—shyly aware that all eyes were upon her.

"In beauty it is finished," the big man sang. "In beauty it is finished."

Leaphorn stood, waiting his turn to join the single file exiting through the hogan doorway. The space was filled with the smell of sweat, wool, earth and piñon smoke from the fire outside. The audience crowded around the blanket, collecting their newly blessed belongings. A middle-aged woman in a pants suit picked up a bridle; a teen-age boy wearing a black felt "reservation hat" took a small slab of turquoise stone and a red plastic floating battery lantern stenciled HAAS; an old man wearing a striped denim Santa Fe Rail-road cap picked up a flour sack containing God knows what. Leaphorn ducked through the door-way. Mixed with the perfume of the piñon smoke there now came the smell of roasting mutton.

He felt both hungry and relaxed. He would eat, and then he would ask around about a man with gold-rimmed glasses and an oversized dog, and then he would resume his conversation with Lis-tening Woman. His mind had started working again, finding a hint of a pattern in what had been only disorder. He would simply chat with Mrs. Cigaret, giving her a chance to know him better. By tomorrow he wanted her to know him well enough even to risk discussing that danger-ous subject no wise Navajo would discuss with a stranger—witchcraft.

The wind died away with evening. The sunset had produced a great flare of fluorescent orange from the still-dusty atmosphere. Leaphorn had eaten mutton ribs, and fry bread, and talked to a dozen people, and learned nothing useful. He had talked with Margaret Cigaret again, getting her to recreate as well as she remembered the sequence of events that led up to the Tso-Atcitty deaths, but he had learned little he hadn't already known from the FBI report and the tape recording. And nothing he learned seemed helpful. Anna Atcitty had not wanted to drive Mrs. Cigaret to her appointment with Hosteen Tso, and Mrs. Cigaret believed that was because she wanted to meet a boy. Mrs. Cigaret wasn't sure of the boy's identity but suspected he was a Salt Cedar Dinee who worked at Short Mountain. A dust devil had blown away some of the pollen which Mrs. Cigaret used in her professional procedure. Mrs. Cigaret had not, as Leaphorn had assumed, done her listening in the little cul-de-sac worn in the mesa cliff just under where Leaphorn had stood looking down on the Tso hogan. Leaphorn had guessed about that, knowing from the FBI report only that she had gone to a sheltered place against the cliff out of sight of the hogan; he had presumed she had been led by Anna Atcitty to the closest such place. But Mrs. Cigaret remembered walking along a goat trail to reach the sand-floored cul-de-sac where she had listened. And she thought it was at least one hundred yards from the hogan, which meant it was another, somewhat smaller drainage cut in the mesa cliff west of where Leaphorn had stood. Leaphorn remembered he had looked down into it and had noticed it had once been fenced off as a holding pen for sheep.

None of these odds and ends seemed to hold any promise, though sometime after midnight Leaphorn learned that the child who had reported seeing the "dark bird" dive into an arm of Lake Powell was one of the Gorman boys. The boy was attending the Kinaalda, but had left with two of his cousins to refill the Endischee water barrels. That involved a round trip of more than twelve miles and the wagon probably wouldn't be back before dawn. The boy's name was Eddie. He was the boy in the black hat and it turned out he wouldn't be back at all after loading the water barrels; he was going to Farmington.

Leaphorn sat through the night-long ceremonial, singing the twelve Hogan Songs, and the Songs of the Talking God, and watching sympathetically the grimly determined efforts of the Endischee girl not to break the rules by falling asleep. When the sky was pink in the east he had joined the others and chanted the Dawn Song, remembering the reverence with which his grandfather had always used it to greet each new day. The words, down through the generations, had become so melded into the rhythm that they were hardly more than musical sounds. But Leaphorn remembered the meaning.

> *"Below the East, she has discovered it,*
> *Now she has discovered Dawn Boy,*
> *The child now he has come upon it,*
> *Where it was resting, he has come upon it,*
> *Now he talks to it, now it listens to him.*
> *Since it listens to him, it obeys him;*
> *Since it obeys him, it grants him beauty.*
> *From the mouth of Dawn Boy, beauty comes forth.*
> *Now the child will have life of everlasting beauty.*
> *Now the child will go with beauty before it,*
> *Now the child will go with beauty all around it,*
> *Now the child will be with beauty finished."*

Then the Endischee girl had gone, trailed again by cousins, and nieces and nephews, to run the final race of Kinaalda. The sun had come up and Leaphorn thought he'd try once more to talk to Mrs. Cigaret. She was sitting in her truck, its door open, listening to those who were about to remove the Kinaalda cake from the fire pit.

Leaphorn sat down beside her. "One thing still troubles me," he said. "You told the FBI man, and you have told me, that the man who was killed said that sand paintings were spoiled. Sand paintings. More than one of the dry paintings. How could that be?"

"I don't know," Mrs. Cigaret said.

"Do you know of *any* sing that has more than one sand painting at a time?" Leaphorn asked. "Is there any singer *anywhere* on the reservation who does it a different way?"

"They all do it the same way, if they do it the way the Talking God taught them to make dry paintings."

"That's what my grandfather taught me," Leaphorn said. "The proper one is made, and when the ceremonial is finished, the singer wipes it out, and the sand is mixed together and carried out of the hogan, and scattered back to the wind. That's the way I was taught."

"Yes," Margaret Cigaret said.

"Then, old mother, could it have been that you did not understand what the man who was your patient said to you? Could he have said one sand painting was spoiled?"

Mrs. Cigaret turned her face from the place where the Endischees had scraped away the hot cinders, and had brushed away a layer of ashes, and were now preparing to lift the Kinaalda cake from its pit oven. Her eyes focused directly on Leaphorn's face; as directly as if she could see him.

"No," she said. "I thought I heard him wrong. And I said so. And he said . . ." She paused, recalling it. "He said, 'No, not just one holy painting. More than one.' He said it was strange, and then he wouldn't talk any more about it."

"Very strange," Leaphorn said. The only place he knew of that a bona fide singer had produced genuine dry paintings to be preserved was at the Museum of Navajo Ceremonial Art in Santa Fe. There it had been done only after much soul-searching and argument, and only after certain elements had been slightly modified. The argument for breaking the rules had been to preserve certain paintings so they would never be lost. Could that be the answer here? Had Standing Medicine found a way to leave sand paintings so a ceremony would be preserved for posterity? Leaphorn shook his head.

"It doesn't make sense," Leaphorn said.

"No," Mrs. Cigaret said. "No one would do it."

Leaphorn opened his mouth and then closed it. It was not necessary to say the obvious. There was no reason to say, "Except a witch." In the metaphysics of the Navajo, these stylized reproductions of Holy People reliving moments from mythology were produced to restore harmony. But this same metaphysics provided that when not done properly, a sand painting would destroy harmony and cause death. The legends of the grisly happenings in witches' dens were sprinkled with deliberately perverted sand paintings, as well as with murder and incest.

Mrs. Cigaret had turned her face toward the fire pit. Amid laughter and loud approval, the great brown cake was being raised from the pit—carefully, to avoid breaking—and the dust and ashes brushed away.

"The cake is out," Leaphorn said. "It looks perfect."

"The ceremony has been perfect," Listening Woman said. "Everything was done just right. In the songs, everybody got the words right. And I heard your voice among the singers."

"Yes," Leaphorn said.

Mrs. Cigaret was smiling now, but the smile was grim. "And in a moment you will ask me if the man who was to die told me anything about skinwalkers, anything about a den of witches."

"I might have asked you that, old mother," Leaphorn said. "I was trying to remember if it is wrong to even ask about witches at a Kinaalda."

"It's not a good thing to talk about," Mrs. Cigaret said. "But in this case it is business, and we won't be talking much about witches, because the old man told me nothing about them."

"Nothing?"

"Nothing. I asked him. I asked him because I, too, wondered about the sand paintings," Mrs. Cigaret said. She laughed. "And all he did was get angry. He said he couldn't talk about it because it was a secret. A big secret."

"Did you ever think that the old man might himself be a skinwalker?"

Mrs. Cigaret was silent. At the hogan door, Mrs. Endischee was cutting portions from the rim of the cake and handing them out to relatives.

"I thought about it," Mrs. Cigaret said. She shook her head again. "I don't know," she said. "If he was, he doesn't hurt anybody now."

Just beyond the Mexican Water chapter house, where Navajo Route 1 intersects with Navajo Route 12, Leaphorn pulled the carryall onto the shoulder, cut the ignition, and sat. The Tuba City district office was 113 miles west, down Route 1. Chinle, and the onerous duty of helping provide Boy Scout security at Canyon De Chelly, lay 62 miles almost due south down Route 12. Desire pulled Leaphorn westward. But when he got to the Tuba City district office what could he tell Captain Largo? He had come up with absolutely nothing concrete to justify the time Largo had bought for him—and damned little that could be described even as nebulous. He should radio Largo that he was calling it all off and then drive to Chinle and report for duty. Leaphorn picked up the Tso-Atcitty file, flipped rapidly through it, put it down again and picked up the thicker file about the search for the helicopter.

The recreated route of the copter still led erratically, but fairly directly, toward the vicinity of the Tso hogan. Leaphorn stared at the map, remembering that another line—drawn from an abandoned Mercedes to a water hole where two dogs had died—would, if extended, pass near the same spot. He flipped to the next page and began reading rapidly the description of the copter, the details of its rental, the pertinent facts about the pilot. Leaphorn stared at the name, Edward Haas. HAAS had been stenciled in white on the red plastic of the battery lantern on the blanket in the Endischee hogan.

"Well, now," Leaphorn said aloud. He thought of dates and places, trying to make connections, and failing that, thought of what Listening Woman had said when he'd asked if Tso might have been a witch. Then he reached down, picked up the radio mike and checked in with the Tuba City headquarters. Captain Largo wasn't in.

"Just tell him this, then," Leaphorn said. "Tell him that a boy named Eddie Gorman was at the Endischee Kinaalda with one of those floating fishermen's lanterns with the name Haas stenciled on it." He filled in the details of description, family, and where the boy might be found. "Tell him I'm going to Window Rock and clear a trip to Albuquerque."

"Albuquerque?" the dispatcher asked. "Largo's going to ask me why you're going to Albuquerque."

Leaphorn stared at the speaker a moment, thinking about it. "Tell him I'm going to the FBI office. I want to read their file on that helicopter case."

ELEVEN

SPECIAL AGENT GEORGE Witover, who ushered Leaphorn into the interrogation room, had a bushy but neat mustache, shrewd light-blue eyes, and freckles. He took the chair behind the desk and smiled at Leaphorn. "Well, Lieutenant—" He glanced down at the note the receptionist had given him. "Lieutenant Leaphorn. We understand you found a flashlight from the Haas helicopter." The blue eyes held Leaphorn's eyes expectantly. "Have a seat." He gestured to the chair beside the desk.

Leaphorn sat down. "Yes."

"Your Window Rock office called and told us a little about it," the man said. "They said you particularly wanted to talk to me. Why was that?"

"I heard somewhere that the man to talk to about the case was Agent George Witover,"

Leaphorn said. "I heard you were the one who was handling it."

"Oh," Witover said. He eyed Leaphorn curiously, and seemed to be trying to read something in his face.

"And I thought about the rule the FBI has about not letting anybody see case files, and I thought about how we have just exactly the same rule, and it occurred to me that sometimes rules like that get in the way of getting things done. So I thought that since we're both interested in that copter, we could sort of exchange information informally."

"You can see the report we made to the U.S. Attorney," Witover said.

"If you're like us, sometimes that report is fairly brief, and the file is fairly thick. Everything doesn't go into the report," Leaphorn said.

"What we heard from Window Rock was that you were at some sort of ceremonial, and saw the flashlight there with the name stenciled on it, but you didn't get the flashlight or talk to the man who had it."

"That's about it," Leaphorn said. "Except it was a battery lantern and a boy who had it."

"And you didn't find out where he'd gotten it?"

Leaphorn found himself doing exactly what he'd decided not to do. He was allowing himself to be irritated by an FBI agent. And that made him irritated at himself. "That's right," he said. "I didn't."

Witover looked at him, the bright blue eyes asking "Why not?" Leaphorn ignored the question.

"Could you tell me why not?" Witover asked.

"When I saw the lantern, I didn't know the name of the helicopter pilot," Leaphorn said, his voice cold.

Witover said nothing. His expression changed from incredulous to something that said: "Well, what can you expect?" "And now you want to read our file," he stated.

"That's right."

"I wish you could tell us a bit more. Any sudden show of wealth among those people. *Anything* interesting."

"In that Short Mountain country, if anybody has three dollars it's a show of wealth," Leaphorn said. "There hasn't been anything like that."

Witover shrugged and fiddled with something in the desk drawer. Through the interrogation room's single window Leaphorn could see the sun reflecting off the windows of the post office annex across Albuquerque's Gold Avenue. In the reception room behind him, a telephone rang once.

"What made you think I was particularly interested in this case?" Witover asked.

"You know how it is," Leaphorn said. "Small world. I just remember hearing somebody say that you'd asked to come out from Washington because you wanted to stay on that Santa Fe robbery."

Witover's expression said he knew that wasn't exactly what Leaphorn had heard.

"Probably just gossip," Leaphorn said.

"We don't know each other," Witover said, "but John O'Malley told me you worked with him on that Cata homicide on the Zuñi Reservation. He speaks well of you."

"I'm glad to hear that." Leaphorn knew it wasn't true. He and O'Malley had worked poorly together and the case, as far as the FBI was concerned, remained open and unsolved. But Leaphorn was glad that Witover had suddenly chosen to be friendly.

"If I show you the file, I'd be breaking the rule," Witover said. It was a statement, but it included a question. What, it asked, do I get in return?

"Yes," Leaphorn said. "And if I found the helicopter, or found out how to find it, our rules would require me to report to the captain, and he'd inform the chief, and the chief would inform Washington FBI, and then they'd teletype you. It would be quicker if I picked up the telephone and called you directly—at your home telephone number—but that would break *our* rules."

Witover's expression changed very slightly. The corners of his lips edged a millimeter upward. "Of course," he said, "you can't be tipping people off on their home telephones unless there's a clear understanding that nobody talks about it later."

"Exactly," Leaphorn said. "Just as you can't leave files in here with me if you didn't know I'd swear it never happened."

"Just a minute," Witover said.

It actually took him almost ten minutes. When he came back through the door he had a bulky file in one hand and his card in the other. He put the file on the desk and handed Leaphorn the card. "My home number's on the back," he said.

Witover sat down again and fingered the cord that held down the file flap. "It goes all the way back to Wounded Knee," he said. "When the old American Indian Movement took over the place in 1973, one of them was a disbarred lawyer from Oklahoma named Henry Kelongy." He glanced at Leaphorn. "You know about the Buffalo Society?"

"We don't get cut in for much of that," Leaphorn said. "I know what I hear, and what I read in *Newsweek*."

"Um. Well, Kelongy was a fanatic. They call him 'The Kiowa' because he's half Kiowa Indian. Raised in Anadarko, and got through the University of Oklahoma law school, and served in the Forty-fifth Division in World War Two, and made it up to first lieutenant and then killed somebody in Le Havre on the way home and lost his commission in the court-martial. Some politics after that. Ran for the legislature, worked for a congressman, kept getting more and more militant. Ran an Indian draft-resisters group during the Vietnam war. So forth. Behind all this he was working as a preacher. Started out as a Church of the Nazarene evangelist, and then moved over into the Native American Church, and then started his own offshoot of that. Kept the Native American peyote ceremony, but tossed out the Christianity. Went back to the Sun God or whatever Indians worship." Witover glanced quickly at Leaphorn. "I mean whatever Kiowas worship," he amended.

"It's complicated," Leaphorn said. "I don't know much about it, but I think Kiowas used the sun as a symbol of the Creator." Actually, he knew quite a bit about it. Religious values had always fascinated Leaphorn, and he'd studied them at Arizona State—but just now he wasn't prepared to educate an FBI agent.

"Anyway," Witover continued, "to skip a lot of the minor stuff, Kelongy had a couple of brushes with the law, and then he and some of his disciples got active in AIM. We're pretty sure they were the ones who did most of the damage when AIM took over the Bureau of Indian Affairs office in Washington. And then at Wounded Knee, Kelongy was there preaching violence. When the AIM people decided to cancel things, Kelongy raised hell, and called them cowards, and split off."

Witover fished a pack of filtered cigarettes from his pocket, offered one to Leaphorn and lit up. He inhaled, blew out a cloud of blue smoke. "Then we started hearing about the Buffalo Society. There was a bombing in Phoenix, with pamphlets left scattered around, all about the Indians killed by soldiers somewhere or other. And some more bombings here and there. . . ." Witover paused, tapping his fingertips on the desktop, thinking. "At Sacramento, and Minneapolis, and Duluth, and one in the South—Richmond, I think it was. And a bank robbery up in Utah, at Ogden, and always pamphlets identifying the Buffalo Society and a bunch of stuff about white atrocities against the Indians." Witover puffed again. "And that brings us to the business at Santa Fe. A very skillful piece of business." He glanced at Leaphorn. "How much you know about that?"

"Nothing much that didn't apply to our part of it," Leaphorn said. "Hunting the helicopter."

"The afternoon before the robbery, Kelongy checked into the La Fonda and asked for a fifth-floor suite overlooking the plaza. You can see the bank from there. Then—"

"He used his own name?" Leaphorn was frowning.

"No," Witover said. He looked slightly sheepish. "We had a tail on him."

Leaphorn nodded, his expression carefully noncommittal. He was imagining Witover trying to write the letter explaining how a man had managed a half-million-dollar robbery while under Witover's surveillance.

"We've pretty well put together exactly what happened," Witover went on. He leaned back in the swivel chair, locked his fingers behind his head, and talked with the easy precision of one practiced in delivering oral reports. The Wells Fargo truck had pulled away from the First National Bank on the northwest corner of Santa Fe Plaza at three-ten. At almost exactly three-ten, barriers were placed across arterial streets, detouring traffic from all directions into the narrow downtown streets. As the armored truck moved away from downtown, traffic congealed in a monumental jam behind it. This both occupied police and effectively sealed off the sheriff's and police departments, both in the downtown district. A man in a Santa Fe police uniform and riding a police-model motorcycle put up a barrier in the path of the armored truck, diverting a van ahead of the truck, the truck itself and a following car into Acequia Madre street. Then the barrier was used to block Acequia Madre, preventing local traffic from blundering onto the impending robbery. On the narrow street, lined by high adobe walls, the armored truck was jammed between the van and the car.

Witover leaned forward, stressing his point. "All perfectly timed," he said. "At about exactly the same time, some sort of car—nobody can remember what—drove up to the Airco office at the municipal airport. The copter was waiting. Reserved the day before in the name of an engineering company—a regular customer. Nobody saw who got out of the car and got into the copter."

Witover shook his head and gestured with both hands. "So the car drove away, and the copter flew away, and we don't even know if the passenger was a man or a woman. It landed on a ridge back in the foothills north of St. John's College. We know that because people saw it landing. It was on the ground maybe five minutes, and we can presume that while it was on the ground, the money from the Wells Fargo truck was loaded onto it—and maybe it took on a couple more passengers."

"But how'd they get into the armored truck?" Leaphorn said. "Isn't that supposed to be damned near impossible?"

"Ah," Witover said. "Exactly." The pale-blue eyes approved Leaphorn's question. "The armored truck is designed with armed robbery in mind and therefore the people on the inside can keep the people on the outside out. So how did the robbers get in? That brings us to the Buffalo Society's secret weapon. A crazy son-of-a-bitch named Tull."

"Tull?" The name seemed vaguely familiar.

"He's the only one we got," Witover said. He grimaced. "It turns out Tull thinks he's immortal. Believe it or not, the son-of-a-bitch claims to think he's already died two or three times and comes back to life." Witover's eyes held Leaphorn's, gauging his reaction. "That's what he tells the federal psychiatrists, and the shrinks tell us they believe he believes it."

Witover got up, and peered through the glass down at Gold Avenue. "He sure as hell acts like he believes it," he continued. "All of a sudden the truckdriver finds himself blocked, front and rear, and Tull jumps out of the van and puts some sort of gadget on the antenna to cut off radio transmission. By the time he gets that done the guard and driver are bright enough to have figured out that a robbery attempt is in progress. But Tull trots around to the rear door and starts stuffing this puttylike stuff around the door hinges. And what the hell you think the guard did?"

Leaphorn thought about it. The guard would have been incredulous. "Yelled at him, probably."

"Right. Asked him what the hell he was doing. Warned him he'd shoot. And by the time he did shoot, Tull had the putty in—and of course it was some sort of plastic explosive with a radio-activated fuse. And then the guard didn't shoot until Tull had it worked in and was running away."

"Then bang!" Leaphorn said.

"Right. Bang. Blew the door off," Witover said. "When the police finally got there, the neighbors were giving first aid. Tull had a bullet through the lung, and the guard and the driver were in pretty bad shape from blast concussions, and the money was gone."

"There must have been a bunch of them," Leaphorn said.

"Altogether probably six. One to put out the detour signs to create the traffic jams, and whoever got on the helicopter, and Kelongy, and the one dressed as a cop who diverted the armored truck and followed it down Acequia Madre, and Tull and the guy driving the car behind the van. And each one of them faded away as his part of the job was done."

"Except Tull," Leaphorn said.

"We got Tull and an identification on the one who wore the police uniform and had the motorcycle. The driver and the guard got a good look at him. He's the guy who called himself Hoski up at Wounded Knee, and something else before then, and a couple of other names since. He's Kelongy's right-hand man."

"This Tull," Leaphorn said. "Was he in on that Ogden bank robbery? If I remember that one, didn't they pull it off because a crazy bastard walked right up to a gun barrel?"

"Same guy," Witover said. "No doubt about it. It was another money transfer. Two guards carrying bags and one standing there with a shotgun and Tull walks right up to the shotgun and the guard's too damned surprised to shoot. You just can't train people to expect something like that."

"Maybe it's a bargain, then," Leaphorn said. "They got a half-million dollars and you got Tull."

There was a brief silence. Witover made a wry

face. "When Tull was in the hospital waiting to get the lung fixed up, we got bond set at $100,000—which is sort of high for a nonhomicide. Figured they were tossing Tull to the wolves, so we made sure Tull knew how much they had from the bank, and how much they needed to bail him out." Witover's blue eyes assumed a sadness. "If they didn't bail him out, the plan was to offer him a deal and get him to cooperate. And sure enough, no bail was posted. But Tull wouldn't cooperate. The shrinks warned us he wouldn't. And he didn't. When no bail was posted, there was a theory that the Buffalo Society had lost the money and that Tull somehow knew it. That explained why they couldn't find the copter. It had crashed into Lake Powell and sunk."

Leaphorn said nothing. He was thinking that the route of the copter, if extended, would have taken it down the lake. The red plastic lantern with HAAS stenciled on it was a floating lantern. And then there was the distorted story that its finder had seen a great bird diving into the lake.

"Yes," Leaphorn said. "Maybe that's it."

Witover laughed, and shook his head. "It sounded plausible. Tull got his lung healed, and they transferred him to the state prison at Santa Fe for safekeeping, and months passed and they talked to him again, told him why be the fall guy, told him it was clear nobody was going to bond him out, and Tull just laughed and told us to screw ourselves. And now"—Witover paused, his sharp blue eyes studying Leaphorn's face for the effect—"and now they show up and bail him out."

It was what Leaphorn had expected Witover to say, but he caused his face to register surprise. Goldrims must be Tull, new to freedom and running to cover before the feds changed their minds and got the bond revoked. That would explain a lot of things. It would explain the craziness. He calculated rapidly, counting the days backward.

"Did they bail him out last Wednesday?"

Witover looked surprised. "No," he said. "It was almost three weeks ago." He gazed at Leaphorn, awaiting an explanation for the bad guess.

Leaphorn shrugged. "Where is he now?"

"God knows," Witover said. "They caught us napping. From what we can find out, it was this one they call Hoski. He made a cash deposit in five Albuquerque banks. Anyway, Tull's lawyer showed up with five cashier's checks, posted bond, got the order, and the prisoner was sprung before anybody had time to react." Witover looked glum, remembering it. "So they didn't lose the money. There goes the theory that the copter sank in the lake. They leave him in all that time, and then all of a sudden they spring him," Witover complained.

"Maybe all of a sudden they needed him," Leaphorn said.

"Yeah," Witover said. "I thought of that. It could make you nervous."

TWELVE

THE RIGHT EYE of John Tull stared directly at the lens, black, insolent, hating the cameramen then, hating Leaphorn now. The left eye stared blindly upward and to the left out of its ruined socket, providing a sort of crazy, obscene focus for his lopsided head. Leaphorn flipped quickly back into the biographical material. He learned that when John Tull was thirteen he had been kicked by a mule and suffered a crushed cheekbone, a broken jaw and loss of sight in one eye. It took only a glance at the photographs to kill any lingering thoughts that Tull and Goldrims might be the same. Even in the dim reflection of the red warning flasher, a glimpse of John Tull would have been memorable. Leaphorn studied the photos only a moment. The right profile was a normally handsome, sensitive face—betraying the blood of

Tull's Seminole mother. The left showed what the hoof of a mule could do to fragile human bones. Leaphorn looked up from the report, lit a cigarette and puffed—thinking how a boy would learn to live behind a façade that reminded others of their own fragile, painful mortality. It helped explain why guards had been slow to shoot. And it helped explain why Tull was crazy—if crazy he was.

The report itself offered nothing surprising. A fairly usual police record, somewhat heavy on crimes of violence. At nineteen, a two-to-seven for attempted homicide, served at the Santa Fe prison without parole—which almost certainly meant a rough record inside the walls. And then a short-term armed-robbery conviction, and after that only arrests on suspicion and a single robbery charge which didn't stick.

Leaphorn flipped past that into the transcripts of various interrogations after the Santa Fe robbery. From them another picture of Tull emerged—wise and tough. But there was one exception. The interrogator here was Agent John O'Malley, and Leaphorn read through it twice.

O'MALLEY: You're forgetting they drove right off and left you.

TULL: I wanted to collect my Blue Cross benefits.

O'MALLEY: You've collected them now. Ask yourself why they don't come and get you. They got plenty of money to make bail.

TULL: I'm not worrying.

O'MALLEY: This Hoski. This guy you call your friend. You know where he is now? He left Washington and he's in Hawaii. Living it up on his share. And his share is fatter because part of it's your share.

TULL: Screw you. He's not in Hawaii.

O'MALLEY: That's what Hoski and Kelongy and the rest of them are doing to you, baby. Screwing you.

TULL: *(Laughs.)*

O'MALLEY: You ain't got a friend, buddy. You're taking everybody's fall for them. And this friend of yours is letting it happen.

TULL: You don't know this friend of mine. I'll be all right.

O'MALLEY: Face it. He went off and left you.

TULL: God damn you. You pig. You don't know him. You don't even know his name. You don't even know where he is. He never will let me down. He never will.

Leaphorn looked up from the page, closed his eyes and tried to recreate the voice. Was it vehement? Or forlorn? The words on paper told him too little. But the repetition suggested a shout.

And the shouting had ended that particular interview.

Leaphorn put that folder aside and picked up the psychiatric report. He read quickly through the diagnosis, which concluded that Tull had psychotic symptoms of schizophrenic paranoia and that he suffered delusions and hallucinations. A Dr. Alexander Steiner was the psychiatrist. He had talked to Tull week after week following his bout with chest surgery and he'd established an odd sort of guarded rapport with Tull, surprisingly soon.

Much of the talk was about a grim childhood with a drunken mother and a series of men with whom she had lived—and finally with the uncle whose mule had kicked him. Leaphorn scanned rapidly through the report, but he lingered over sections that focused on Tull's vision of his own immortality.

STEINER: When did you find out for sure? Was it that first time in prison?

TULL: Yeah. In the box. That's what they called it then. The box. *(Laughs.)* That's what it was, too. Welded it together out of boiler plate. A hatch on one side so you could crawl in and then they'd bolt it shut behind you. It was under the floor of the laundry building in the old prison—the one they tore down. About five foot square, so you couldn't stand up but you could lay down if you lay with your feet in one corner and your head in the other. You know what I mean?

STEINER: Yes.

TULL: Usually you got into that for hitting a guard or something like that. That's what I done. Hit a guard. *(Laughs.)* They don't tell you how long you're going to be in the box, and that wouldn't matter anyway because it's pitch black under that laundry and it's even blacker in the box, so the only way you could keep track of the days passing is because the steam pipes from the laundry make more noise in the daytime. Anyway, they put me in there and bolted that place shut behind me. And you keep control pretty good at first. Explore around with your hands, find the rough places and the slick places on the wall. And you fiddle with the buckets. There's one with drinking water and one you use as a toilet. And then, all of a sudden, it gets to you. It's closing in on you, and there ain't no air to breathe, and you're screaming and fighting the walls and . . . and . . . *(Laughs.)* Anyway, I smothered to death in there. Sort of drowned. And when

I came alive again, I was laying there on the floor, with the spilled water all cool and comfortable around me. I was a different person from that boy they put in the box. And I got to thinking about it and it came to me that wasn't the first time I'd died and come alive again. And I knew it wouldn't be the last time.

STEINER: The first time you died. Was that when the horse kicked you?

TULL: Yes, sir, it was. I didn't know it then, though.

STEINER: And then you feel as if you died again when this truck guard shot you at Santa Fe?

TULL: You can feel it, you know. There's a kind of a shock when the bullet hits—a numb feeling. And it hurts a little where it went in and came out. Lot of nerves in the skin, I guess. But inside, it just feels funny. And you see the blood running out of you. (Laughs.) I said to myself, "Well, I'm dyin' again and when I come alive in my next life, I'm going to have another face."

STEINER: You think about that a lot, don't you? Having another face?

TULL: It happened once. It'll happen again. This wasn't the face I had the first time I died.

STEINER: But don't you think that if they had taken you to the right kind of surgeon he could have straightened it out after you got kicked?

TULL: No. It was different. It wasn't the one I had.

STEINER: When you look in a mirror, though. When you look at the right side of your face, isn't that the way you always looked?

TULL: The right side? No. I didn't really look like that in my first life. *(Laughs.)* You got a cigarette?

STEINER: Pall Malls.

TULL: Thanks. You know, Doc, that's why the pigs is so wrong about my buddy. The one they call Hoski. They don't even know his real name. He's like me. He told me once that he's immortal, too. Just let it slip out, like he wasn't supposed to tell anyone. But it don't make any difference to me if everybody knows. And there's another way I can tell he's like me. When he looks at me, he sees me. Me. You know. Not this goddamned face. He sees right through the face and he sees me behind it. Most people they look and they see this crazy eyeball, and they flinch, like they was looking at something sick and nasty. But—but my buddy . . . *(Laughs.)* I almost let his real name slip out there. The first time he looked at me, he didn't see this face at all. He just grinned and said "Gladtameetcha," or something like that, and we sat there and drank some beer, and it was just as if this face had peeled away and it was me sitting there.

STEINER: But the police think this man sort of took advantage of you. Left you behind and all that.

TULL: They think bullshit. They're trying to con me into talking. They think I'm crazy, too.

STEINER: What do you think about that?

TULL: You ought to see the Kiowa. He's the crazy one. He's got this stone. Claims it's a sort of a god. Got feathers and fur and a bone hanging from it. Hangs it from this goddamn bamboo tripod and sings to it. *(Laughs.)* Calls it Boy Medicine, and Talyda-i, or some damn thing like that. I think it's a Kiowa word. He told us there at Wounded Knee that if those AIM people was willin' to start shootin' to kill, then this Boy Medicine would help them. The white man was goin' to be wiped out and the Buffalo would cover the earth again. *(Laughs.)* How about *that* for crazy shit?

STEINER: But isn't that the leader of the orga-

nization? The one you're supposed to be following?

TULL: The Kiowa? Shit. My buddy, he was
workin' with him, and I'm workin' with my
buddy. Following? We don't follow nobody.
Not my buddy and me.

Leaphorn skipped back and reread the para-
graph about the Kiowa. What was it they had
learned in his senior graduate seminar on Native
American Religions? The sun was personified by
the Kiowas, as he remembered it, and the sun
had lured a Kiowa virgin into the sky and impregnated her and she had borne an infant boy.
Much like the Navajos' own White Shell Maiden,
being impregnated by Sun and Water and bear-
ing the Hero Twins. And the Kiowa maiden had
tried to escape from the sun, and had lowered
the boy to earth and escaped after him. But the
sun had thrown down a magic ring and killed
her. Then the boy had taken the ring, and struck
himself with it, and divided himself into twins.
One of the twins had walked into the water and
disappeared forever. The other had turned himself into ten medicine bundles and had given
himself to his mother's people as a sort of Holy
Eucharist. Nobody seemed to know exactly what
had happened to these bundles. Apparently they

had been gradually lost in the Kiowas' endless cavalry war for control of the High Plains. After the battle of Palo Duro Canyon, when the army herded the rag-tag remainders of these Lords of the Plains back into captivity at Fort Sill, at least one of the bundles had remained. The army had made the Kiowa watch while the last of the tribe's great horse herd was shot. But according to the legend, this Boy Medicine still remained with his humiliated people. The Kiowas had tried to hold their great annual Kado even when captive on the reservation, but they had to have a bull buffalo for the dance. Warriors slipped away to the King Ranch in Texas to buy one, but they came back empty-handed. And after that, the old people taught, Boy Medicine had left the Kiowas and the last of the medicine bundles had disappeared.

Leaphorn thought about it. Could Kelongy actually have come into possession of one of the sacred medicine bundles? He had preached a revival of the Buffalo religion. He promised the return of utopia, the white men exterminated, and Native Americans again living in a free society. The Buffalo then would again spring from the earth in their millions and nurture the children of the sun.

Leaphorn became aware of heat against his finger—his cigarette burning too close to the skin. He took a final drag, stubbed it out, and studied the smoke trickling slowly upward from his lips. He felt a vague uneasiness. Some thought struggling to be remembered. Something nameless tugging at him. He tried to let it surface and found himself thinking vaguely of witchcraft, remembering incongruously something that had no connection at all with what he had been reading, remembering Listening Woman telling him that more than one of the holy sand paintings had been desecrated in the place where Hosteen Tso had been. And remembering that it had occurred to Listening Woman, as it had occurred to him, that Hosteen Tso might have been involved in some sort of perverted ritual of a coven of Navajo Wolves.

The door to the interrogation room opened. A youngish man in a seersucker suit came in, glanced curiously at Leaphorn, said "Excuse me," and left. Leaphorn stretched and yawned, put the Tull folder back into the accordion file that held it, and resumed his fishing expedition through the remaining material.

The helicopter pilot seemed straight. He had flown copters in Vietnam. He had a wife and two children. There was no criminal record. The only question the FBI had been able to raise about his character referred to "three trips to Las Vegas over the past two years, after two of which he told informants he had won small amounts of money."

Kelongy had a much thicker file, but it added nothing substantial to Leaphorn's knowledge. Kelongy was a violent man, and a bitter one, and a dreamer of deadly dreams. Three of the other "minimum of six" participants in the Santa Fe robbery remained nameless and faceless. There was a short file for a Jackie Noni, a young part-Potawatomi with a brief but violent police record, who apparently drove the car that blocked the armored truck.

That left Tull's buddy, the one the FBI called Hoski. There was nothing standard about Hoski.

The FBI had no real idea who he was. It listed him as Frank Hoski, also known as Colton Hoski, a.k.a. Frank Morris, a.k.a. Van Black. The only photograph in the file was a grainy blowup obviously taken with a telephoto lens in bad light. It showed a trim but slightly stocky man, face partially averted, coming through a doorway. The man's hair was black, or very dark, and he looked Indian, possibly Navajo or Apache, Leaphorn thought, or possibly something else. He reminded Leaphorn vaguely of the uneasiness that had been troubling him, but he could dredge up absolutely nothing. The legend under the photo guessed Hoski's weight at "about 190," and his height at about five foot eleven, his race as "probably Indian, or part Indian," and his identifying marks as "possible heavy scar tissue under hairline above right cheek."

Not much was known of Hoski's career. He had first appeared at Wounded Knee, where informers listed him as one of the "violents" and as a right-hand man of Kelongy. A man who fit his description and used the name Frank Morris was seen by witnesses at the Ogden robbery and FBI informers confirmed that Hoski and Morris were identical. What was known about him was mostly pieced together from FBI informers who had infiltrated AIM. He was believed to be a Vietnam war veteran. Three informers identified him as army, two of the three as a demolitions expert, the other as an infantry company radioman. He occasionally smoked cigars, was a moderate drinker, was pugnacious (having engaged in fistfights on three occasions with other AIM members), often told jokes, had once lived in Los Angeles, had once lived in Memphis, and possibly once lived in Provo, Utah. Had no known homosexual tendencies, had no known relationships with females, had only one known close friend, a subject identified as John Tull. He had been identified again, on a "most likely" basis, as the man wearing the police uniform who had diverted the Wells Fargo truck into the robbery trap at Santa Fe. He came into view again in

Washington, D.C., where he was working as a janitor for a company identified as Safety Systems, Inc., which dealt in burglary alarms, locking systems and other security devices.

Leaphorn opened the last section of the report. The FBI, he was thinking, was in an enviable situation relative to Hoski. They had spotted him without Hoski's knowing he was spotted. A string tied to a key man in the Buffalo Society would almost inevitably lead eventually to other members of the terrorist group. The agency would put its best people on the surveillance team. It wouldn't risk either tipping Hoski or allowing him to slip away.

Leaphorn read. The head of the team of the FBI's best people, assigned to keep Hoski on the FBI string, was George Witover. And that, of course, was why Witover had been sent back to the Albuquerque agency, and why Witover was willing to break a rule. Hoski had cut the string under Witover's eyes.

Leaphorn read on. Until the very end, Witover's operation had seemed to go flawlessly. Hoski had been located more than a month after the Santa Fe robbery. He followed a routine. Each weekday afternoon about 6 P.M., Hoski would emerge from his utility apartment, walk two blocks to a bus stop and catch a bus to his job at Safety Systems, Inc., where he was employed under the name

Theodore Parker. On the premises, he would eat a midnight lunch, carried from his apartment in a sack, with a black fellow janitor. At about 4:30 A.M. he would leave the Safety Systems, Inc. building, walk five blocks to a bus stop and catch the bus back to his apartment. He would reemerge from the apartment in the early afternoon, to do grocery shopping, take care of his laundry at a neighborhood coin-operated laundromat, take long walks, or sit in a park overlooking the Potomac. The routine had rarely varied and never in any important degree—until March 23. On that date he was observed at the laundromat engaging in a lengthy conversation with a young woman, subsequently identified as Rosemary Rita Oliveras, twenty-eight, divorced, an immigrant from Puerto Rico. On March 30, the two had again met at the laundromat, engaged in conversation, and later gone for a wandering walk which lasted more than three hours. On April 1, a Saturday, Hoski had surprised his surveillance by emerging from his apartment before noon and walking to the boardinghouse where Mrs. Oliveras resided. The two thereupon walked to a cafe, lunched and went to a movie. Subsequently Hoski spent most of his free time with Mrs. Oliveras. Otherwise, nothing changed.

The mail cover on Hoski continued turning up one outgoing letter every week, either left for the mailman or dropped in a letter slot. The letter was invariably addressed to an Eloy R. Albertson, General Delivery, West Covina, California, and invariably contained the same message: "Dear Eloy: Nothing new. Hoski."

No one had ever appeared at the West Covina post office to claim the letters.

The second variation in the pattern of Hoski's behavior came on March 11. A taxicab had pulled up to his address at about 1 P.M. and had taken Hoski to an urban renewal demolition district two blocks from the Potomac. He left the cab at a street corner, walked through a mixture of wind-driven rain and sleet to a telephone booth and made a brief call. He then walked down the street into the sheltered doorway of an abandoned storefront across the street from the Office Bar. Approximately twenty minutes later, at 2:11 P.M., a taxi discharged a passenger at the entrance of the Office Bar. The passenger was subsequently identified as Robert Rainey, thirty-two, a former activist in the Students for a Democratic Society, and a former AIM member, with a three-rap demonstration-related arrest record. He immediately entered the bar. The FBI agent watching Hoski notified his control that a meeting seemed impending. A second agent was dispatched. The second agent arrived twenty-one minutes after Rainey entered the bar. Informed that Hoski was still waiting across the street from the Office Bar, the second agent parked his van down the street. To avoid suspicion, he left the vehicle and took up a position out of sight in the doorway of an empty storefront. About three minutes after he did so, Hoski walked down the street to the doorway, spoke to the agent about "getting in out of the weather," and then walked back up the street and into the Office Bar. The second agent thereupon checked and discovered that the alley exit from this bar was closed off by a locked garbage-access gate. Since the second agent had been seen, the first agent entered the bar to determine whether Hoski was making a contact. Hoski was sitting in a booth with Rainey. The agent ordered a beer, drank it at the bar and left—there being no opportunity to overhear the conversation between Hoski and Rainey. Hoski left the bar about ten minutes later, walked to the telephone booth at the end of the block, made a brief telephone call, and then returned to his apartment by bus. He emerged again, as was usual, to take a bus to his job.

"It is presumed that Rainey delivered a message," the report said.

Leaphorn rubbed his eyes. A messenger, of course, but how had the meeting been arranged? Not by mail, which was covered. Not by telephone, which was tapped. A note hand-delivered to Hoski's mail slot, perhaps. Or handed to him on a bus. Or a prearranged visit to a pay-phone information drop. There were any of a thousand ways to do it. That meant Hoski either knew he was being watched, or suspected he was, or was naturally cautious. Leaphorn frowned. That made Hoski's behavior relative to the meeting inconsistent. The bar was outside Hoski's regular territory, broke his routine, was sure to attract FBI attention. And so, certainly, was his behavior—the long wait outside the bar, all that. Leaphorn frowned. The frown gradually converted itself to a smile, to a broad, delighted grin, as Leaphorn realized what Hoski had been doing. Still grinning, Leaphorn leaned back in the chair and stared at the wall, reconstructing it all.

Hoski had known he was being followed and had gone to considerable pains to keep the FBI from knowing that he knew. The weekly letters to California, for example. No one would ever pick them up. Their only purpose was to assure the FBI that Hoski suspected nothing. And then the message had come. Probably a note to call a telephone number. From a pay phone. Hoski had picked an isolated bar and a meeting time which would guarantee low traffic and high visibility. He had picked a bar without a back entrance to assure that no one could enter without being seen by Hoski. He had notified the messenger of the meeting place only after he was in position to watch the front door. Then he had waited to watch the messenger arrive—and to watch the FBI reaction to the arrival and Hoski's other unorthodox behavior. Why? Because Hoski didn't know whether the messenger was a legitimate runner of the Buffalo Society or an FBI informer. If the messenger was not FBI, the agency would quickly send someone to tail the messenger. Thus Hoski had waited for the second tail to arrive. And when the van had parked down the street, Hoski had walked over to make sure the driver was in fact FBI, watching from the doorway, and not someone with a key and business inside. Then, with the legitimacy of the messenger confirmed by the FBI reaction, he'd gone into the bar and received his message.

What next? Leaphorn resumed reading. The following day the agency had doubled its watch on Hoski. The day was routine, except that Hoski had walked to a neighborhood shopping center and, at a J. C. Penney store, had bought a blue-and-white-checked nylon windbreaker, a blue cloth hat and navy-blue trousers.

The next day the routine shattered. A little after 3 P.M. an ambulance arrived at Hoski's apartment building. Hoski, holding a bloody bath towel to his face, was helped into the vehicle and taken to the emergency room at Memorial Hospital. The ambulance attendants reported that they found Hoski sitting on the steps just inside the entrance waiting for them. The police emergency operator revealed that a man had called fifteen minutes earlier, claimed he had cut himself and was bleeding to death, and asked for an ambulance. At the hospital, the attending physician reported that the patient's right scalp had been slashed. Hoski said he had slipped with a bottle in his hand and fallen on the broken glass. He was released with seventeen stitches closing the wound, and a bandage which covered much of his face. He took a cab home, called Safety Systems, Inc., and announced that he had cut his head and would have to miss work for two or three days.

At mid-morning the next day, he emerged from the apartment wearing the clothing purchased at J. C. Penney and carrying a bulging pillowcase. He walked slowly, with one rest at a bus stop, to the Bendix laundromat where he had routinely done his laundry. In the laundry, Hoski washed the contents of the pillowcase, placed the wet wash in a dryer, disappeared into the rest room for about four minutes, emerged and waited for the drying cycle to be completed, and then carried the dried laundry in the pillowcase back to his apartment.

Two days later, a young Indian, who hadn't been observed entering the apartment building, emerged and left in a taxi. This had aroused suspicion. The following day, Hoski's apartment was entered and proved to be empty. Evidence found included a new blue-and-white-checked nylon windbreaker, a blue cloth hat, navy-blue trousers and the remains of a facial bandage, which—since it was not stained by medications—was presumed to have been used as a disguise.

Leaphorn read through the rest of it rapidly. Rosemary Rita Oliveras had appeared two days later at Hoski's apartment house, and had called his employer, and then had gone to the police to report him missing. The FBI statement described her as "distraught—apparently convinced that subject is the victim of foul play." The rest of it was appendix material—interviews with Rosemary Rita Oliveras, the transcripts of tapped telephone calls, odds and ends of accumulated evidence. Leaphorn read all of it. He sorted the materials into their folders, fitted the folders back into the accordion file, and sat staring at nothing in particular.

It was obvious enough how Hoski had done it. When the FBI's reaction had proved the messenger legitimate, he had gone to a department store and bought easy-to-recognize, easy-to-match clothing. Then he had called a friend. (Not a friend, Leaphorn corrected himself. He had called an accomplice. Hoski had no friends. In all those months in Washington he had seen no one except Rosemary Rita Oliveras.) He had told the accomplice exactly which items to buy, and to have his face bandaged as if his right scalp had been slashed open. He had told him to come early and unobserved to the laundromat, to lock himself into a toilet booth and to wait. When Hoski had appeared, this man had simply assumed Hoski's role—had carried the laundry back to Hoski's apartment and waited. And inside the men's room booth, Hoski had dressed in a set of clothing the man must have brought for him, and removed the bandage, and covered his sewn scalp with a wig or a hat, and vanished. Away from Washington, and from FBI agents, and from Rosemary Rita Oliveras. He must have been tempted to call her, Leaphorn thought. The only thing that Hoski hadn't planned on was falling in love with this woman. But he had. Something in those telephone transcripts said he had. They were terse, but you found love somehow in what was said, and left unsaid. But Hoski hadn't contacted her. He had left Rosemary Rita Oliveras without a word. The FBI would have known if he had tipped her off. She was an uncomplicated woman. She couldn't have faked the frantic worry, or the hurt.

Leaphorn lit another cigarette. He thought of the nature of the man the FBI called Hoski; a man smart enough to use the FBI as Hoski had done and then to arrange that clever escape. What had that taken? Leaphorn imagined how it must have been done. First, the call to the ambulance to minimize the risk. Then the broken glass gripped carefully, placed against the cringing skin. The brain telling the muscle to perform the act that every instinct screamed against. God! What sort of man was Hoski?

Leaphorn turned back to the file. The last items were three poorly printed propaganda leaflets left at the scenes of various Buffalo Society crimes. The rhetoric was uncompromising anger. The white man had attempted genocide against the Buffalo People. But the Great Power of the Sun was just. The Sun had ordained the Buffalo Society as his avenger. When seven symbolic crimes had been avenged, white men everywhere would be stricken. The earth would be cleansed of them. Then the sacred buffalo herds and the people they nourished would again flourish and populate the land.

The crimes were listed, with the number of victims, in the order they would be avenged. Most of them were familiar. The Wounded Knee Massacre was there, and the ghastly slaughter at Sand Creek, and the mutilation of Acoma males after their pueblo stronghold fell to the Spanish. But the first crime was unfamiliar to Leaphorn.

It was an attack on a Kiowa encampment in West Texas by a force of cavalry and Texas Rangers. The pamphlet called it the Olds Prairie Murders, said it came when the men were away hunting buffalo, and listed the dead as eleven children and three adults. That was the smallest casualty total. The death toll increased down the list, culminating with the "Subjugation of the Navajos." For that, the pamphleteer listed a death toll of 3,500 children and 2,500 adults. Probably, Leaphorn thought, as fair a guess as any. He put the pamphlet aside and found a sort of anxious uneasiness again intruding into his thoughts. He was overlooking something. Something important. Abruptly he knew it was related to what Mrs. Cigaret had told him. Something about where she had sat, with her head against the stone, while she had listened to the voices in the earth. But what had she said? Just enough to let Leaphorn know that he had guessed wrong about which of the cul-de-sacs in the mesa cliff she had used for this communion with the stone. She had not used the one closest to the Tso hogan. Anna Atcitty had led her up a sheep trail beside the mesa.

Leaphorn closed his eyes, grimaced with concentration, remembering how he had stood on the mesa rim, looking down on the Tso hogan, on the wagon track leading to it, on the brush arbor. There had been a cul-de-sac below him and another perhaps two hundred yards to his left, where sheep had once been penned. Leaphorn could see it again in memory—the sheep track angling gradually away from the wagon road. And then he was suddenly, chillingly aware of what his subconscious had been trying to tell him. If Listening Woman had sat there, she would have been plainly visible to the killer as he approached the hogan down the wagon track—and even more obvious as he left. Did that mean Mrs. Cigaret had lied? Leaphorn wasted hardly a second on that. Mrs. Cigaret had not lied. It meant the wagon road was not the way the killer had come and gone. He had come out of the canyon, and departed into it. And that meant that if he emerged again, he would find Father Tso and Theodora Adams just where he had found Hosteen Tso and Anna Atcitty.

THIRTEEN

THE NUCLEUS OF the cloud formed about noon over the Nevada-Arizona border. By the time it trailed its dark-blue shadow across the Grand Canyon, it had built into a tower more than a mile from its sparkling white top to its flat, dark base. It crossed the southern slopes of Short Mountain at midafternoon, growing fast. Fierce internal updrafts pushed its cap above thirty thousand feet. There the mist droplets turned to ice, and fell, and melted, and were caught again in updrafts and soared into the frigid stratosphere, only to fall again—increasing in size with this churning and producing immense charges of static electricity which caused the cloud to mutter and grumble with thunder and produce occasional explosive bolts of lightning. These linked cloud with mountain or mesa top for brilliant seconds, and sent waves of echoes booming down the canyons below. And finally, the icy droplets glittering at the cloud-top against the deep-blue sky became too heavy for the winds, and too large to evaporate in the warm air below. Then thin curtains of falling ice and water lowered from the black base of the cloud and at last touched the ground. Thus, east of Short Mountain, the cloud became a "male rain."

Leaphorn stopped the carryall, turned off the ignition and listened to it coming. The sun slanted into the falling water, creating a gaudy double rainbow which seemed to move steadily toward him, narrowing its arch as it came in accordance with rainbow optics. There was sound now, the muted approaching roar of billions of particles of ice and water striking stone. The first huge drop struck the roof of Leaphorn's carryall. Plong! Plong-plong! And a torrent of rain and hail swept over the vehicle. The screen of falling water dimmed the landscape for a moment, the droplets reflecting the sun like a rhinestone curtain. And then the light was drowned. Leaphorn sat, engulfed in sound. He glanced at his watch, and waited, enjoying the storm as he enjoyed all things right and natural—not thinking for a moment about any of the unnatural affairs that involved him. He put aside the sense of urgency that had brought him down this wagon track much faster than it could wisely be driven. It took a fraction over seven minutes for the storm to pass Leaphorn's carryall. He started the engine and drove through the diminishing shower. A mile short of the Tso place, runoff water flashing down an arroyo had cut deeply into its bank. Leaphorn climbed out of the carryall and examined the road. A couple of hours with a shovel would make it passable again. Now it was not. It would be quicker to walk.

Leaphorn walked. The sun emerged. In places the sandstone landscape was littered with hail. In places the hot stone steamed, the cold rain water evaporating to form patches of ground mist. The air was cold, smelling washed and clean. The Tso hogan, as Leaphorn approached it, appeared deserted.

He stopped a hundred yards short of the buildings and shouted, calling first for Tso and then for the girl. Silence. The rocks steamed. Leaphorn shouted again. He walked to the hogan. The door stood open. He peered into its dark interior. Two bedrolls, side by side. Theodora Adams's overnight case and duffel bag. The scant luggage of Father Tso. A box of groceries, cooking utensils. Everything was neat. Everything in order. Leaphorn turned from the doorway and surveyed the surroundings. The rain had swept the ground clean of tracks, and nothing had been here since the rain had stopped. Father Tso and Theodora had left the hogan before the storm arrived. And they had been too far afield to return to its shelter when the rain began. But where could they go? Behind the hogan, the wall of the mesa rose. It was mostly cliff, but breaks made it easy enough to climb in half a dozen places. To the north, northwest and northeast, the ground fell away into a labyrinth of vertical-walled canyons which he knew drained, eventually, into the San Juan River. The track he had taken circled in from the south, through a wilderness of eroded stone. Tso and the girl had probably climbed the mesa, or wandered southward, though the canyons would make forbidding, and dangerous, walking.

A faint breeze stirred the air and brought the distant sound of thunder from the retreating storm. The sun was low now, warm against the side of Leaphorn's face. He looked down the wagon track toward the place where Listening Woman had seen her vision and had been, for some reason, herself unseen by a murderer. So the murderer had not used the only easy exit route. If he had climbed the mesa, it, too, would have offered him an open view of the woman. That left only the canyons. Which made no sense.

Leaphorn looked northward. A reasonably agile man could climb down off this bench to the canyon floor, but canyons would lead him nowhere.

Only into an endless labyrinth—deeper and deeper into the sheer-walled maze.

Leaphorn turned suddenly, ducked through the hogan door and sorted through Tso's supplies. His groceries included about twenty cans of meats, fruits and vegetables, two-thirds of a twenty-pound sack of potatoes, and an assortment of dried beans and other staples. Tso had come, obviously, for a long stay. Leaphorn checked the girl's duffel bag, and the priest's suitcases, and found nothing that seemed helpful.

Then as he looked toward the hogan door, he saw marks on the floor which were almost too faint to register. They were visible only because of the angle of light between Leaphorn and the doorway. They were nothing more than the damp pawprints of a very large dog left on the hard-packed earthen floor. But they were enough to tell Leaphorn that he had failed in carrying out his instructions to take care of Theodora Adams.

Leaphorn studied the hogan floor again, his cheek to the packed earth as he examined the stirred dust against the light. But he learned little. The dog had evidently come here during the rain or immediately after it. And someone had been with the dog, since several of its damp footprints had been scuffed. That could have been Goldrims, or Tso and Adams, or perhaps all three. The dog might even have arrived pre-rain, and have run out into the rain, and returned wet-footed. And all had left while enough rain was still falling to erase their tracks.

He stood at the door. Too much coincidence. Leaphorn didn't believe in it. He believed nothing happened without cause. Everything intermeshed, from the mood of a man, to the flight of the corn beetle, to the music of the wind. It was the Navajo philosophy, this concept of interwoven harmony, and it was bred into Joe Leaphorn's bones. There had to be a reason for the death of Hosteen Tso, and it had to be connected with why Goldrims—or at least Goldrims's dog—had been drawn to the Tso hogan. Leaphorn tried to think it through. He knew Listening Woman had sensed some unusual evil behind the troubled spirit of Hosteen Tso. She had decided to recommend that a Mountain Way be performed for the old man, and that the Black Rain Chant also should be done. It was an unusual prescription. Both of the curing ceremonials were ritual recreations of a portion of the myths that taught how the Dinee had emerged from the underworld and become human clans. The Mountain Way would have been intended to restore Hosteen Tso's psyche with the harmony that had been disrupted by his witnessing some sort of sacrilegious taboo violation—the disrespect to the holy sand paintings probably. But why the Black

Rain Chant? Leaphorn should have asked her more about that. It was an obscure ritual, rarely performed. He remembered that its name came from the creation of rain. First Coyote had a role in it, Leaphorn recalled. And a fire played a part somehow. But how could that be involved with the curing of Hosteen Tso? He leaned against the hogan doorframe, recalling the lessons of his boyhood. Hosteen Coyote had visited Fire Man, and had tricked him, and had stolen a bundle of burning sticks and escaped with the treasure tied to his bushy tail. And in running, he had spread flames all across Dinetah, and the Holy Land of the People was burning, and the Holy People had met to consider the crisis. Something clicked suddenly into place. The hero of this particular myth adventure was First Frog. Hosteen Frog had used his magic, inflated himself with water, and—carried aloft by First Crane—had produced black rain to save Dinetah from fire. And Listening Woman had mentioned that Hosteen Tso had killed a frog—or caused it to be killed by a falling rock. Leaphorn frowned again. Killing a frog was a taboo, but a minor one. A personal chant would cure the guilt and restore beauty. Why had the death of this frog been weighted so heavily? Because, Leaphorn guessed, Tso associated it with the other, grimmer sacrilege. Had there been frogs near the place where the sand paintings were desecrated?

Leaphorn glanced again at the mesa, where his common sense suggested that Father Tso and Theodora Adams must have gone—and away from the dead-end waste of canyons which led absolutely nowhere except—if you followed them far—under the drowning waters of Lake Powell. Yet, Leaphorn thought, if the man who had killed Hosteen Tso had failed to see Listening Woman, he must have gone into the canyons. And if there was a secret place nearby where the sand paintings and the medicine bundle of the Way to Cure the World's End had waited out the generations, it might well be in a deep, dry cave and caves again meant the canyons. Finally, the mesa offered no water, and thus no possibility of frogs. Leaphorn—walking fast—headed for the canyon rim.

The branch canyon that skirted past the Tso hogan was perhaps eighty vertical feet from the cap rock to its sandy bottom. The trail that connected the two had been cut by goats at a steep angle and at the bottom Leaphorn found tracks which proved to him he had guessed right. The rocks were dry now and the humans—humanlike—had avoided the rainwater puddles between them. But the dog had not. At several places Leaphorn found traces left by its wet paws. They led down the narrow slot, and here a narrow strip of sand was wet. Two persons had stepped in it—perhaps three. Large feet and a small foot. Adams and Father Tso? Adams and Goldrims? Had the party included a third member, who had stepped from rock to rock and left no footprints? Leaphorn turned to the spring. It was little more than a seep, emerging from a moss-covered crack and dripping into a catch basin which Tso had probably dug out. There were no frogs here, and no sign of a rock slide. Leaphorn tasted the water. It was cold, with a slightly mineral taste. He drank deeply, wiped his mouth, and began walking as quietly as he could down the hard-packed sand of the canyon bottom.

FOURTEEN

LEAPHORN HAD BEEN walking almost three hours, slowly, cautiously, trying to follow tracks in the gathering darkness, when he heard the sound. It stopped him, and he held his breath, listening. It was a soprano sound, made by something living—human or otherwise. It came from a long distance, lasted perhaps three or four seconds, cut off abruptly in midnote, and was followed by a confusion of echoes. Leaphorn stood on the sand of the canyon bottom, analyzing the diminishing echoes. A human voice? Perhaps the high-pitched scream of a bobcat? It seemed to come from the place where this canyon drained into a larger canyon about 150 yards below him. But whether it originated up or down the larger canyon, or across it, or above it, Leaphorn could only guess. The echoes had been chaotic.

He listened a moment longer and heard nothing. The sound seemed to have startled even the insects and the insect-hunting evening birds. Leaphorn began to run as quietly as he could toward the canyon mouth, the whisper of his bootsoles on the sand the only sound in an eerie silence. At the junction he stopped, looking right and left. He had been in the canyons long enough to develop an unusual and unsettling sense of disorientation—of not knowing exactly where he was in terms of either direction or landmarks. He understood its cause: a horizon which rose vertically overhead and the constant turning of the corridors sliced through the stone. Understanding it made it no more comfortable. Leaphorn, who had never been lost in his life, didn't know exactly where he was. He could tell he was moving approximately northward. But he wasn't sure he could retrace his way directly back to the Tso hogan without wasting steps. That uncertainty added to his general uneasiness. Far overhead, the clifftops still glowed with the light of the sunset's afterglow, but here it was almost dark. Leaphorn sat on a boulder, fished a cigaret out of a package in his shirt pocket, and held it under his nose. He inhaled the aroma of the tobacco, and then slipped it back into the pack. He would not make a light. He simply sat, letting his senses work for him. He was hungry. He put that thought aside. On earth level the breeze had died, as it often did in the desert twilight. Here, two hundred feet below the earth's surface, the air moved down-canyon, pressed by the cooling atmosphere from the slopes above. Leaphorn heard the song of insects, the chirping of rock crickets, and now and then the call of an owl. A bullbat swept past him, hunting mosquitoes, oblivious of the motionless man. Once again Leaphorn became aware of the distant steady murmur of the river. It was nearer now, and the noise of water over rock was funneled and concentrated by the cliffs. No more than a mile and a half away, he guessed. Normally the thin, dry air of desert country carries few smells. But the air at canyon bottom was damp, so Leaphorn could identify the smell of wet sand, the resinous aroma of cedar, the vague perfume of piñon needles, and a dozen scents too faint for identification. The afterglow faded from the clifftops.

Time ticked away, bringing to the waiting man sounds and smells, but no repetition of the shout, if shout it had been, and nothing to hint at where Goldrims might have gone. Stars appeared in the slot overhead. First one, glittering alone, and then a dozen, and hundreds, and millions. The stars of the constellation Ursa Minor became visible, and Leaphorn felt the relief of again knowing his direction exactly. Abruptly he pushed himself upright, listening. From his left, down the dark canyon, came a faint rhythm of sound. Frogs greeting the summer night. He walked slowly, placing his feet carefully, moving down the canyon toward the almost imperceptible sound of the frogs. The darkness gave him an advantage. While it canceled sight, the night magnified the value of hearing. If it had kept Tso's secrets for a hundred years, the cave must be hidden from sight. But if there were people in it, they would—unless they slept—produce sound. The darkness would hide him, and he could move almost without noise down the sand of the canyon floor.

But there was also a disadvantage. The dog. If the dog was out in the canyon, it would smell him two hundred yards away. Leaphorn assumed that the cave would be somewhere up the cliff wall, as caves tended to be, and in this damp air, his scent would probably not rise. If the dog was in the cave, Leaphorn could go undetected. Nevertheless, he drew his pistol and walked with it in his hand, its hammer held on half cock and the safety catch off. He walked tensely, stopping every few yards both to listen and to make sure that his breathing remained slow and low.

He heard very little: the faint sound of his own bootsoles placed carefully on the sand, the distant barking of a coyote hunting somewhere on the surface above, the occasional call of a night bird, and finally, as the evening breeze rose, the breathing of air moving around the rocks, all against the background music of frog song. Once he was startled by a sudden scurrying of a rodent. And then, midstride, he heard a voice.

He stood motionless, straining to hear more. It had been a man's voice—coming from somewhere down the canyon, saying something terse. Three or four quick words. Leaphorn looked around him, identifying his location. Just down the canyon bottom, he could make out the shape of a granite outcropping. The canyon bent here, turning abruptly to the right around the granite. To his left, at his elbow, the cliff wall split, forming a narrow declivity in which brush grew. Checking his surroundings was an automatic precaution, typical of Leaphorn—making sure that he could find this place again in daylight. That done, he renewed his concentrated listening.

He heard in the darkness the sound of running, and of panting breath. It was coming directly toward him. In a split second the adrenal glands flooded his blood. Leaphorn managed to thumb back the pistol hammer to full cock, and half raise the .38. Then looming out of the darkness came the bulk of the dog, eyes and teeth reflecting the starlight in a strange wet whiteness. Leaphorn was able to lunge sideways toward the split cliff, and jerk the trigger. Amid the thunder of the pistol shot, the dog was on him. It struck him shoulder-high. Because of Leaphorn's lunge, the impact was glancing. Instead of being knocked on his back, the animal atop him, he was spun sideways against the cliff. The beast's teeth tore at his jacket instead of his throat, and the momentum of its leap carried it past him. Leaphorn found himself in the crevasse, scrambling frantically upward over boulders and brush. The dog, snarling now for the first time, had recovered itself and was into the crevasse after him. Leaphorn pulled himself desperately upward, with the dog just below him—far enough below him to make Leaphorn's dangling legs safe by a matter of perhaps a yard. He gripped a root of some sort with his right hand and felt carefully with his left and found a higher handhold. He squirmed upward, reaching a narrow shelf. There the dog couldn't possibly reach him. He turned and looked down. In this crevasse, the darkness of the canyon bottom became total. He could see nothing below him. But the animal was there; its snarl had become a frustrated yipping. Leaphorn took a deep breath, held it a moment, released it—recovering from his panic. He felt the nausea of a system overloaded with adrenaline. There was no time for sickness, or for the anger which was now replacing fear. He was safe for the moment from the dog, but he was totally exposed to the dog's owner. He made a quick inventory of his situation. His pistol was gone. The animal had struck him as he swung it upward and had knocked it from his hand. He hadn't, apparently, hit the dog, but the blast of the shot must have at least surprised and deafened it—and given Leaphorn time. No worry about concealment now. He unhooked his flashlight from his belt and surveyed his situation. The dog was standing, its forepaws against the rock, just below him. It was as huge as Leaphorn expected. He was neither knowledgeable nor particularly interested in dogs, but this one, he guessed, was a mongrel cross between some of the biggest breeds; Irish wolfhound and Great Dane perhaps. Whatever the mix, it had produced a shaggy coat, a frame taller than a man's when the dog stood as it now stood, on its hind legs, and a massive, ugly head. Leaphorn inspected the declivity into which he had climbed. It slanted steeply upward, apparently an old crack opened by an earth tremor in the cliff. Runoff water had drained down it, debris had tumbled into it, and an assortment of cactus, creosote bush, rabbit brush and weeds had taken root amid the boulders. It had two advantages—it offered a hiding place and was too steep for the dog to climb. Its disadvantage overrode both of these. It was a trap. The only way out was past the dog. Leaphorn felt around him for a rock of proper throwing size. The one he managed to pull loose from between the two boulders on which he was perched was smaller than he wanted—about the size of a small, flattened orange. He shifted the flashlight to his left hand and the rock to his right, and examined his target. The dog was snarling again. Its teeth and its eyes gleamed in the reflected light. He must hit it in the forehead, and hit it hard. He hurled the rock.

It seemed to strike the dog between its left eye and ear. The animal yelped and retreated down the slope.

At first he thought the dog had disappeared. Then he saw it, eyes reflecting the light, just outside the mouth of the crack. Still within accurate rock range. He fished behind him for another rock, and then quickly flicked off the light. On the canyon floor behind the dog he saw a glimmer of brightness—a flashlight beam bobbing with the walking pace of the person who held it.

"There's the dog," a voice said. "Don't put the light on it, Tull. The son-of-a-bitch has a gun."

The flashlight beam abruptly blinked out. Leaphorn eased himself silently upward. He heard the same voice talking quietly to the dog. And then a second voice:

"He must be up in that crack there," the man called Tull said. "The dog's treed him."

The first voice said, "I told you that dog would earn his keep."

"Up to now he's been a pain in the butt," Tull said. "The son-of-a-bitch scares me."

"No reason for that," the first voice said. "Lynch trained him himself. He was the pride of Safety Systems." The man laughed. "Or he was before I started slipping him food."

"Hell," Tull said. "Look what I just stepped on. It's his gun! The dog took the bastard's gun away from him."

There was a brief silence.

"It's the right one all right. It's been fired," Tull said.

The flashlight went on again. Leaphorn's reaching hand was exploring an opening between the boulders. He pulled himself further into the slot, stood cautiously and looked downward. He could see a circle of yellow light on the sandy canyon bottom and the legs of two men. Then the light flashed upward, its beam moving over the rocks and brush below him. He ducked back. The beam flashed past, lighting the space in which he stood with its reflection. To the left of where he was crouching, and above him, an immense slab had split away from the face of the cliff. Behind it there would be better cover and the faint possibility of a route to climb upward.

The first voice was shouting up toward him.

"You might as well come on down," the voice said. "We'll hold the dog."

Leaphorn stood silent.

"Come on," the voice said. "You can't get out of there and if you don't come down we're going to get sore about it."

"We just want to talk to you," the Tull voice said. "Who the hell are you and what are you doing here?"

The voices paused, waiting for an answer. The words echoed up and down the canyon, then died away.

"It's a police-issued pistol," the first voice said. "Thirty-eight revolver. There's just one shot fired. The one we heard."

"A cop?"

"Yeah, I'd guess so. Maybe the one that came nosing around the old man's hogan."

"He's not going to come down," Tull said. "I don't think he's coming down."

"No," First Voice said.

"You want me to go up and get him?"

"Hell, no. He'd brain you with a rock. He's above you and you couldn't see it coming in the dark."

"Yeah," Tull said. "So we wait for morning?"

"No. We're going to be busy in the morning," First Voice said. There was silence then. The flashlight beam moved up the crevasse, back and forth, to Leaphorn's hiding place, and then above it. Leaphorn turned and looked up. Far above his head the yellow light reflected from sections of unbroken cliff. But the cleft, he saw, went all the way to the top.

Four cautious steps into the opening and the flash caught him. He scrambled desperately, blinded by the beam, toward the crevasse behind the slab. There was a sudden explosion of gunshots, deafening in the closed space, and the sound of bullets whining off the stones around him. Then he was behind the slab, panting, the flashlight beam reflecting off the cliff.

"What do you think?" Tull asked.

"Damn. I think we missed him."

"He's sure not going to come down now," Tull said.

"Hey, buddy," First Voice said. "You're stuck in a box. If you don't come down, we're going to set this brush on fire here at the bottom and burn you out. Hear that?"

Leaphorn said nothing. He was considering alternatives. He was sure that if he came out they would kill him. Would they build the fire? Maybe. Could he survive it? This slot would give him some protection from the flame, but the fire would roar up the crevasse much like a chimney, exhausting the oxygen. If the heat didn't kill him, suffocation would.

"Go ahead and start it," First Voice said. "I told you he's not coming down."

"Well, hell," Tull said. "Don't a fire draw a crowd out here?"

Voice One laughed. "The only light that'll get out of this canyon will reflect straight up," he said. "There's nobody in forty miles to see it, and by morning the smoke will be all gone."

"Here's some dry grass," Tull said. "Once it gets going, the damp stuff will catch. It's not that wet."

Leaphorn had made his decision without consciously doing so. He would not climb down to be shot. The men below him started the blaze in a mat of brush and canyon-bottom driftwood caught at the crevasse opening. In moments, the smell of burning creosote bush and piñon resin reached Leaphorn's nostrils. The fire below would be interfering with the men's vision. He looked down at them. The dog stood behind them, backed nervously away from the blaze, but still looking up—its pointed ears erect and its eyes reflecting yellow in the firelight. To its left stood a large man in jeans and a denim jacket. He was holding a military-model automatic rifle cradled over his arm and using the other hand to shield his face from the heat. The face looked lopsided, somehow distorted, and the one eye Leaphorn could see stared upward toward him curiously. Tull. The second man was smaller. He wore a long-sleeved shirt and no jacket, his hair was black and cut fairly short, and the firelight glittered off gold-rimmed glasses. And behind the glasses Leaphorn saw a bland Navajo face. The light was weak and flickering, the glimpse was momentary, and the gold-rimmed glasses might have tricked the imagination. But Leaphorn found himself facing the fact that the man trying to kill him looked like Father Benjamin Tso of the Order of Friars Minor.

FIFTEEN

THE PROBLEM WOULD be flame, heat and lack of oxygen. Behind this slab, the flames would not reach him unless they were drawn in by some freakish draft. That left heat, which could kill him just as surely. And suffocation. The light from the fire below grew, flickering at first and then steady. Leaphorn worked his way further behind the slab, away from the light. His boot-sole suddenly splashed into water. The slab had formed a catch basin which had trapped the day's rain water as it poured down the cliff face. Behind him now the flames were making a steady roar as brush higher up the crevasse heated and exploded into fire. He pulled himself into the water. It was cool. He soaked his shirt, his pants, his boots. Through the slot behind him now he could see only fire. A gust of heat struck him, a searing torch on his cheek. He ducked his face into the water, held it there until his lungs cried for air. When he raised his face, he drew in a breath slowly and cautiously. The air was hot now, and his ears were filled with the roar of the fire. As he looked through slitted eyes, weeds in the lip of the slot wilted suddenly, then exploded into bright yellow flame. His denims were steaming. He splashed more water on them. The heat was intense, but his lungs told him it would be suffocation that would kill him unless he could find some source of oxygen. He climbed frantically between the cliff face and the inner surface of slab, working his way away from the fire. The first breath he took seared his lungs. But there was a draft now, sucking past his face. It came not from the flames but from somewhere below, pulled through the slot by the heat-caused vacuum. Leaphorn forced himself into the increasingly narrow gap—away from the furnace and toward this source of blessed air. Finally he could go no farther. His head was jammed in a vise of stone. The heat varied, now unbearably intense, now merely scalding. He could feel steam from his soaked pants legs hot on his inner thighs. The fire was making its own wind, sucking air—extremely hot air—past his face. If the draft changed, it would pull fire up this slot and char him like a moth. Or when his clothing dried and ignited, this draft of oxygen would turn him into a torch. Leaphorn shut this thought out of his mind and concentrated on another thought. If he stayed alive, he would get his rifle, and he would kill the dog and the man with the lopsided face and, most of all, he would kill Goldrims. He would kill Goldrims. He would kill Goldrims. And thus Joe Leaphorn endured.

The time came when the roar of fire diminished, and the draft of air around his face faded, and the heat rose to a furnace intensity. Leaphorn thought, then, that he would not survive. Consciousness slipped away. When it returned, the noise of burning was nothing more than a crackling, and he could hear voices. Sometimes they sounded faint and far away, and sometimes Leaphorn could understand the words. And finally the voices stopped, and time passed, and it was dark again. Leaphorn decided he would try to move, and found that he could, and inched his head out of the crevasse. His nostrils were filled with the smell of heat and ashes. But there was little fire. Most of the light here came from a log which had tumbled into the crack from above. It burned fitfully a hundred yards overhead. Leaphorn eased himself downward, toward the pool of water. It was warm now, almost hot, and much of it had evaporated. Leaphorn put his face into what remained and drank greedily. It tasted of charcoal. Hot as the fire had been it had not been enough to substantially raise the temperature of the massive living stone of the cliff which was still cool and made the temperature here bearable. In the flickering light, Leaphorn sat and inspected himself. He would have blisters, especially on one ankle where the skin had been exposed, and perhaps on his wrists and neck and face. His chest felt uncomfortable but there was no real pain. He had survived. The problem now was just as it had been—how to escape this trap.

He eased his way to the edge of the slab and peered around it. Below, logs and brush were still burning at a dozen places, and hot coals glowed at a hundred others. He could see neither dog nor man. Perhaps they were gone for good. Perhaps they were merely waiting for the fire to cool enough to climb the crevasse and make sure he was dead. Leaphorn thought about it. It must have seemed impossible, seen from below, for any living thing to survive in that flame-filled crevasse. Yet he couldn't quite convince himself that the two men would take the risk. He would try to climb out.

He burned himself a half-dozen times before he learned to detect and avoid the hot spots left by the fire. But by the time he was 150 feet above the canyon floor heat was no longer the problem. Now the cleft had narrowed but the climb was almost vertical. Climbing involved inching upward a few feet and then an extended pause to rest muscles aching with fatigue. The climb used up the night. He finally pulled himself onto the cap rock in the gray light of dawn and lay, utterly spent, with his face against the cold stone. He allowed himself a few minutes to rest and then moved into the cover of a cliff-side juniper.

There he extracted his walkie-talkie from its case on his belt, switched on the receiver and sat, getting his bearings. His transmission range was perhaps ten miles—hopelessly short for reaching any Navajo Police receiver. But Leaphorn tried it anyway. He broadcast his location and a call for help. There was no response. The Arizona State Police band was transmitting a description of a truck. The New Mexico State Police transmitter at Farmington was silent. He could hear the Utah Highway Patrol dispatcher at Moab, but not well enough to understand anything. The Federal Law Enforcement channel was sending what seemed to be a list of identifications. The Navajo State Police dispatcher at Tuba City, like the ASP radio, was giving someone a truck description—a camper truck, a big one apparently, with tandem rear wheels.

Leaphorn had himself placed now. The mesa that overlooked the Tso hogan was on the southwestern horizon, perhaps three miles away. Beyond that was his carryall, with his rifle and a radio transmitter strong enough to reach Tuba City. But at least two canyons cut the plateau between him and the hogan. Getting there would take hours. The sooner he started the better.

If there was any life on this segment of the plateau it wasn't visible in the early morning light. Except for whitish outcrops of limestone, the cap rock was a dark red igneous rock which supported in its cracks and crevasses a sparse growth of dry-country vegetation. A few hundred yards west, a low mesa blocked off the horizon. Leaphorn examined it, wondering if he'd have to cross it to reach his vehicle.

From the radio the pleasant feminine voice of the Tuba City dispatcher came faintly. It completed the description of the camper truck, lapsed into silence, and began another message. Leaphorn's mind was concentrating on what his eyes were seeing—seeking a way up the mesa wall. But it registered the word "hostages." Suddenly Leaphorn was listening.

The radio was silent again. He willed it to speak. The rim of the horizon over New Mexico was bright now with streaks of yellow. A morning breeze moved against his face. The radio spoke faintly, with the meaning lost in the moving air. Leaphorn squatted behind the juniper and held the speaker against his ear.

"All units," the voice said. "We have more

information. All units copy. Confirming three men involved. Confirming all three were armed. Witnesses saw one rifle and two pistols. In addition to the Boy Scouts, the hostages are two adult males. They are identified as—Discontinue this. Discontinue this. All units. All police units are ordered to evacuate the area of the Navajo Reservation north of U.S. Highway 160 and east of U.S. Highway 89, south of the northern border of the reservation, and west of the New Mexico border. We have instructions from the kidnappers that if police are seen in that area the hostages will be killed. Repeating. All police units are ordered . . ."

Leaphorn was only half conscious of the voice repeating itself. Could this explain what Goldrims was doing? Had he been setting up a Buffalo Society kidnapping? Preparing its base—a hiding place for hostages? Why else would police be ordered out of this section of the reservation?

The radio completed its repetition of the warning and finished its interrupted description of the male adult hostages, both leaders of a troop of Scouts from Santa Fe. It launched into a description of the hostage boys.

"Juvenile subject one is identified as Norbert Juan Gomez, age twelve, four feet, eleven inches tall, weight about eighty pounds, black hair, black eyes. All juvenile subjects wearing Boy Scout uniforms.

"Juvenile subject two is Tommy Pearce, age thirteen, five feet tall, weight ninety, brown hair, brown eyes.

"Juvenile subject three . . ."

They all sound pretty much alike, Leaphorn thought. Turned into statistics. Changed by exposure to violence from children into juvenile subjects three, four, five and six, to be measured in pounds and inches and color of hair.

"Juvenile subject eight, Theodore middle initial F. Markham, age thirteen, five feet two inches, weight about one hundred pounds, blond hair, blue eyes, pale complexion."

Leaphorn converted juvenile subject eight into a pale blond boy he had noticed last summer watching a rodeo at Window Rock. The boy had stood at the arena enclosure, one foot on the bottom rail, his hair bleached almost white, his face peeling from old sunburn, his attention on the efforts of a Navajo cowboy trying to tie the forelegs of a calf he had bulldogged.

"Juvenile subject nine is Milton Richard Silver," the radio intoned, and Leaphorn's mind converted nine into Leaphorn's own nephew, who lived in Flagstaff, whose blue jeans were chronically disfigured with plastic model cement and whose elbows were disfigured from the scars of skateboard accidents. And that thought led to another one. Tuba City would remember he had gone to the

Tso hogan. They'd be trying to reach him to call him out of the prohibited zone. But that didn't matter. Goldrims knew he was here. Knew he had been here before the warning. What mattered was to get moving. To get his rifle.

Leaphorn walked rapidly, flinching at first from the stiffness in calves and ankles. He considered dropping his equipment belt, leaving binoculars, radio, flashlight and first-aid kit behind to save the weight. But though the radio and binoculars were heavy, he might need them. The radio had completed its descriptions of the hostage Scouts with juvenile subject eleven and was engaged in responding to questions and transmitting orders. From this Leaphorn pieced together a little more of what had happened. Three armed men, all apparently Indians, had appeared the night before at one of the many Boy Scout troop encampments scattered around the mouth of Canyon de Chelly. They had arrived in two trucks—a camper and a van. They had herded the two Scout leaders and eleven of the boys into the camper and had left two more adults and seven other Scouts tied and locked in the van.

Leaphorn frowned. Why take some hostages and leave others? And why that number? The question instantly answered itself. He remembered the propaganda leaflet in the FBI file at Albuquerque. First on the list of atrocities to be avenged was the Olds Prairie Murders, the victims of which had been three adults and eleven children. The thought chilled him. But why hadn't they taken three adults? Theodora Adams. Was she the third? The Buffalo Society evidently had planned to dramatize the deaths of eleven Kiowa children from a century ago by taking eleven Boy Scouts hostage. They'd known this would launch an international orgy of news coverage, would make for nationwide suspense. There would be television interviews with weeping mothers and distraught fathers. The whole world would be watching this one. The whole world would be asking if an Indian named Kelongy simply wanted to recall an old atrocity or if his sense of justice would demand a perfect balance. Leaphorn was wondering about this himself when he heard the dog.

It came from above him on the cap of the mesa—an angry, frustrated sound something between a snarl and a bark. He had forgotten the dog. The sound stopped him in his tracks. Then he saw the animal almost directly above him. It stood with its front paws on the very edge of the rimrock, shoulders hunched, teeth bared. It barked again, then turned abruptly and ran along the cliff away from him, then back toward him, apparently looking frantically for a way down. The creature was even bigger than he remembered it, looming in the yellow firelight of the night before. At any minute it would find a way down—a rock slide, a deer trail, almost any break in the cliff which would lead to the talus slope below. Leaphorn became aware of a cold knot of fear in his stomach. He looked around him, hoping to see something he could use for a club. He broke a limb from a dead juniper, although it was hopelessly inadequate to stop the animal. Then he turned and ran stiffly back toward the mainstem canyon. It was the only place where having hands could give him an advantage over an adversary with four legs and tearing canine teeth. He stopped at a twisted little cedar rooted into the rock about six feet from the lip of the cliff. Behind it he hurriedly unlaced his boots. He knotted the laces securely together, doubled them, and tied the strings around the trunk of the bush. Then he whipped off his belt, looped it, and tied it to the doubled bootstrings. As he tested its strength, he saw the dog. It had worked its way along a crack in the cap rock, and was bounding down the talus slope toward him, baying again. Last night it had attacked without a sound, as attack dogs are trained to strike, and even after it had cornered him had only snarled. But he must have hurt it with a rock and it had apparently forgotten at least a little of its training. Leaphorn hoped fervently that in its hate for him it had forgotten everything. He picked up his juniper stick and trotted out across the cap toward the dog, his untied boots flapping on his ankles. Then he stopped. The worst mistake would be going too far, waiting too long, and being caught away from the edge of the cliff. He stood, the stick gripped at his side, waiting. Within seconds, the dog appeared. It was perhaps a hundred fifty yards away, running full out, looking for him.

Leaphorn cupped his hands. "Dog," he shouted. "Here I am."

The animal changed direction with an agility that caused Leaphorn's jaw muscles to tighten. His idea wasn't going to work. In a matter of seconds he would be trying to kill that huge animal with a stick and his bare hands. Still, the cliff edge was his best hope. The dog was racing directly toward him now, no longer barking, its teeth bared. Leaphorn waited. Eighty yards now, he guessed. Now sixty. He had a sudden vision of his laceless boots tripping him, and the nightmare thought of falling, with the dog racing down on him. Forty yards. Thirty. Leaphorn turned and ran desperately in his flapping boots toward the cedar. He knew almost at once that he had waited too long. The dog was bigger and faster than he had realized. It must weigh nearly two hundred pounds. He could hear it at his heels. The race now seemed almost dreamlike, the looped belt hanging forever outside his reach. And then with a last leap his hand was grabbing the leather, and he felt the dog's teeth tearing at his hip, and his momentum flung him sideways around the bush, holding with every ounce of his strength to the belt, feeling the dog fly past him, its jaws still ripping at his hip—knowing with a sense of terror that their combined weight would pull his grip loose from the belt, or the nylon strings loose from the tree, and both of them would slide over the cliff and fall, the dog still tearing at him. They would fall, and fall, and fall, tumbling, waiting for the hideous split second when their bodies would strike the rocks below.

And then the teeth tore loose.

In some minuscule fraction of a second Leaphorn's senses told him he was no longer connected to the dog, that his grip on the belt still held, that he would not fall to his death. A second later he knew that his plan to send the animal skidding over the cliff had failed. The dog's hold on Leaphorn's hip had saved it. The animal's back legs had slid over the edge as it had turned, but its body and its front legs were still on the cap rock and it was straining to pull itself to safety.

There was no time to think. Leaphorn flung himself at the animal, pushing desperately at its front feet. The hind paws dislodged stones as the beast kicked for lodging. It snapped viciously at Leaphorn's hand. But the effort cost it an inch. Leaphorn pushed again at a forepaw. This time the dog's teeth snapped shut on his shirt sleeve. The creaure was moving backward, pulling Leaphorn over the edge. Then the cloth tore loose. For a second the animal stood vertically against the cliff, supported by its straining front legs and whatever grip its hind paws had found on the stone face of the canyon wall. It was snarling, its straining efforts aimed not at saving itself but at attacking its victim. And then the hind paws must have slipped for the broad, ugly head disappeared. Leaphorn moved cautiously forward and looked over the edge. The animal was cartwheeling slowly as it fell. Far down the cliff it struck a half-dead clump of rabbit brush growing out of a crack, bounced outward, and set off a small rain of dislodged rocks. Leaphorn looked away before it struck the canyon bottom. But for luck, his body too might be suffering that impact. He pulled himself back to the cedar and inspected the damage.

His pants were bloody at the hip, where the dog's teeth had snapped through trousers, shorts, skin and muscle and had torn loose a flap of flesh. The wound burned and was bleeding copiously. It was a hell of a place to fix. No possibility of a tourniquet, and putting on a pressure bandage would require securing it around both hip and waist. He took tape from his first-aid kit and bandaged the tear as best he could. His other wounds were trivial. A bitten place on his right wrist from which a small amount of blood was oozing, and a gash, probably caused by the dog's teeth, on the back of his left hand. He found himself wondering if the dog had been given rabies shots. The idea seemed so incongruous that he laughed aloud. Like giving shots to a werewolf, he thought.

The laugh died in his throat.

On the mesa, not far from where he had first seen the dog, sunlight flashed from something. Leaphorn crouched behind the cedar, straining his eyes. A man was standing back from the mesa rim, scanning the rocky shelf along the canyon with binoculars. Probably Goldrims, Leaphorn thought. He would have been following his dog. He would have heard barking, and now he would be looking for the animal and for its prey. Leaphorn contemplated hiding. With the dog out of the picture he might succeed, if he could find a place under the rim of the cap rock where he could hang on. And then he realized the man had already seen him. The binoculars were turned directly on Leaphorn's cedar. There would be no hiding. He could only run, and there was no place to run. He would climb down the cleft again. That would delay the inevitable and perhaps in the cover and loose boulders of that steep slope the odds would improve for an unarmed man. Improve, Leaphorn thought grimly, from zero to a hundred to one.

The man didn't seem to have a rifle, but Leaphorn kept under cover as well as he could in reaching the place where the canyon wall was split. As he lowered himself over the cap rock, he saw the man emerging on the talus slope under the mesa, using the same route the dog had taken. Leaphorn had maybe a five-minute lead, and he used it recklessly—taking chance after chance with his injured leg, with precarious handholds on fire-blackened brush, with footholds on stones that might not hold. He had no accurate sense of time. At any moment Goldrims might appear at the top of the slot above him and end this one-sided contest with a pistol shot. But the shot didn't come. Leaphorn, soot-blackened, reached the sheltered place where he had survived the fire. He would give Goldrims as much excitement as he could for his money. He would climb once again up behind that great slab of stone to the place where he had lain when the fire was burning. Goldrims would have to climb after him to kill him. And while he was climbing, Goldrims might leave himself momentarily vulnerable to something thrown from above.

A small cascade of stones slid down the cleft with a clatter. Goldrims was beginning his descent. It would be slower than his own, Leaphorn knew. Goldrims had no reason to be taking chances. That left a little time. Leaphorn looked around him for rocks of the proper size. He found one, about as big as a grapefruit. The binoculars would also make a missile, and so would the flashlight. He began to climb.

It was easy enough. The face of the cliff and the inner surface of the slab were less than a yard apart. He could brace himself between them as he worked his way upward. The surfaces were relatively smooth, the stone polished by eons of rain and blowing sand since some ancient earthquake had fractured the plateau. Above him Leaphorn saw the narrow shelf where he had jammed himself and huddled away from the fire. His heart sank. It was too narrow and too cramped to offer any hope at all of defense. He couldn't throw from there expecting to hit anything. And it offered no cover from below. Goldrims would simply shoot him and the game would be over.

Leaphorn hung motionless for a moment, looking for a way out. Could he squeeze his way to that source of air which had kept him breathing during the fire? He couldn't. The gap narrowed quickly and then closed completely. Leaphorn frowned. Then where had that draft of fresh air originated? He could feel it now, moving faintly against his face. But not from ahead. It came from beneath him.

Leaphorn moved downward, crabwise, as rapidly as he could shift his elbows and knees. It was cooler here, and there was dampness in the air. His boots touched broken rocks. He was at the bottom of the split. Or almost at the bottom. Here the stones were whitish, eaten with erosion. They were limestone, and seeping water had dissolved away the calcite. Below Leaphorn's feet the split sloped away into darkness. A hole. He kicked a rock loose and listened to it bouncing downward. From above and behind him came the sound of other rocks falling. Goldrims had noticed the crack behind the slab and was following him. Without a backward glance, Leaphorn scrambled downward into the narrow darkness.

SIXTEEN

THE WATCH HANDS and numerals were suspended, luminous yellow against the velvet blackness. It was 11:03 A.M. Almost fourteen hours since the dog had first attacked him on the canyon floor, more than twenty-four hours since he had eaten, and two hours since the thundering fall of the boulders Goldrims had dislodged to block his exit. Resting, Leaphorn had used those two hours to assess his situation and work on a plan. He wasn't happy with either. He was caught in a cave. Two quick inspections with his flashlight told him that the cave was extensive, that it sloped sharply downward, and that—like most large caves—it had been leached out of a limestone deposit by ground water. Leaphorn understood the process. Rain water draining through soil containing decaying vegetation became acidic.

The acid quickly ate away the calcite in limestone, dissolving the stone and forming caverns. Here when the canyon formed it had drained away the water, and checked the process. Then an earth tremor had cracked open an entrance to the cave. Since air flowed through it, there must be another entrance. Leaphorn could feel the movement now: a cool current past his face. His plan was simple—he would try to find another exit. If he couldn't, he would return here and try to dig his way out. That would involve dislodging the boulders that Goldrims had rolled into the hole, causing them to tumble downward. Doing that without being crushed would be tricky. Doing it without noise would be impossible, and Goldrims would probably be waiting.

Leaphorn flicked on the flashlight again and began edging downward. As he did, a blast of air struck him, and with the concussion, a deafening explosion of sound. It knocked him from his feet and sent him tumbling down the limestone slope, engulfed in a Niagara of noise. He lay on the cool stone, his ears assaulted with slamming echoes and the sound of falling rock. What the hell had happened? His nostrils told him in a second as the stench of burned dynamite reached them. The flashlight had been knocked from his hand, but it was still burning just below him. He retrieved it and aimed its beam upward. The air above was a fog of limestone dust and blue smoke. Goldrims had dropped dynamite into the cave entrance to kill the policeman with concussion, or crush him, or seal him in. There'd be damn little hope now of getting out the way he'd come in. His hope, if there was hope, lay in finding the source of the air which had moved upward through this cavity.

Leaphorn moved cautiously downward, his ears still ringing with the aftereffects of the blast. At least there was no worry now of Goldrims or Tull following him. He was, from their point of view, dead or neutralized. The thought was small consolation, because Leaphorn's common sense told him such a theory was probably accurate.

The cavity sloped at about sixty degrees, angling toward the face of the canyon cliff. As he lowered himself deeper into it, it widened. At places now the space overhead rose at least a hundred feet. The luminous dial of his wristwatch read a little after three when he first detected reflected light. It originated from a side cavern which led upward and to his right. Leaphorn climbed up it far enough to conclude that the light leaked in from some sort of split in the canyon cliff. The approach to it was too narrow for anything larger than a snake to navigate. Leaphorn let his head slump against the stone and stared longingly toward the unattainable light. He felt no panic—only a sense of helpless defeat. He would rest for a while and then he would begin the long, weary climb back up to the entrance Goldrims had dynamited. There'd be almost no chance he could dig his way out. The blast must have dislodged tens of tons of stone. But it was the only possibility. He backed out of the crack into the cavern itself, and sat thinking. The silence was complete. He could hear his heart beating and the breath moving past his lips. The air was cool. It pressed against his left cheek, smelling fresh and clean. It should smell of burned dynamite, Leaphorn thought. Why doesn't it? It doesn't because at this time of day, air would be moving upward through the cave, pushing the fumes out. The air was still moving. Did that mean that the exit hadn't been entirely sealed by the blast? Leaphorn felt a stirring of hope. But no. The air was moving in the wrong direction. It was moving past his face into the crack—toward the light source. Leaphorn thought about what that implied, and felt another stirring of hope. There must be another source of air, deeper in the cavern. Perhaps this eroded cavity intersected with the cliff wall somewhere below.

At 6:19 P.M., Leaphorn reached a bottom. He

squatted, savoring the unaccustomed feel of level flatness under his bootsoles. The floor here had been formed by sediment. It was calcite dissolved out of the limestone walls, but over the calcite there was a thin layer of gritty sand. Leaphorn examined it with the flashlight. It seemed to be the same sort of sand one would find at the canyon bottom outside—a mixture of fine particles of granite, silica, limestone and sandstone. He flashed the light around. This flat surface seemed to extend from the declivity he had been descending along the length of this long, narrow compartment. The sand must have washed in from below or blown in on the wind. Either way, he should be able to see daylight. He turned off the flashlight and stood, seeing nothing but blackness. But there was still the moving air—the faint feeling of pressure against his face which seemed characteristic of this cave. He moved into the air movement now, as he had ever since he had entered the cave. For the first time, the going was relatively easy—a matter of walking instead of climbing. He saw that originally the cave had continued its downward plunge here—but an invasion of water had filled it with a sedimentary floor. The floor was level, but the ceiling sloped toward his head. He had to stoop now, to pass a cluster of stalactites. Beyond them his flashlight beam prodded to the inevitable point of intersection—where slanted ceiling met level floor. Leaphorn squatted under the lowering roof, moving forward. He advanced on hands and knees. Finally, he crawled. The angle between floor and ceiling narrowed everywhere to nothing. Leaphorn let his forehead rest against the calcite, fighting off the first nudgings of panic. How much longer would the flashlight last? It was a subject he hadn't allowed himself to consider. He moved the tip of his nose through the film of gritty dust and was reassured. His reason told him this sandy stuff must have been carried in from the outside—from the world of light. But here in this cul-de-sac there was no air movement. He began crawling backward. He would find the moving air again and try to follow it.

But the air current was dying. At first Leaphorn thought he had simply been unable to find the area through which it moved. And then he realized that it must be nearing that time of day when this earthly breathing stops—the moment near the margin of daylight and dark when the heating/cooling process briefly reaches balance, when warm air no longer presses upward and cool air is not yet heavy enough to sink. Even in this slanting cavern, where narrowness of passageway multiplied the effect, there would be two periods—morning and evening—when the draft would be dead.

Leaphorn collected a pinch of the fine-grained sand between thumb and forefinger and sifted it out into the beam of his flashlight. It fell almost perpendicularly. Almost—but not quite. Leaphorn moved toward the source of air, repeating the process. And the fifth time he bent to replenish his supply of dust, he saw the footprint of the dog.

He squatted, looking at the print and digesting what it meant. It meant, first, that he was not doomed to die entombed in this cave. The dog had found a way in. Leaphorn could find a way out. It meant, second, that the cavity Leaphorn had been following down from high up the cliff must be connected to a cavern that opened on the canyon bottom. As the thought came, Leaphorn flicked off the flashlight. If the dog had been in this cave, it was probably the hiding place of Goldrims.

Even though he now used the flashlight only cautiously, following the dog's tracks was relatively easy. The animal had roamed through a labyrinth of rooms and corridors, but had quickly exhausted its curiosity.

At about 8 P.M. Leaphorn detected a dim reflection of light. Exulting in the sight, he moved toward it slowly, stopping often to listen. He had a single advantage and he intended to guard it: Goldrims and Tull believed he was dead and out of the game. As long as they didn't know he was inside their sanctuary, he had surprise on his side. He became aware of sounds now. First there was a vague purring, which began suddenly and stopped just as abruptly about five minutes later. It sounded like a small, well-muffled internal-combustion engine. A little later Leaphorn heard a metallic clatter, and after that, when he had edged perhaps a hundred yards toward the source of light, a thumping noise. The light was general now. Still faint but enough so that Leaphorn—his pupils totally dilated by hours of absolute darkness—could forgo the flashlight entirely. He moved past one of the seemingly endless screens of stalagmites into another of the series of auditorium-sized cavities which water seepage had produced at this level. Just around the screen, Leaphorn stopped. The light here reflected and shimmered from the irregular ceiling far overhead. At the end of this room, he could see water. He edged toward it. An underground pool. Its surface was about three feet lower than the old calcite deposit which formed the cavern floor. He knelt beside it and dipped in a finger. It was cool, but not cold. He tasted it. Fresh, with none of the alkaline flavor he had expected. He looked down its surface, toward the source of light. And then he realized that this water must be part of Lake Powell—backing into the cave as the lake surface rose with spring runoff and draining out as the level fell with autumn and winter. He drank thirstily.

The dog tracks led Leaphorn away from the water into the next room. At its far end, Leaphorn saw, it, too, opened onto the lake surface. The light here was still indirect—seemingly reflecting out of the water—but it was brighter. There were sounds, blurred by echoes. Voices. Whose? Goldrims and Tull? Father Goldrims and Theodora Adams? And how had a doctor's daughter and a Franciscan priest become involved in this violent affair? He thought of the face of Father Tso as it had looked magnified through binoculars—the eyes intent on the elevated host, the expression rapt. And the face in the reflected glow of the flashlight at the canyon bottom—the man in the gold-rimmed glasses calmly discussing with Tull how to burn Leaphorn to death. Had his eyes tricked him in the flickering light? Could they be the same man?

The hunger cramps which had bothered him earlier were gone now. He hadn't eaten for thirty-three hours and his digestive system seemed to have adjusted to the oddity. He felt only a sort of lethargic weakness—the product, he guessed, of low blood sugar. An intermittent throbbing had joined the ache in his hip—probably the symptom of an infection beginning in the dog bite. That was something he could think about much later. Now the problem was to find a way out of here.

As he thought that, a beam of yellow light flashed across his face.

Before Leaphorn could react, the light was gone. He stood looking frantically for a place to hide. And then he realized that whoever was behind the light apparently hadn't noticed him. He could see the light only indirectly now, reflecting off the limestone far down the cavern. It swung and bobbed with the movement of the person who carried it. Leaphorn moved toward it as swiftly as he could without risking noise. The flat calcite floor deposit quickly gave way to rougher going—a mixture of stalagmite deposits jutting upward and outcrops of some sort of darker non-limestone extrusions which had resisted the dissolving water. The light disappeared, then its reflection appeared again between a high ridge of lime deposit and the cavern ceiling. Leaphorn climbed the ridge gingerly. He peered over the top. Below him, a thin man wearing a blue shirt and a red sweatband around his forehead was squatting beside a pile of cartons, gathering an armload of boxes and cans. The man rose and turned. He clutched his burden to his chest with his right arm, awkwardly retrieved an electric lantern with his left, and walked quickly from Leaphorn's view the same way he had come. The bobbing light of his lantern faded away. Leaphorn lay a moment, listening. Then he slid over the limestone barrier and climbed quietly down to the boxes.

They contained groceries—canned vegetables, canned meats, cartons of crackers and cookies, pork and beans, canned peaches. Sufficient, Leaphorn guessed, to feed a family for a month. He made a quick estimate of the missing cans and boxes. About enough gone to amount to thirty or forty man-days of eating. Either this cave had been occupied by one person a month or more, or by several persons for a shorter period. Near the cache of groceries was a row of five-gallon gasoline cans. Eight of them. Leaphorn checked. Five were full of gasoline and three were empty. Beyond them was a wooden crate. The word EX-PLOSIVES was stenciled across the loosened lid. Leaphorn lifted it and looked inside. Dynamite sticks, neatly packed. Six of the twenty-four sticks were missing. He replaced the lid. Beside the dynamite case was a padlocked metal tool-box and two cardboard cartons. The smaller one contained a roll of blue insulated wire. The larger one originally had held a pair of Justin boots. Now it held what looked like the works of a large clock—a timing device of some sort. Leaphorn put it back and rearranged the paper padding as he had found it. He squatted on his heels. What might he do with dynamite and a timing device? He could think of absolutely nothing useful, beyond committing suicide. The detonators seemed to be kept somewhere else—a healthy habit developed by those who worked with explosives. Without the blasting caps the stuff could be fired by impact—but it would take a heavy blow. He left the dynamite and selected a box of crackers and an assortment of canned meats and vegetables from boxes where they seemed least likely to be missed. Then he hurried back into the darkness. He would hide, eat, and wait. With food and water, time was no longer an enemy. He would wait for night, when darkness would spread from the interior of the cave to its mouth. Then he could learn more about what lay between him and the exit.

Even during the long days of August, darkness came relatively early at the bottom of a canyon. By 9 P.M. it was dark enough. His bootsoles and heels were rubber and relatively noiseless, but he cut the sleeves from his shirt and wrapped the boots carefully to further muffle the sound of his footsteps. Then he began his careful prowling.

A little before 11 P.M. he had done as much exploring as caution permitted. He had learned that his escape would certainly involve getting wet, and would probably involve getting shot.

He had found the cave mouth by edging his way down the waterline, wading at times where the limestone formations forced him into the water. Just around one such outcropping, he had seen a wide arch of opalescent light. The night outside, dark as it was, was immensely brighter than the eyeless blackness of the cave. The cave mouth showed as an irregular, flattened arch of light. This bright slope was bisected by a horizontal line. Leaphorn studied this optical phenomenon a moment before he understood its cause. Most of the mouth of the cave was submerged in the lake. Only a few feet at the top were open to the air. Leaving the cave would involve swimming—simple enough. It would also involve swimming past two men. A butane lantern on a shelf of stone to the left of the cave entrance illuminated the men. One was Tull. In the dim light, he was sprawled against a bedroll, reading a magazine. The other man had his back to Leaphorn. He was kneeling, working intently at something. Leaphorn extracted his binoculars. Through them he saw the man was working on what seemed to be a radio transceiver, apparently adjusting something. His shoulders were hunched and his face hidden, but the form and clothing were familiar. Goldrims. Leaphorn stared at the man, pulled optically almost into touching distance by the lenses. Was it the priest? He felt his stomach tighten. Fear, or anger, or both. The man had tried to kill him three times. He stared at the man's back, watching his shoulders move as he worked. Then he shifted the binoculars to Tull, seeing the undamaged side of his face in profile. From this angle the deformity was not apparent. The face, softly lit by the yellow flare of the lantern, was gentle, engrossed in whatever he was reading. The lips suddenly turned up in a smile, and the face turned toward Father Goldrims and mouthed something. Leaphorn had seen the ruined face before in the flickering firelight. Now he saw it more clearly—the crushed cheekbone, the mouth pulled forever awry by the improperly healed jawbone, the misshapen eye socket. It was the sort of face that made those who saw it flinch.

Suddenly Tull's lips stopped moving. He swung his head slightly to the left, frowning, listening. Then Leaphorn heard the sound that had attracted Tull's attention. It was faint and made incoherent by echoes, but it was a human sound. Tull said something to Goldrims, his face angry. Goldrims glanced toward the source of the sound, his face in profile now to Leaphorn's binoculars. He shook his head, said something, and went back to work. Leaphorn lowered the binoculars and concentrated on listening. The sound was high-pitched, shrill and excited. A female voice. Now he knew in what direction he would find Theodora Adams.

SEVENTEEN

LEAPHORN MOVED CAREFULLY back into the labyrinth, circling to his right beyond the cache of supplies into another arm of the cavern. The calcite floors here were at several levels—dropping abruptly as much as four or five feet from one flat plane to another—suggesting that the cavern had flooded, drained and reflooded repeatedly down through geological time. The darkness was virtually total again and Leaphorn felt his way cautiously, not risking the flashlight, less fearful of a fall than of giving away his only advantage. The distant sound of the voices pulled him on. There was a hint of light from ahead, elusive as the sound, which echoed and reflected, seeming no closer. Leaphorn stopped, as he had a dozen times, trying to locate the source exactly.

As he stood, breath held, ears straining, he heard another sound.

It was a rubbing, scraping sound, coming from his right. At first it defied identification. He stared into the blackness. The sound came, and came again, and came again—rhythmically. It became louder, and clearer, and Leaphorn began to distinguish a pattern to it—a second of silence before the repetition. It was something alive dragging itself directly toward him. Leaphorn had a sudden hideous intuition. The dog had tumbled down the cliff. But he hadn't seen it hit the bottom. It was alive, crippled, dragging itself inexorably after Leaphorn's scent. For a second, reason reasserted itself in Leaphorn's logical mind. The dog couldn't have fallen three hundred feet down the face of that cliff and survived. But then the sound came again, closer now, only a few yards away from his feet, and Leaphorn was again in a nightmare world in which men became witches, and turned themselves into wolves; in which wolves didn't fall, but flew. He pointed the flashlight at the sound, like a gun, and pushed the button.

There was, for a moment, nothing but a blaze of blinding light. Then Leaphorn's dilated pupils adjusted and the shape illuminated in the flashlight beam became Father Benjamin Tso. The priest's eyes were squeezed shut against the light, his face jerked away from the beam. He was sitting on the calcite floor, his feet stretched in front of him, his arms behind him. His ankles were fastened with what appeared to be a strip of nylon.

Now Tso squinted up into the flashlight beam.

"All right," he said. "If you'll untie my ankles, I'll walk back."

Leaphorn said nothing.

"No harm trying," the priest said. He laughed. "Maybe I could have got away."

"Who in the hell are you?" Leaphorn asked. He could hardly get the words out.

The priest frowned into the light, his face puzzled. "What do you mean?" he asked. Then he frowned again, trying to see Leaphorn's face through the flashlight beam. "I'm Benjamin Tso," he said. "Father Benjamin Tso." He paused. "But aren't you . . . ?"

"I'm Leaphorn. The Navajo cop."

"Thank God," Father Tso said. "Thank God for that." He swung his head to the side. "The others are back there. They're all right. How did you . . . ?"

"Keep your voice down," Leaphorn said.

He snapped off the light and listened. In the cave now there was only a heavy, ear-ringing total silence.

"Can you untie my hands?" Father Tso whispered. "They've been numb for a long time."

Leaphorn switched on the flash again, holding his hand over the lens to release only the dimmest illumination. He studied the priest's face. It was a lot like the face of the man he had seen with Tull and the dog, the face of the man who had tried to burn him to death in the canyon.

Father Benjamin Tso glanced up at Leaphorn, and then away. Even in the dim light Leaphorn could see the face change. It became tired and older.

"I guess you've met my brother," he said.

"Is that it?" Leaphorn asked. "Yes, it must be. He looks something like you."

"A year older," Father Tso said. "We weren't raised together." He glanced up at Leaphorn. "He's in the Buffalo Society. My returning didn't help his plans."

"But what made you . . . how did you get here?" Leaphorn asked. "I mean, to your grandfather's hogan?"

"It was a long trip. I flew back from Rome, and then to Phoenix. And then I took a bus to Flagstaff and then to Kayenta, and then I caught a ride."

"And where's the Adams girl?"

"He came to the hogan and got us," Tso said. "My brother and that dog he has." Father Tso stopped. "That dog. He's around here and he'll find us. Are there other police with you? Have you arrested them?"

"The dog's dead. Just tell me what happened," Leaphorn said.

"My brother came to the hogan and brought us to this cave," Father Tso said. "He said we'd have to stay until some sort of operation was over. Then later . . ." He shrugged and looked apologetic. "I don't know how much later. It's hard to keep track of time in here and I can't see my wrist watch. Anyway, later, my brother and a man called Tull and three other men brought a bunch of Boy Scouts and put them in with us. I don't understand it. What do you know about it?"

"Just what I heard on the radio," Leaphorn said. He knelt behind Tso and examined the bindings on his wrists. "Keep talking," Leaphorn said. "And keep it at a whisper." He fished out his pocket knife and sawed through the strips, a type of disposable handcuff developed for use by police in making mass arrests. The BIA police had bought some during the early stages of the American Indian Movement troubles, but they'd been junked because if the subject struggled, they tightened and cut off circulation. Tso's hands were ice cold and bloodless. It would be a while before he could use them.

"I just know what I heard, too," Father Tso was saying. "And what the Scout leader told us. I guess we're involved in some sort of symbolic kidnapping."

Leaphorn had the strips cut from Tso's ankles now. Tso tried to massage them, but his numb hands dangled almost uselessly from his wrists.

"It takes a while for the circulation to come back," Leaphorn said. "When it does, it hurts. Can you tell me more?"

Tso began rubbing his hands briskly against his chest. "Every couple of hours or so Tull or my brother comes back and they have two questions they ask the Scout leader or one of the boys. It's to prove everyone is still alive or something. It seems they told the police they have to stay completely out of this part of the reservation. I think the deal is if they see any police they say they'll kill the hostages. Otherwise the police get to broadcast questions every couple of hours, and he—"

"Questions? What sort of questions?"

"Oh, one was where did the Scout leader meet his wife. And one was why he was late for a trip, and where was the telephone in his home. Trivial stuff that no one else could know." Father Tso grimaced suddenly and inspected his hands. "I see what you mean about hurting."

"Keep rubbing them. And keep talking. Do you know the timetable?" Leaphorn asked. "Did you hear anything about that?"

"They told the Scouts they'd probably be here

about two or three days. Maybe less. Until they get the ransom."

"Do you know how many are involved? I've seen three in the cave. Are there more than that?"

"I've seen at least five," Father Tso said. "When my brother brought us back, first there was just a young man here they call Jackie. Just my brother and Jackie. Then when they brought the Boy Scouts there were three more of them. One with an awfully disfigured face, called Tull. He's still here, I think. But I haven't seen the other two again."

"This Jackie. How was he dressed?" Leaphorn asked.

"Jeans," Father Tso said. "Denim shirt. Red sweatband around his forehead."

"Yes, I've seen him," Leaphorn said. "Where are the other hostages? And how'd you get away?"

"They've got a sort of cage welded together out of reinforcing rods or something," Tso said. "Set back in a part of the cave way back there. That's where they put Theodora and me at first, and then they brought the Boy Scouts in. Then a couple of hours ago they took me out and moved me into another part of the cave." Tso pointed behind him. "A sort of big room back in that direction, and they put these things on my wrists and ankles and they sort of anchored me to a stalagmite." Tso laughed. "Tied a rope around it."

"How'd you get loose?"

"Well, they warned me that if I moved around too much with these nylon things on they'd tighten up and cut off my circulation, but I found that if you didn't mind a little of that, you could work the strip around so that the knot was where you could get at it."

Leaphorn remembered trying on the nylon cuffs when the department was considering them, and how quickly pulling against them caused them to cut into your wrists. He glanced at Tso, remeasuring him.

"The people who invented those things counted on people not wanting to hurt themselves," Leaphorn said.

"I guess so," Father Tso said. He was massaging his ankles now. "Anyway, these calcite deposits are too soft to cut anything. I thought maybe I could find some sort of outcropping—granite or something—where I could cut the nylon off."

"Is the feeling coming back?" Leaphorn asked. "Good. I don't think we want to waste any time if we can help it. I don't have a gun." He helped Tso to his feet and supported him. "When they come to the cage to get the questions answered, who comes? Just one of them?"

"The last time it was just the one with the red headband. The one they called Jackie."

"You okay now? Ready to move?"

Father Tso took a step, and then a smaller one, and sucked in his breath sharply. "Just give me a second to get used to it." The breath hissed through gritted teeth. "What are we going to do?" he whispered.

"We're going to be there when they come back to the cage. If you can find a place for me to hide. If two come, we won't try anything right now. But if just one of them comes, then you step out and confront him. Make as much noise as you can to cover me coming, and I'll jump him."

"As I remember it, there's not much to hide behind," Tso said doubtfully. "Not close anyway."

They moved slowly through the dark, the priest limping gingerly, Leaphorn supporting part of his weight.

"There's one other thing," Tso said. "I don't think this Tull is sane. He thinks he dies and comes back alive again."

"I've heard about Tull," Leaphorn said.

"And my brother," Tso said. "I guess you'd have to say he's sort of crazy, too."

Leaphorn said nothing. They moved silently toward the light, feeling their way. From ahead, suddenly, there came the sound of a woman's voice—distant, and as yet undecipherable.

"This is terrible for Theodora," Father Tso said. "Terrible."

"Yes," Leaphorn said. He was remembering Captain Largo's instructions. He flicked the flash on—getting direction—and quickly off.

"My brother," Tso said. "He stayed with my father, and my father was a drunk." Tso's whisper was barely audible. "I didn't ever live with them. All I know is what I've heard, but I heard it was bad. My father died of a beating in Gallup." The whisper stopped and Leaphorn began thinking of other things, of what his tactics would have to be.

"My brother was about fourteen when it happened," Father Tso said. "I heard my brother was there when they beat him, and that it was the police that did it."

"Maybe," Leaphorn said. "There're some bad cops." He flicked the light on again, and off.

"That's not what I'm talking about," Father Tso said. "I'm telling you because I don't think there'll be any hostages released." He paused. "They've gone too far for that," the voice whispered. "They're not sane. None of them. Poor Theodora."

They could hear the voice of Theodora Adams again, a matter more of tones echoing than of words. Leaphorn was suddenly aware that he was exhausted. His hip throbbed steadily now, his burn stung, his cut hand hurt. He felt sick and frightened and humiliated. And all this merged into anger.

"God damn it," he said. "You say you're a priest? What were you doing with a woman anyway?"

Tso limped along silently. Leaphorn instantly regretted the question.

"There are good priests and bad ones," Tso said. "You get into it because you tell yourself somebody needs help. . . ."

"Look," Leaphorn said. "It's none of my business. I'm sorry. I shouldn't have—"

"No," Father Tso said. "That's fair enough. First you kid yourself somebody needs you—which is easy to kid yourself about, because that's why you thought you had the vocation to start with. That's what the fathers tell you at St. Anthony's Mission, you know: Somebody needs you. And then it's all reversed: a woman comes along who needs help. And then she's an antidote for loneliness. And then she's most of everything you're giving up. And what if you're wrong? What if there's no God? If there's not, you're letting your life tick away for nothing. It gets complicated. So you get your faith back. . . ." He stopped, glanced at Leaphorn in the brief glow of the flash. "You do get it if you want it, you know. And so you try

to get out of it. You run away." Father Tso stopped.
Then he began again. "But by then, she really does
need you. So what are you running away from?"
Even whispered, the question was angry.

"So that's why you came—trying to get away
from her?" Leaphorn asked.

"I don't know," Father Tso said. "The old man
asked me to come. But mostly I was running,
I guess."

"And you got tangled with your brother?"

"We're the Hero Twins." Father Tso made a
sound a little like laughing. "Maybe we're both
saving the People from the Monsters. Different
approaches, but about equal success."

Now the voice of Theodora Adams was close
enough so that they could understand an occasional word. The cavern narrowed again, and
Leaphorn stood against the wall, one hand holding the priest's elbow, and stared toward reflected
light. The light was harsh and its source was
low—probably a lantern of some sort placed on
the calcite floor. Here a hodgepodge of stalagmites rose in crooked lines from the level floor
and curtains of stalactites hung down toward
them. The light cast them in relief—black against
the dim yellow.

"The cage is just back around that corner," Tso
whispered. "That light's from a butane lamp sitting outside."

"Does the guard have to come past this way?"

"I don't know," Tso said. "It's confusing in here."

"Let's get closer, then," Leaphorn said softly. "But keep it absolutely quiet. He might be there already."

They edged through the darkness, keeping in the cover of a wall of stalagmites. Leaphorn could see part of the cage now, and the butane lantern, and the head and shoulders of Theodora Adams sitting in its corner. Close enough, he thought. Somewhere near here he would stage his ambush.

"I wonder why they took me out of there," Father Tso whispered.

Leaphorn didn't answer. He was thinking that maybe with Father Tso subtracted, the cage held the symbolic number—eleven children and three adults. Father Tso would have spoiled the symmetry of revenge. But there must be more reason than that.

In the darkness, time seemed to take on another dimension. After three exhausting days and nights virtually without sleep, Leaphorn was finding it took much of his concentration simply to stay awake. He shifted, moving his weight from his left side to his right. In this new position, he could see most of Theodora Adams. The lantern light gave her face a sculptured effect and left her eye sockets dark. He could see two other hostages of the Buffalo Society. A man who must be one of the Scout leaders lay on his side, his head cushioned on his folded coat, apparently asleep. He was a small man, perhaps forty-five years old, with dark hair and a delicate doll-like face. There was a dark smudge on his forehead, rubbed into a brown streak across his cheek. Dried blood from a head cut, Leaphorn guessed. The man's hands lay relaxed and limp against the floor. The other person was a boy, perhaps thirteen, who slept fitfully. Theodora Adams spoke to someone out of Leaphorn's vision.

"Is he feeling any better?"

And a precise, boyish voice said, "I think he's almost asleep."

After that, no one said anything. Leaphorn longed for a conversation to overhear. For anything to help him fight off the dizzying assault of sleep. He forced his mind to consider the furious activity this kidnapping must be creating. The rescue of this many children would have total, absolute priority. Every man, every resource, would be made available for finding them. The reservation would be aswarm with FBI agents, and every variety of state, federal, military and Indian cop. Leaphorn caught himself slipping into a dream of the bedlam that must be going on now at Window Rock, and shook his head furiously.

He *couldn't* allow himself to sleep. He forced his mind to retrace what must have been the sequence of this affair. Why this cave was so important was clear to him now. On the surface of the earth, there was no way an operation like this could remain undetected. But this cave was not only a hiding hole under the earth; it was one whose existence was hidden behind a century of time and the promises made to a holy man's ghost. Old Man Tso must have learned that the sacred cave was being used—and desecrated— when he came to take care of the medicine bundles left by Standing Medicine. That seemed now to be what was implied in the story Tso had told Listening Woman. And the Buffalo Society either knew he had found them, or had learned he used the cave. And that meant he could not be left alive. A dream of the murder of Hosteen Tso began merging with reality in Leaphorn's mind. He ground his chin deliberately against the stone, driving away sleep with pain.

And the police would never find this cave. They would ask the People. The People would know nothing. The cave would have been entered only by water—on which no tracks can be followed. From outside, the cave mouth would seem only one of a hundred thousand dark cliff overhangs into which the water lapped. They would ask Old Man McGinnis, who usually knew everything, and McGinnis would know nothing. Leaphorn fought back sleep by diverting his thoughts into another channel. The same "fade-away" tactics employed in the Santa Fe robbery were probably being used here. Those who seized and delivered the hostages would have run for cover. They would have gone safely away long before the crime was discovered. Only enough men would have been left here to handle the hostages and collect the ransom. Probably only three men. But how would *they* get away? Everyone had escaped, except three. Tull and Jackie and Goldrims. They would have set up a way to relay and rebroadcast the radio message that kept the police away. Easy enough to rig, Leaphorn guessed. It wouldn't take much—if the transmissions were kept brief—to confuse radio directional finders. But how did the Society plan to extricate the final three when the ransom arrived? How could they be given time to escape? No one except the hostages would have seen them. If the hostages were killed, there would be no witnesses. Still, Goldrims would need running time—an hour or two to get far enough away from here to become just another Navajo. How could he provide himself with that time? Leaphorn thought of the dynamite, and the timing device, and of John Tull, who believed himself to be immortal.

Leaphorn caught himself dozing again and shook his head angrily. If he hoped to leave this cave alive, he must stay awake until Goldrims, or Tull, or Jackie came alone to check on the hostages, or ask the ritual questions of one of the Scouts. He must be awake and alert for an opportunity at ambush, at overpowering the guard, at getting a gun and changing the odds. To accomplish this he had to stay awake. To go to sleep would be to wake up dead. Thinking that, Lieutenant Joe Leaphorn fell asleep.

Leaphorn's dream had nothing at all to do with the cave, or kidnapping, or Goldrims, or Hosteen Tso. It was involved with winter and with punishment, and was motivated by the cold of the stone beneath his side and the pain in his hip. Despite his exhaustion, this discomfort kept dragging him back toward consciousness, and finally to a voice which was saying:

"All right. Wake him up."

For a moment the words were nothing but an incomprehensible part of a chaotic dream. And then Leaphorn was awake.

"Let's not waste any time," the voice was saying, and it was the voice of Goldrims. "I need the one named Symons." A panicky second passed before Leaphorn realized that Goldrims was standing by the cage door and the words were not directed at him.

"You're Symons?" Goldrims asked. The voice was loud and the words echoed through the cavern. "Wake up. I need to know your birth date and what your wife gave you for your last birthday."

Leaphorn could hear Symons's voice, but not his answer.

"May third and what? May third and a sweater. Okay."

"Are you going to let us go?" It was Theodora Adams's voice, but she had moved out of the corner now and out of Leaphorn's vision.

"Sure," Goldrims said. "When we get what we're asking, you're free as a bird." The voice sounded amused.

"What have you done with Ben?" she asked.

Goldrims said nothing. Leaphorn could see his back and his right profile, silhouetted against the reflected lantern light. Far behind him, at the edge of the darkness, John Tull stood. The lantern light glistened on the shotgun Tull held casually by his side. The shadow converted his ruined face into a gargoyle shape. But Leaphorn could see Tull was grinning. He could also see there was no chance for an ambush.

"What have I done with Ben?" Goldrims asked. He moved abruptly to the cage's gate, and there was the click of the padlock opening. Goldrims disappeared inside. "What have I done with

Ben?" he asked again. The voice was fierce now and there was the sudden violent sound of a blow struck. Near him in the darkness, Leaphorn heard a sharp intake of breath from where Father Tso was standing, and there was a muffled scream from the Adams woman.

"You bitch," Goldrims was saying. "You tell me what Whitey has done to Ben. It got him crawling on his belly to a white man's church, giving himself up to the white man's God, and then a white bitch comes along . . ." Goldrims's voice broke, and halted. And when it began again its words were paced, tense, controlled. "I know how it works," Goldrims said. "When I heard that this thing that claims to be my brother had become a priest, I got a book and read about it. They made him lay on his face, and promise to stay away from women. And then the first slut that comes after him, he breaks his promise."

Goldrims's voice halted. He reappeared in Leaphorn's view, opening the gate. Leaphorn could hear Theodora Adams crying, and a whimpering sound from one of the Boy Scouts. Tull was no longer grinning. His grotesque face was somber and watchful. Goldrims closed the gate behind him.

"Slut," he said. "You're the kind of woman who eats men."

And with that, Goldrims clicked the padlock

shut and walked angrily across the cave floor, with Tull two steps behind him. The lantern Goldrims carried illuminated them only from the waist down—four legs scissoring, out of step and out of cadence. Leaphorn told Father Tso where to wait for a second chance at an ambush two hours later. And then he followed the now distant legs through the darkness. It was like tracking a strange uncoordinated beast through the night.

EIGHTEEN

"NO, NO," GOLDRIMS was saying. "Look. It goes in like this."

They were squatted beside the radio transceiver, Tull and Goldrims, with the one they called Jackie sprawled on the bedroll, motionless.

"Like this?" Tull asked. He was doing something with the transmitter—changing the crystal or making some sort of antenna adjustment, Leaphorn guessed. From where he stood behind the stalagmites that formed the nearest cover, the acoustics of the cave carried the voices clearly through the stillness, but Leaphorn was too far away to hear everything. Tull said something else, unintelligible.

"All right, then," Goldrims said. "Run through it again." There was a pause. "Right," Goldrims said. "That's right. Put the speaker of the tape recorder about three inches from the mike. About like that."

"I've got it," Tull said. "No sweat. And right at 4 A.M. Right?"

"That's right—4 A.M. for the next one. If I'm not back by then. Just a second and we'll get this one broadcast." He studied his watch, apparently waiting for the proper second. Then he took the microphone, flicked a series of switches. "Whitey," he said. "Whitey, this is Buffalo Society. We have your answers and instructions."

The radio said: "Go ahead, Buffalo, ready to record."

"Your answers are May the third and a sweater," Goldrims said. "And now we're ready to wrap this up. Here are your orders." Goldrims leaned toward the microphone and Leaphorn could hear only part of the instructions. There were references to map coordinates, a line drawn between them, one man in a helicopter, references to times, a flashed signal from the ground. Obviously instructions for the ransom drop, and like everything else about this operation, it seemed meticulously planned. No way to set a trap if the drop site wasn't known until the copter reached it. In all, the instructions took only a minute. And then the radio was off, and Goldrims was standing, facing directly toward Leaphorn, talking to Tull, going over it again. They walked away together, away from the pool of lantern light toward the water, still talking. Then the purring sound of a heavily muffled engine started. Not a generator, as he had thought, but almost certainly a muffled boat engine. The sound moved and faded toward the dim light of the cave mouth.

Leaphorn waited long enough to make absolutely sure that the man returning with the bobbing flashlight was John Tull. Then he moved quietly away from the stalagmites, back into the darkness. It would be at least an hour, he guessed, before the next questions were radioed in and the next answers extracted to prove the hostages still alive. Leaphorn intended to use that hour well. He had not seen the boat. He planned to make sure there was nothing else hidden in this darkness that he didn't know about.

The dynamite was gone. Leaphorn flicked the flashlight beam quickly across the cartons of supplies to make sure he hadn't simply forgotten where the wooden case had been. Even as he did, logic told him the dynamite, and the small boxes containing the timer and the electrical wire, would be missing. He had expected it. It fit into the pattern Leaphorn's mind was trying to make of this affair—of the relationship between Tull and Goldrims and between what seemed to be too many coincidences, and too many unanswered questions. He snapped off the flashlight and stood in the darkness, concentrating on arranging what he knew of Goldrims and the Buffalo Society, and of what was happening here, into some order. He tried to project, and understand, Goldrims's intentions. The man was extremely smart. And he was Navajo. He could easily vanish in the immense empty canyon country around Short Mountain, no matter how many people were hunting him. If he had another well-stocked hideaway like this, he could stay holed up for months. But finally he would run out of time. He would be the country's most wanted man. There seemed to be no real possibility of escape for Goldrims. That seemed out of character. A fatal loose end. Goldrims would leave no loose ends, Leaphorn thought. There must be something Leaphorn was overlooking.

The dynamite and the timer must have something to do with it. But Leaphorn couldn't see how blowing up the cave would solve Goldrims's problem. He glanced at his watch. In about forty-five minutes, the next set of questions would be broadcast and brought to the Boy Scouts for the time-buying answers. When that time came, Leaphorn had to be in position to jump whoever came with the tape recorder. In the meantime, he had to find the dynamite.

Leaphorn did find some of the dynamite. But first he discovered what had to be Hosteen Tso's tracks, undisturbed in the quiet dust for months. They were moccasin prints scuffed across the white floor. Mixed with them were boot tracks which Leaphorn had long since identified as Gold-rims's. They led into what seemed to be a dead-end cavern. But the cavern turned, and dropped, and widened into a room with a ceiling which soared upward into a ragged hanging curtain of stalactites. Leaphorn examined it quickly with his flashlight. In several places the calcite surface was piled deep with ashes of old fires. Leaphorn took two steps toward the old hearths and stopped abruptly. The floor here was patterned with sand paintings. At least thirty of them, each a geometric pattern of the colors and shapes of the Holy People of the Navajos. Leaphorn studied them—recognizing Corn Beetle, the Sacred Fly, Talking God, and Black God, Coyote and others. He could read some of the stories told in these pictures-formed-of-colored-sand. One of them he recognized as part of the Sun Father Chant, and another seemed to be a piece of the Mountain Way. Leaphorn came from a family rich in cere-monial people. Two of his uncles were singers, and a grandfather; a nephew was learning a cur-ing ritual, and his maternal grandmother had been a Hand-Trembler famous in the Toadlena–Beautiful Mountain country. But some of these dry paintings were totally unfamiliar to him. These must be the great heritage Standing Medicine had left for the People—the Way to start the world again.

Leaphorn stood staring at them, and then past them at the black metal case that sat on the cave floor beyond them. His flashlight beam glittered from the glass face of dials and from shiny metal knobs. Leaphorn squatted beside it. A trademark on its side read HALLICRAFTERS. It was another radio transmitter. Wires ran from it, disappearing into the darkness. Connecting to an antenna, Leaphorn guessed. Taped securely to its top was a battery-powered tape recorder, and wired to both tape recorder and radio was an enameled metal box. Leaphorn was conscious now of a new sound, a sort of electric whirring which came from the box—another timer. The dial on its top showed its pointer had moved past seven of the fifty markings on its face. There was no way of telling whether each mark represented a minute or an hour. It was obviously adjustable. Behind the radio a paper sack sat on the floor—also linked to terminals on the timer box. Leaphorn opened the sack gingerly. In it were two dynamite sticks, held together around a blasting cap with black friction tape. Leaphorn rocked back on his heels, frowning. Why dynamite a radio? He studied the timer again. It seemed to be custom-made. Sequential, he guessed. First it would turn on the radio, and then the tape recorder, and when the recording was broadcast, it would detonate the dynamite.

Leaphorn extracted his pocket knife and carefully removed the screws that attached the dynamite wires to the timer. Then he cut the tape recorder free, sat on the floor and pushed the play button.

"You were warned. But our people—"

The words boomed out into the cave. Leaphorn stabbed the off button down. The voice was that of Goldrims. But he couldn't risk playing it now. Sound carried too well in this cavern. He shoved the recorder under his shirt. He would play the tape later.

As it happened, Leaphorn had cut it close. He found Father Benjamin Tso waiting where he had left him, hidden among a cluster of stalagmites close to the cage door. He told the priest what he had learned, of Goldrims's leaving to pick up the ransom, and of the radio and the time bomb in the cave room where Father Tso had been left.

"I saw the radio," Father Tso said. "I didn't

know what was in the sack." He paused. "But why would he want to blow me up?" The voice was incredulous. Leaphorn didn't attempt an answer. Far back in the darkness a tiny dot of light had appeared, bobbing with the walk of whoever carried it. Leaphorn prayed it was Jackie, and only Jackie. He motioned Father Tso back out of sight and climbed quickly onto a calcite shelf, from which he could watch and launch his ambush. He was still trying to control his breathing when the yellow light of a battery lantern joined the glow of the butane light at the cage.

"Time to talk again." The voice was Jackie's. "Got questions for two of these boys." He hooked his lantern on his belt, shifted the shotgun he was carrying to his left hand and fished a piece of paper from his shirt pocket.

Leaphorn moved swiftly. He had the walkie-talkie out of its case, holding it like a club as he came around the wall of stalagmites. Then he hesitated. Once he jumped down to the lower calcite floor, there was no cover. For thirty yards he would be in the open and clearly visible. It was much too far. Jackie would have him. He could spin around and shoot Leaphorn dead.

But Father Tso was there, walking toward Jackie.

"Hey," Jackie said. He swung the shotgun toward Tso. "Hey, how'd you get loose?"

"Put down the gun!" Father Tso shouted it, and the cavern echo-boomed: *"Gun . . . gun . . . gun . . . gun."* He walked toward Jackie. "Put it down."

"Hold it," Jackie said. "Hold it or I'll kill you." He took a step backward. "Come on," he shouted. "Jesus, you're as crazy as Tull."

"I'm as immortal as Tull," Father Tso shouted. He walked toward Jackie, hands outstretched, reaching for the shotgun.

Leaphorn was running now—knowing what would happen, knowing how Father Tso planned it to happen, knowing it was the only way it could work.

"God forgive—" Father Tso was shouting and that was all Leaphorn heard. Jackie fired from a crouch. The gunshot boomed like a bomb, surrounding Leaphorn with a blast of sound.

The impact knocked Father Tso backward. He fell on his side. Only after Father Tso lay still did Jackie hear through the booming echoes the sound of Leaphorn running, and spin with his catlike quickness so that the walkie-talkie struck not the back of his head, where Leaphorn had aimed it, but across his temple. Jackie seemed to die instantly, the shotgun spinning from his hand as he fell. Father Tso lived perhaps a minute. Leaphorn picked up the shotgun—it was a Remington automatic—and knelt beside Tso. Whatever the priest was saying, Leaphorn couldn't understand it. He put his ear close to Father Tso's face, but now the priest was saying nothing at all. Leaphorn could hear only the echoes of the gunshots dying away and over that the sound of Theodora Adams screaming.

There was no time to plan anything. Leaphorn moved as quickly as he could. He felt rapidly through Jackie's pockets, finding the padlock key but no additional ammunition for the shotgun. He glanced at the cage. A quick impression of a dozen frightened faces staring at him—and of Theodora Adams, sobbing in the corner.

"The other one's going to be coming and I'm going to take him," Leaphorn said. "Get every-body to sit back down. Don't give him any hint I'm out here." And with that, Leaphorn ran back into the darkness.

He stopped behind the stalagmites and stared in the direction from which Tull would come. Nothing but blackness. But Tull would surely come. The sound of the shot would have reached him at the cave entrance. And he would have heard the Adams woman screaming. If he came at a run, he should be arriving now. Leaphorn held the shotgun ready, looking down its barrel into the darkness. He swung it toward the glow of light, noticing with satisfaction that the bead sight was lined exactly in the V of the rear sight.

He could hear Theodora Adams's sobbing—less hysterical now and more the sound of simple sorrow. For the first time, Leaphorn became conscious of the smell of burned gunpowder. As soon as Tull came well between him and the light—as soon as he could line up the sights on his silhouette—he would shoot for the center of the body. There'd be no warning shout. In this darkness, Tull was far too dangerous for that. Leaphorn would simply try to kill him. Time ticked silently away.

But where was Tull? Leaphorn was belatedly conscious that he had underestimated the man. Tull had not jumped to the obvious conclusion that Jackie had shot someone and come running to see about it. If Tull was coming at all, he was coming quietly, with his light turned off, stalking the lighted place to learn what had happened. Leaphorn lowered himself slightly behind the stony barrier, aware that Tull might be somewhere behind him—looking for Leaphorn's shape against the glow exactly as Leaphorn had looked for Tull's. But even as he crouched, even as he registered this increased respect for John Tull as an adversary, Leaphorn felt a fierce exultant certainty of the outcome. No matter how cautious Tull was, the odds had shifted now. Tull would see Jackie and Father Tso on the cave floor and the surviving hostages in the cage. That would account for everyone. He would have to come into the light to get the answers. And he would want to find out what had happened, how Jackie and Tso had died. With his weapon ready, with everyone accounted for, there'd be no reason for him to hold back.

"Hey." Tull's voice came from Leaphorn's right— well out of the periphery of the lantern light. "What happened?" The voice echoed, and died away, and silence resumed.

"They fought." It was the voice of the scout leader named Symons. "The priest attacked your man and I think they killed each other."

A good answer, Leaphorn thought. Smart.

"Where's Jackie's gun?" Tull shouted. "Where's the shotgun?"

"I don't know," Symons said. "I don't see it."

A bright light blinked on suddenly, its beam emerging from behind a screen of stalagmites far beyond the cage. It played over the bodies, searching.

Leaphorn felt a sick disappointment. Tull was even smarter than he'd guessed.

"You son-of-a-bitch," Tull shouted. "You've got the shotgun in there. Throw it out. If you don't, I'm going to start shooting people."

The light had blinked quickly off, but Leaphorn

had him located now. A hint of reflected light, perhaps one hundred yards away. Leaphorn tried to line his sights on it, then lowered the gun. The odds of an effective hit at this range were terrible.

"We don't have the gun," Symons shouted.

In the dim light, Leaphorn could see Tull had already—without a word—raised his pistol.

It was still a high-odds shot, but there was no choice now. Leaphorn steadied the gun, trying to keep the dim form visible over the bead. He squeezed the trigger.

The muzzle flash was blinding. Leaphorn wanted desperately to know if he had hit Tull, but he could see only the whiteness burned on his retina and hear nothing but the reverberating thunder of the gunshot booming down the corridors of the cavern. Then there was the sound of another shot. Tull's pistol. Leaphorn crouched behind the stone barrier, waiting for sight and hearing to return. He became aware that the butane lantern was out. The darkness here now was total. Tull must have shot out the light. A quick-thinking man. Leaphorn stared into the darkness. What would Tull do? The gunman would know now that another person had somehow gotten into the cave. He might guess that the person was the Navajo policeman. He'd know the policeman had Jackie's shotgun and . . . how many rounds of ammunition? Leaphorn opened the magazine, poured three shells out into his hand, and carefully reloaded them. A round in the chamber and three in the magazine. Knowing this, what would Tull do? Not, Leaphorn thought, stand and fight in this blackness with a pistol against a shotgun. The darkness minimized the effect of the pistol's range and magnified the effect of the shotgun's scattered pattern. Tull would head for the entrance, for the light and the radio. He would call Goldrims for help. And would Goldrims come? Leaphorn thought about it. Goldrims had probably intended to radio to the copter as it passed and order it to land, order the pilot out, and then, if he could fly a copter, fly a few miles, abandon the aircraft and begin a well-planned escape maneuver. If he couldn't fly a copter, he'd disable it and its radio, fix the pilot so he couldn't follow, and run. Why return to the cave? Leaphorn could think of no reason. Would he come back to help Tull in the cave? Leaphorn doubted it. Tull had been expendable at the Santa Fe robbery. Why wouldn't he be expendable now? The contest in this cave would be between John Tull and Joe Leaphorn. Leaphorn felt along the top of the rocky ledge for a flat place, put his flashlight on it, aimed it at the place where Tull had been, and flicked it on. He ducked three long steps to his right and then looked over the top. The flashlight beam shone through a blue haze of gun-powder smoke into a gray-white emptiness. Where Tull had been, there was nothing now. Leaphorn slipped back to the flashlight, flicked it off, aimed it at the place the hostages had been kept, and snapped it on again. The beam fell directly on the body of Father Benjamin Tso and illuminated Theodora Adams, kneeling inside the cage. She covered her eyes against the glare. Leaphorn turned off the flash, and felt his way through the blackness to the cage. He unlocked the padlock with the key he had taken from Jackie's pocket.

"Get the lantern off Jackie's body," he said. "Get everybody away from this place. Find a place to hide until I call for you." He didn't wait to answer any questions.

The speed with which Leaphorn followed John Tull toward the cave's mouth was reduced by a healthy respect for Tull. He skirted far to the left of the direct route, carrying the shotgun at ready. When he finally reached the area where light from the entrance turned the blackness into mere dimness, he found droplets of blood on the gray-white calcite floor. At another point, a smear of reddish brown discolored a limestone outcrop. Leaphorn guessed it was where Tull had put a bloody hand against the stone. Leaphorn hadn't missed. The shotgun blast had hit Tull, and hit him hard.

Leaphorn paused and digested this. In a sense, time was now on his side. A shotgun would make a multiple wound, hard to stop bleeding—and Tull seemed to be bleeding freely. As time passed, he would weaken. But was the crucial measurement of time here being made by Tull's pumping heart or by a clockwork mechanism attached to about twenty sticks of dynamite still unaccounted for? Leaphorn decided he couldn't wait. Somewhere in the darkness around him, Leaphorn was sure that missing timer—and perhaps other timers he had never seen—was counting away the seconds.

He found Tull where he thought he would find him—at the radio. The man had moved the butane lantern some fifty feet back into the cave from the place where Leaphorn had first seen him and Goldrims, and he'd turned on a battery lantern and adjusted its beam toward part of the cavern. The range of light thus extended substantially beyond the effective range of the shotgun. Leaphorn circled, trying to find an approach that offered some close-in cover. There wasn't one. The floor here was as dead level as a ballroom. From it ragged rows of stalagmites rose like a patchwork of volcanic islands from the surface of a still, white sea. Tull had moved the radio behind one such island and the lantern was beside it—giving Tull the advantage of deep shadow. From there, he could have a clear shot at anyone trying to get out of the cave mouth via the water. The lake protected one flank and the cave wall another. Approaching him meant walking into the lantern light and into the barrel of his pistol.

Leaphorn glanced at his watch, and considered. His hip now throbbed with a steady pain.

"Hey, Tull," he shouted. "Let's talk."

Perhaps five seconds passed.

"Fine," Tull said. "Talk."

"He's not coming back, you know," Leaphorn said. "He'll take the money and run. You get stuck."

"No," Tull said. "But I tell you what. You throw that shotgun out there where I can see it, and we'll just make you one more hostage. When we cut out of here, you're a free man. Otherwise, when my friend gets back, he's going to be behind you, and I'm going to move in from the front, and we're going to kill you."

And that was about the way it would work, if Goldrims did come back, Leaphorn thought. He would be fairly easy to handle by two men—even with the shotgun. But he didn't think Goldrims would be coming back.

"Let's quit kidding each other," Leaphorn said. "Your friend is taking the ransom and running.

And you're supposed to wait around for some more broadcasts, and then you'll run. And when you run, you're blowing this place up."

Tull said nothing.

"How bad did I hit you?"

"You missed," Tull said.

"You're lying. I hit you and you've been losing blood. And that's another reason you're not going to get out of here unless we make a deal. I can keep you in here, and you can keep me in here. It's a Mexican standoff, and we can't afford a standoff because your boss has a bomb set to go." Leaphorn paused, thinking about where he had found the bomb and the circumstances. "He didn't tell you about the bomb, did he?"

"Screw you," Tull said.

No, Leaphorn thought, he didn't tell you about the radio setup and the bomb in the room with the sacred paintings. Tull's tracks hadn't shown up there, and six sticks of dynamite had been missing when Leaphorn had first found the cache. Probably that bomb had been set up separately. This was a Buffalo Society operation, but part of it, Leaphorn was increasingly certain, might be a very private affair of Goldrims himself.

"I'm going to play a tape recording for you," Leaphorn said. He took the recorder from under his shirt and adjusted it. "Haven't heard it myself yet, so we can listen to it together. It was fastened to a Hallicrafters radio transceiver way back in a side room. There was this radio, with a timer set to turn it on to broadcasting, and let it warm up and then turn on this tape recorder. And after the tape ran, the timer was set to detonate some dynamite in a sack there. You ready for it?"

There was silence. Seconds ticked away.

"Okay," Tull said. "Let's hear it. If it exists."

Leaphorn pushed the on button. Goldrims's voice boomed out again.

". . . have seen policemen in the territory you agreed would be kept clear of police. You have broken your promise. The Buffalo Society never breaks a promise. Remember this in the future. Remember and learn. We promised that if police came into this corner of the Navajo Nation, the hostages would die. They will now die, and we warriors of the Buffalo Society will die with them. You will find our bodies in our sacred cavern, the mouth of which opens into the San Juan River arm of Lake Powell less than a mile below the present lake-level mouth of the river, approximately twenty-three miles east by northeast of Short Mountain, and exactly at north latitude 36, 11, 17, and west longitude 110, 29, 3. To those of the Buffalo Society who seized these white hostages, know that we three warriors kept our honor and our promise. To the white man, come to this cave and recover the bodies of three of your adults and eleven of your young. They died to avenge the deaths of three of our adults and eleven children in the Olds Prairie Murders. With them will be bodies of three warriors of the Buffalo Society: Jackie Noni of the Potawatomi Nation, and John Tull, of the Seminole, and myself, whom the white men call Hoski, or James Tso, a warrior of the Navajo Nation. May our memories live in the glory of the Buffalo Society."

The clear, resonant voice of Goldrims stopped and there was only the faint hiss of the blank tape winding into the take-up reel.

Leaphorn pushed the off button and rewound the tape. He felt numb. His logic had told him that Goldrims might kill the hostages to eliminate witnesses, but now he realized that he hadn't really believed it. The impact of hearing Goldrims's pleasant, unemotional voice declare this mass murder/mass suicide was stunning. And in that split second, he also became aware that the name of Father Benjamin Tso was missing from the catalog of the dead. He confronted the implications of that gap in the roster. It meant that Goldrims had planned even better than Leaphorn had guessed.

"You want to hear it again?" Leaphorn shouted. "From the beginning this time."

Tull said nothing. Leaphorn pushed the on button. "You were warned," the tape began. "But our people have seen policemen in the territory . . ." When the recorder reached the list of bodies, Leaphorn stopped it. "I want you to notice," he shouted to Tull, "there's a name missing from this list. Notice it's the name of your buddy's brother. I want you to think about that."

Leaphorn thought of it himself. Bits of the puzzle fell into place. He knew now who had written the letter summoning Father Benjamin Tso to his grandfather's hogan. Goldrims had written it himself. He felt a chill admiration for the mind that had conceived such a plan. Hoski had realized he could not escape from the manhunt. It would be massive and inexorable. So he had devised a way to abort it. What the dynamite left of his brother, as Hoski had arranged it, would be found with the shattered radio and identified as Hoski's body. Everyone would thus be accounted for. There would be no one left to hunt. As he realized this, Leaphorn also realized that his own problem had been multiplied. Goldrims would have to respond to Tull's radioed call for help. He couldn't risk having Leaphorn, or anyone who had seen Father Tso, escape from the cave. Hoski would have to come back.

Leaphorn pushed the play button again, ran the tape, pushed stop, pushed rewind. He was awed by it. Perfect. Flawless. Impeccable. It left nothing to chance. The big score for James Tso would not just be the ransom. The big score would be a new life, free from surveillance, free from hiding. There would be no reason to question the identity of the body. Hoski had never been arrested or fingerprinted. And no one knew the priest was here. No one, that is, who would remain alive. And there was a family resemblance.

"Hey, Tull," Leaphorn yelled. "Have you counted the bodies? There's Jackie, and all those Boy Scouts, and the woman, and one of the Tso brothers, and you. You're there on the list of dead, Tull. But your friend Hoski is going to be alive and well. And wealthy, too."

Tull said nothing.

"Goddamn it, Tull," Leaphorn shouted. "Think! He's screwing you. He's screwing the Buffalo Society. Kelongy won't see a dollar of that ransom. Hoski's going to disappear with it."

Leaphorn listened and heard nothing but the echoes of his own voice dying in the cave. He hoped Tull was thinking. Hoski would disappear. And someday a man with another name and another identity would appear in Washington, and contact a woman named Rosemary Rita Oliveras. And somewhere, wherever he was hiding, a madman named Kelongy would wonder what went wrong with his crazy scheme and perhaps he would mourn his brilliant lieutenant. But there was no time to think of that now. Leaphorn glanced at his wrist watch. It was 2:47 A.M. In an hour and thirteen minutes it would be time to broadcast the answers that would keep the law at bay for another two hours. What had been Hoski's timing? He had called the helicopter to deliver the ransom at 4 A.M. Probably he would have picked up the money about two-thirty. When was the Hallicrafters set timed to broadcast its tape, and to detonate its bomb? Since Hoski would want to make sure that broadcast was recorded, he'd probably time it at one of the regular two-hour broadcasts. But how soon? Leaphorn tried to concentrate, to shut out the throbbing of his hip, the aching fatigue, the damp, mushroom smell of this watery part of the cave. It would be soon. Hoski would need very little running time. An hour or two of darkness would be enough to get well clear of the cave and its neighborhood. Because there'd be no search once that tape was aired. There would only be a great flocking of everybody to find this point on the map—the smoking mouth of a cave. There would be chaos. The hunted would have been found. Hoski/Goldrims, safely outside the circle of confusion, would simply walk away. Leaphorn was suddenly confident he understood the timing of Hoski's plan.

TONY HILLERMAN

"Tull," Leaphorn shouted. "Can't you see the son-of-a-bitch set you up? Use your head."

"No," Tull said. "Not him. You made that tape up."

"It's his voice," Leaphorn shouted. "Can't you recognize his voice?"

Silence.

"He didn't tell you why he moved his brother away from the Boy Scouts, did he?" Leaphorn shouted. "He didn't tell you about this tape. He didn't tell you about the bomb."

"Hell, man," Tull said. "I helped him put them together. I've got one right here with me, by this radio set here. And when the time comes, it's going to blow you to hell."

"You and me together, Tull," Leaphorn said. And as he said it, he heard the muffled purring of an outboard motor.

"You weren't here when he made one of those bombs," Leaphorn said. "And he didn't tell you about it. Or about that tape. Or about broadcasting it over that spare radio. Come on, Tull. You were the sucker in Santa Fe. You think you're immortal, but don't you get tired of being the one who gets screwed?"

Tull said nothing. Over the echoes of his own words, Leaphorn could hear the purring motor.

"Think," he shouted. "Count the dynamite sticks. There were twenty-four in the box. He used some to seal the other end of the cave. And some in a bomb to wipe out the Scouts, and you probably have a couple there. So does it all add up to twenty-four?"

Silence. It wasn't going to work. The tone of the outboard motor had changed now. It was inside the cave.

"You said there was dynamite in a sack by that Hallicrafters," Tull said. "Is that what you said?" His voice sounded weak now, pained. "How many sticks did you say?"

"Two sticks," Leaphorn said.

"How many dynamite caps?"

"Just one," Leaphorn said. "I think just one. With a wire connected." The purring of the outboard stopped.

"I'll bet Hoski set the timers himself," Leaphorn said. "I'll bet he told you that bomb with you there will go off about six o'clock. You're going to make the four o'clock broadcast and then cut out and run for it. But he set the timer a couple of hours early."

"Hey, Jimmy," Tull yelled. "He's over here."

"What's he have?" Hoski yelled. "Just Jackie's shotgun? Is that all?" Hoski's voice came from the water's edge, still a long way off.

"God damn it, Tull," Leaphorn shouted. "Don't be stupid. He's screwing you again, I tell you. He's got you listed among the dead on that tape, so you gotta be dead when they get here."

"He just has the shotgun," Tull shouted. "Move around behind him."

"He set the timer up on that bomb you have," Leaphorn shouted. "Can't you understand he has to kill you, too?"

"No," Tull said. "Jimmy's my friend." It was almost a scream.

"He left you at Santa Fe. He didn't tell you about that tape. He's got you listed with the dead. He set the timer . . ."

"Shut up," Tull said. "Shut up. You're wrong, damn you, and I can prove it." Tull's voice rose to a scream. "God damn you, I can prove you're wrong."

The tone, the hysteria, told Leaphorn more than the words. He knew, with a sick horror, exactly what Tull meant when he said he could prove it.

"He's talking crap," Goldrims was shouting, his voice much closer now. "He's lying to you, Tull. What the hell are you doing?"

Leaphorn was scrambling to his feet.

Tull's voice was saying: "I can just move this little hour hand up to . . ."

"Don't," Goldrims screamed, and Tull's voice was cut off by the sound of a pistol shot.

Leaphorn was running as fast as heart and legs and lungs would let him run, thinking that each

yard of distance from the center of the blast increased his chances for survival. From behind
him came the sound of Goldrims screaming
Tull's name, and another shot.

And then the blast. It was bright, as if a thousand flash bulbs lit the gray-white interior of the
cavern. Then the shock wave hit Leaphorn and
sent him tumbling and sliding over the calcite
floor, slamming finally into something.

Leaphorn became aware that he could hear
nothing and see nothing. Perhaps he had lost
consciousness long enough for the echoes to die
away. He noticed his nose was bleeding and felt
below his face. There were only a few drops of
wetness on the stony floor. Little time had passed.

He sat up gingerly. When the flash blindness
subsided enough so that he could read his watch,
it was 2:57. Leaphorn hurried. First he found his
flashlight behind the rocks where he had left
it, with the shotgun nearby. Next he found two
boats—a small three-man affair with an outboard engine, and a flat-bottomed fiberglass
model with a muffled inboard. In its bottom was
a green nylon backpack and a heavy canvas bag.
Leaphorn zipped the bag open. Inside were doz-
ens of small plastic packages. Leaphorn fished
one out, opened it and shone his flashlight onto
tight bundles of twenty-dollar bills. He returned

the pouch and carried the backpack and bag into the cave. Near the blackened area where James Tso and John Tull had died, he stopped, swung the heavy bag and sent the ransom money sliding down the cave floor into the darkness.

By the time he had everyone in the boats it was after 3 A.M.

At ten minutes after three, both boats purred out of the cave mouth and into open water. The night seemed incredibly bright. It was windless. A half moon hung halfway down the western sky. Leaphorn quickly got his directions. It was probably eighty miles down the lake to the dam and the nearest telephone—at least four or five hours. Leaphorn's hip throbbed. To hell with that, he thought. There would surely be aerial surveillance. Let someone else do some work. He picked up the spare gasoline can, screwed off the cap, floated it on the lake surface, and—as it drifted away—blasted it with his shotgun. It erupted into flame and burned, a bright blue-white beacon reflecting from the water, lighting the cliff walls around them, lighting the dirty, exhausted faces of eleven Boy Scouts. Normally it wouldn't be noticed in this lonely country. But tonight it would be. Tonight anything would be noticed.

At three-forty-two he heard the plane. High at

first, but circling. Leaphorn pointed his flashlight up. Blinked it off and on. The plane came low, buzzed the boat with landing lights on. It looked like an army reconnaissance craft.

Now Leaphorn was keeping his eye on the dark shape where cliff and water met—and the darkness that hid the cave mouth. The second hand of his watch swept past 4 A.M. Nothing happened. The hand swept down, and up, and down again. At 4:02 the blackness at the cliff base became a blinding flash of white light. Seconds passed. A tremendous muffled thump echoed across the water, followed by a rumbling. Slabs of rocks falling inside the cave. Too many rocks for the white men to remove to clear the path to Standing Medicine's sand paintings, Leaphorn thought. But not too many rocks to remove to salvage a canvas bag heavy with cash. A foot-high shock wave from the blast spread rapidly toward them across the mirrorlike surface of the lake. The reflected stars rippled. It reached the boat, rocked it abruptly, and moved down the lake.

They sat, waiting.

Leaphorn stared over the side, into the clear, dark water. Somewhere down below would be the hiding place of the helicopter, and the grave of Haas. He imagined how it happened. Haas with a gun in his ribs hovering the craft over this same boat, the bank loot being lowered into it, the passengers climbing down. Had they shot him then, or left a bomb aboard to be triggered when the copter was a safer fifty yards away? Whatever method, it left a trail impossible to follow.

From down the lake came the sound of another helicopter, traveling low and fast toward them.

How many, like Haas, had died to make Goldrims's trail impossible to follow? Hosteen Tso and Anna Atcitty, certainly, and almost certainly Frederick Lynch. Leaphorn considered how it must have happened. Goldrims had been told of the secret cavern as the oldest son. He had stocked it as the base for this operation, and killed his grandfather to keep the secret safe. Then he must have returned to Washington. Why Washington? Kelongy must be there with the Buffalo Society's funds from the Santa Fe robbery. And when the time came for the kidnapping, Goldrims had returned to Safety Systems, Inc., and taken the dog he had coveted and corrupted and his ex-employer's car, and left Frederick Lynch in no condition to report the theft and in no place where he would ever be found again. That crime, Leaphorn guessed, would have been as much personal vendetta as motivated by actual need.

As for Tull, he was simply something useful. And as for Benjamin Tso . . .

Theodora Adams interrupted his thoughts. "Why did Ben do that?" she asked, in a choked voice. "It was like he knew he would be killed. Did he do it to save me?"

Leaphorn opened his mouth and closed it. Ben did it to save himself, he thought. But he didn't say it. It wasn't something he could explain to her if she didn't already understand it.

As Tony's home state paper,
the *Oklahoma City Oklahoman,* says,
"Readers who have not discovered Hillerman
should not waste one minute more."
Find out what you've been missing
with Leaphorn and Chee . . .

A dead reporter's secret notebook implicates a senatorial candidate and political figures in a million-dollar murder scam.

THE FLY ON THE WALL

John Cotton was a simple man with one desire: to write the greatest story of his life and have enough life left to read all about it. He knows what to do when he finds a great story, but he is a little afraid when a big story begins to find him. It starts when a fellow reporter is murdered, and his notebook, filled with information about a tax scam, ends up in John's hands. Not long afterward, a body is discovered in John's car. Then John's car ends up in the river, a bomb is found in his apartment, and his girlfriend drops out of sight. It's up to John to unravel the mystery of the notebook and why anyone would kill for the information it contains.

"Fascinating . . . breathless suspense."
Minneapolis Tribune

"Explosive . . . sensational . . . excellent."
Cleveland Plain Dealer

An archaeological dig, a steel hypodermic needle, and the strange laws of the Zuñi complicate the disappearance of two young boys.

DANCE HALL OF THE DEAD

Two young boys suddenly disappear. One of them, a Zuñi, leaves a pool of blood behind. Lieutenant Joe Leaphorn of the Navajo Tribal Police tracks the brutal killer. Three things complicate the search: an archaeological dig, a steel hypodermic needle, and the strange laws of the Zuñi. Compelling, terrifying, and highly suspenseful, *Dance Hall of the Dead* never relents from first page till last.

"High entertainment, an aesthetically satisfying glimpse of the still-powerful tribal mysteries."
New York Times

"Riveting descriptions of Zuñi religious rites."
Newsweek

A baffling investigation of murder, ghosts, and witches can be solved only by Lieutenant Leaphorn, a man who understands both his own people and cold-blooded killers.

LISTENING WOMAN

The state police and FBI are baffled when an old man and a teenage girl are brutally murdered. The blind Navajo Listening Woman speaks of ghosts and of witches. But Lieutenant Leaphorn of the Navajo Tribal Police knows his people as well as he knows cold-blooded killers. His incredible investigation carries him from a dead man's secret to a kidnap scheme, to a conspiracy that stretches back more than one hundred years. Leaphorn arrives at the threshold of a solution— and is greeted with the most violent confrontation of his career.

"Hillerman's mysteries are special . . .
Listening Woman is among the best."
Washington Post

"A good exciting mystery that has everything."
Pittsburgh Press

An assassin waits for Officer Chee in the desert to protect a vision of death that for thirty years has been fed by greed and washed in blood.

PEOPLE OF DARKNESS

Who would murder a dying man? Why would someone steal a box of rocks? And why would a rich man's wife pay $3,000 to get them back? These questions haunt Sergeant Jim Chee of the Navajo Tribal Police as he journeys into the scorching Southwest. But there, out in the Bad Country, a lone assassin waits for Chee to come seeking answers, waits ready and willing to protect a vision of death that for thirty years has been fed by greed and washed in blood.

"Hillerman . . . is in a class by himself."
Los Angeles Times

"Great suspense."
Chicago Tribune

Sergeant Jim Chee becomes trapped in a deadly web of a cunningly spun plot driven by Navajo sorcery and white man's greed.

THE DARK WIND

A corpse whose palms and soles have been "scalped" is only the first in a series of disturbing clues: an airplane's mysterious crash in the nighttime desert, a bizarre attack on a windmill, a vanishing shipment of cocaine. Sergeant Jim Chee of the Navajo Tribal Police is trapped in a deadly web of a cunningly spun plot driven by Navajo sorcery and white man's greed.

"Hillerman is first-rate . . . fresh, original, and highly suspenseful."
Los Angeles Times

"A beauty of a thriller . . . exotic and compelling reading."
Cleveland Plain Dealer

A photo sends Officer Chee on an odyssey of murder and revenge that moves from an Indian hogan to a deadly healing ceremony.

THE GHOSTWAY

Old Joseph Joe sees it all. Two strangers spill blood at the Shiprock Wash-O-Mat. One dies. The other drives off into the dry lands of the Big Reservation, but not before he shows the old Navajo a photo of the man he seeks. This is enough to send Tribal Policeman Jim Chee after a killer . . . and on an odyssey of murder and revenge that moves from an Indian hogan and its trapped ghost, to the dark underbelly of L.A., to a healing ceremony whose cure could be death.

"A first-rate story of suspense and mystery."
The New Yorker

"Fresh, original and highly suspenseful."
Los Angeles Times

Three shotgun blasts in a trailer bring Officer Chee and Lieutenant Leaphorn together for the first time in an investigation of ritual, witchcraft, and blood.

SKINWALKERS

Three shotgun blasts explode into the trailer of Officer Jim Chee of the Navajo Tribal Police. But Chee survives to join partner Lieutenant Joe Leaphorn in a frightening investigation that takes them into a dark world of ritual, witchcraft, and blood — all tied to the elusive and evil "skinwalker." Brimming with Navajo lore and sizzling suspense, *Skinwalkers* brings Chee and Leaphorn, Hillerman's best-selling detective team, together for the first time.

"Full of mystery, intrigue, and
dangerous magic."
Ross Thomas

"Hillerman is unique and *Skinwalkers*
is one of his best."
Los Angeles Times

Stolen ancient goods and new corpses at an ancient burial site confound Leaphorn and Chee. They must plunge into the past to unearth the truth.

A THIEF OF TIME

A noted anthropologist vanishes at a moonlit Indian ruin where "thieves of time" ravage sacred ground for profit. When two corpses appear amid stolen goods and bones at an ancient burial site, Navajo Tribal Policemen Lieutenant Joe Leaphorn and Officer Jim Chee must plunge into the past to unearth the astonishing truth behind a mystifying series of horrific murders.

"Skillful. Provocative. The action never flags."
New York Times Book Review

"Vintage Tony Hillerman: suspenseful, compelling! Hillerman transcends the mystery genre and this is one of [his] best."
Washington Post Book World

A grave robber and a corpse reunite Leaphorn and Chee in a dangerous arena of superstition, ancient ceremony, and living gods.

TALKING GOD

As Leaphorn seeks the identity of a murder victim, Chee is arresting Smithsonian conservator Henry Highhawk for ransacking the sacred bones of his ancestors. As the layers of each case are peeled away, it becomes shockingly clear that they are connected, that there are mysterious others pursuing Highhawk, and that Leaphorn and Chee have entered into the dangerous arena of superstition, ancient ceremony, and living gods.

"Woven as tightly as a Navajo blanket."
Newsweek

"Suddenly now Hillerman has become a national literary and cultural sensation . . . it does not take too much to determine why Hillerman has become so popular. He is a solid, down-to-earth storyteller."
Los Angeles Times

*When a bullet kills Officer Jim Chee's good friend
Del, a Navajo shaman is arrested for homicide, but
the case is far from closed.*

COYOTE WAITS

The car fire didn't kill Navajo Tribal Policeman Del-
bert Nez, a bullet did. Officer Jim Chee's good friend
Del lies dead, and a whiskey-soaked Navajo shaman
is found with the murder weapon. The old man is
Ashie Pinto. He's quickly arrested for homicide and
defended by a woman Chee could either love or loathe.
But when Pinto won't utter a word of confession or
denial, Lieutenant Joe Leaphorn begins an investigation. Soon, Leaphorn and Chee unravel a complex plot
of death involving a historical find, a lost fortune . . .
and the mythical Coyote, who is always waiting, and
always hungry.

Officer Chee attempts to solve two modern murders by deciphering the sacred clowns' ancient message to the people of the Tano pueblo.

SACRED CLOWNS

During a Tano kachina ceremony, something in the antics of the dancing *koshare* fills the air with tension. Moments later the clown is found brutally bludgeoned in the same manner that a reservation schoolteacher was killed just days before.

In true Navajo style, Officer Jim Chee and Lieutenant Leaphorn of the Navajo Tribal Police go back to the beginning to decipher the sacred clowns' message to the people of the Tano pueblo. Amid guarded tribal secrets and crooked Indian traders, they find a trail of blood that links a runaway schoolboy, two dead bodies, and the mysterious presence of a sacred artifact.

"This is Hillerman at his best, mixing human nature, ethnicity and the overpowering physical presence of the Southwest."
Newsweek

"[Hillerman's] affection for his characters and for the real world in which they live and work has never been more appealingly demonstrated."
Los Angeles Times Book Review

A man met his death on Ship Rock Mountain eleven years ago, and with the discovery of his body by a group of climbers, Chee and Leaphorn must hunt down the cause of his lonely death.

THE FALLEN MAN

Sprawled on a ledge under the peak of Ship Rock Mountain for eleven years lies an unknown body, now only bones. At Canyon de Chelly, three hundred miles across the Navajo reservation, a sniper shoots an old canyon guide who has always walked that pollen path in peace. At his home in Window Rock, Joe Leaphorn, newly retired from the Navajo Tribal Police, connects skeleton and sniper, and remembers an old puzzle he could never solve. At his office in Shiprock, Acting Lieutenant Jim Chee is too busy to take much interest in the case—until it hits too close to home. Bringing the beauty and mystery of the Southwest to vivid life once again, Tony Hillerman has reunited Joe Leaphorn and Jim Chee in an evocative mystery in which the past and the present join forces in a most unholy union.

"The personal tensions add another facet to the story, which continues the author's fascination with the savagery that men do to themselves and to the land they claim to hold sacred."
New York Times Book Review

When Acting Lieutenant Jim Chee catches a Hopi poacher huddled over a butchered Navajo Tribal Police officer, he has an open-and-shut case—until his former boss, Joe Leaphorn, blows it wide open.

THE FIRST EAGLE

Now retired from the Navajo Tribal Police, Leaphorn has been hired to find a hot-headed female biologist hunting for the key to a virulent plague lurking in the Southwest. The scientist disappeared from the same area the same day the Navajo cop was murdered. Is she a suspect or another victim? And what about a report that a skinwalker—a Navajo witch—was seen at the same time and place too? For Leaphorn and Chee, the answers lie buried in a complicated knot of superstition and science, in a place where the worlds of native peoples and outside forces converge and collide.

"Surrendering to Hillerman's strong narrative voice and supple storytelling techniques, we come to see that ancient cultures and modern sciences are simply different mythologies for the same reality."
New York Times Book Review

Hunting Badger *finds Navajo Tribal Police officers Joe Leaphorn and Jim Chee working two angles of the same case—each trying to catch the right-wing militiamen who pulled off a violent heist at an Indian casino.*

HUNTING BADGER

Three armed men raid the Ute tribe's gambling casino, and then disappear in the maze of canyons on the Utah-Arizona border. The FBI takes over the investigation, and agents swarm in with helicopters and high-tech equipment. Making an explosive situation even hotter, these experts devise a theory of the crime that makes a wounded deputy sheriff a suspect — a development that brings in Tribal Police Sergeant Jim Chee and his longtime colleague, retired Lieutenant Joe Leaphorn, to help.

Chee finds a fatal flaw in the federal theory and Leaphorn sees an intriguing pattern connecting this crime with the exploits of a legendary Ute hero bandit. Balancing politics, outsiders, and missing armed fugitives, Leaphorn and Chee soon find themselves caught in the most perplexing—and deadly—crime hunt of their lives . . .

"Hillerman soars."
Boston Globe

"Hillerman continues to dazzle . . .
A standout."
Washington Post Book World

A haunting tale of obsessive greed—of lost love and murder—as only the master, Tony Hillerman, can tell it.

THE WAILING WIND

Officer Bernadette Manuelito found the dead man slumped over the cab of a blue pickup abandoned in a dry gulch off a dirt road—with a rich ex-con's phone number in his pocket and a tobacco tin filled with tracer gold. It's her initial mishandling of the scene that spells trouble for her supervisor, Sergeant Jim Chee of the Navajo Tribal Police—but it's the echoes of a long-ago crime scene that call the legendary former Lieutenant Joe Leaphorn out of retirement. Years earlier, Leaphorn followed the trail of a beautiful, young, and missing wife to a dead end, and his failure has haunted him ever since. But ghosts never sleep in these high, lonely Southwestern hills. And the twisted threads of craven murders past and current may finally be coming together, thanks to secrets once moaned in torment on the desert wind.

"Enough to give anyone the shivers."
New York Times Book Review

"Grade A . . . Thrilling, chilling . . .
another Hillerman treasure."
Denver Rocky Mountain News

Leaphorn and Chee must battle the feds and a clever killer in a case that will take them from the tribe's Four Corners country all the way south to the Mexican border and the Sonoran Desert.

THE SINISTER PIG

Sergeant Jim Chee is troubled by the nameless corpse discovered just inside his jurisdiction, at the edge of the Jicarilla Apache natural gas field. More troubling still is the FBI's insistence that the Bureau take over the case, calling the unidentified victim's death a "hunting accident."

But if a hunter was involved, Chee knows the prey was intentionally human. This belief is shared by the legendary Lieutenant Joe Leaphorn, who once again is pulled out of retirement by the possibility of serious wrongs being committed against the Navajo nation by the Washington bureaucracy. Yet it is former policewoman Bernadette Manuelito, recently relocated to Customs Patrol at the U.S.-Mexico border, who possibly holds the key to a fiendishly twisted conspiracy of greed, lies, and murder—and whose only hope for survival now rests in the hands of friends too far away for comfort.

"Riveting . . . This *Pig* flies!"
People

"An extraordinary display of
sheer plotting craftsmanship."
New York Times Book Review

In 1956, an airplane crash left the remains of 172 passengers scattered among the majestic cliffs of the Grand Canyon—including an arm attached to a briefcase containing a fortune in gems. Half a century later, one of the missing diamonds has reappeared . . . and the wolves are on the scent.

SKELETON MAN

Former Navajo Tribal Police Lieutenant Joe Leaphorn is coming out of retirement to help exonerate a slow, simple kid accused of robbing a trading post. Billy Tuve claims he received the diamond he tried to pawn from a mysterious old man in the canyon, and his story has attracted the dangerous attention of strangers to the Navajo land—one more interested in a severed limb than in the fortune it was handcuffed to, another willing to murder to keep lost secrets hidden. But nature herself may prove the deadliest adversary, as Leaphorn and Sergeant Jim Chee follow a puzzle—and a killer—down into the dark realm of Skeleton Man.

Retirement has never sat well with former Navajo Tribal Police Lieutenant Joe Leaphorn. Now the ghosts of a still-unsolved case are returning to haunt him . . .

THE SHAPE SHIFTER

Joe Leaphorn's interest in the case is reawakened by a photograph in a magazine spread of a one-of-a-kind Navajo rug—a priceless work of woven art that was supposedly destroyed in a suspicious fire many years earlier. The rug, commemorating one of the darkest and most terrible chapters in American history, was always said to be cursed, and now the friend who brought it to Leaphorn's attention has mysteriously gone missing.

With newly wedded officers Jim Chee and Bernie Manuelito just back from their honeymoon, the legendary ex-lawman is on his own to pick up the threads of a crime he'd once thought impossible to untangle. And they're leading him back into a world of lethal greed, shifting truths, and changing faces, where a cold-blooded killer still resides.

"Hillerman scores. . . . Atmospheric and suspenseful. . . . With *The Shape Shifter*, Hillerman once again proves himself the master of Southwest mystery fiction."
Santa Fe New Mexican